A FIRE THAT STILL BURNS

Denise M. McShane
&
Betty Lynn Nye

ISBN: 979-8-218-14486-9

"The sheer horror of Boston's Cocoanut Grove nightclub fire can't be captured in death tolls and statistics. To do honor to the multiple people impacted—the dead, the injured and those who somehow escaped the inferno—authors Denise M. McShane and Betty Lynn Nye have created a compelling work of historical fiction about that fateful night of November 28, 1942, from the events leading up to it to the aftermath. Mixing historical fact with imagination, the authors weave together the individual stories of a memorable cast of characters and reveal the factors that led to the fire and the quirks of fate that saved some and doomed many. Meticulously researched, the novel adds to our collective knowledge of the fire and its lingering effect. *A Fire that Still Burns* helps us imagine the unimaginable."

—Stephanie Schorow, author
The Cocoanut Grove Nightclub Fire: A Boston Tragedy

"The sheer horror of Boston's Cocoanut Grove nightclub fire can't be captured in death tolls and statistics. To do honor to the multiple people impacted—the dead, the injured and those who somehow escaped the inferno—authors Denise M. McShane and Betty Lynn Nye have created a compelling work of historical fiction about that fateful night of November 28, 1942, from the events leading up to it to the aftermath. Mixing historical fact with imagination, the authors weave together the individual stories of a memorable cast of characters and reveal the factors that led to the fire and the quirks of fate that saved some and doomed many. Meticulously researched, the novel adds to our collective knowledge of the fire and its lingering effect. *A Fire that Still Burns* helps us imagine the unimaginable."

—Stephanie Schorow, author
The Cocoanut Grove Nightclub Fire: A Boston Tragedy

This novel, while a work of fiction, is based on fact. There were thousands of reports and anecdotes about the Cocoanut Grove Fire and rescue efforts. As with all eyewitness accounts, the details differ from one person's recollection to that of another's. We researched a myriad of books, newspaper articles, documentaries, and firsthand accounts. Ultimately, we chose to include the events that were the most well-known and for which there appeared to be the greatest consensus. The fictional main characters we created allowed us the opportunity to present not only the experience of the fire but the circumstances leading up to it. We also paid honor to individuals who were actually in the club that night by telling their stories respectfully.

We wrote this book with the hope that the tragedy of the Cocoanut Grove Fire will never be forgotten.

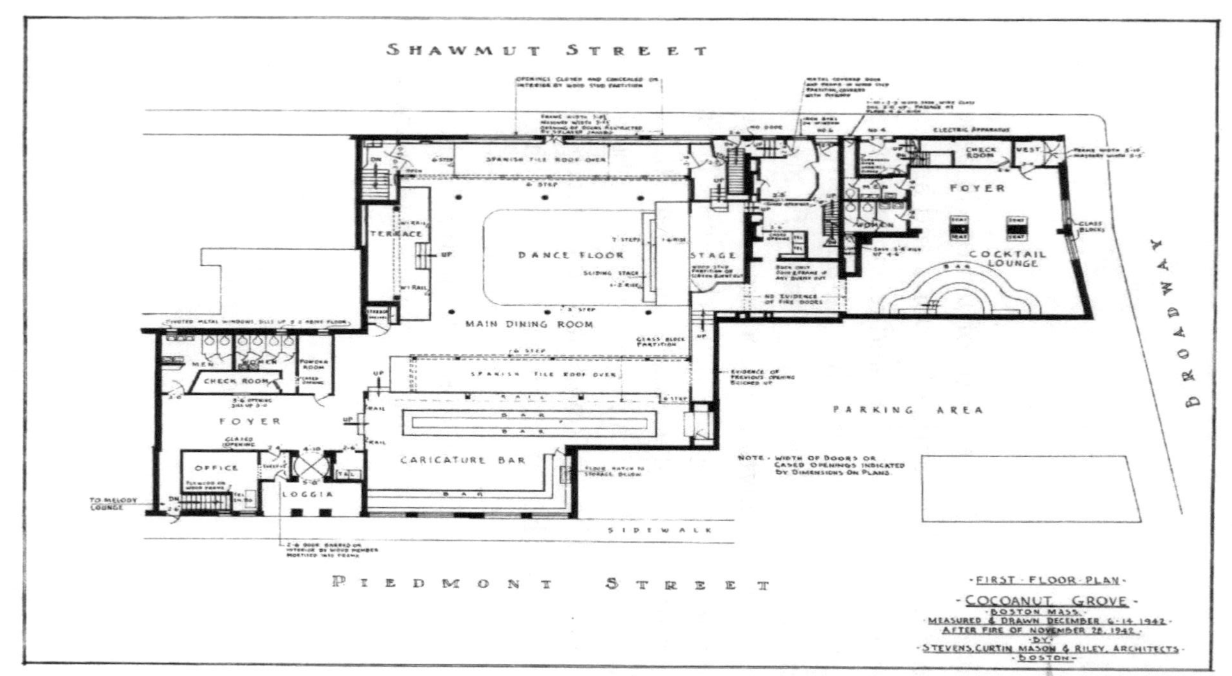
SHAWMUT STREET
BROADWAY
PIEDMONT STREET
SIDEWALK
PARKING AREA
SPANISH TILE ROOF OVER
DANCE FLOOR
STAGE
TERRACE
MAIN DINING ROOM
CARICATURE BAR
BAR
FOYER
CHECK ROOM
MEN
WOMEN
POWDER ROOM
OFFICE
LOGGIA
TO MELODY LOUNGE
COCKTAIL LOUNGE
WEST
NOTE - WIDTH OF DOORS OR CASED OPENINGS INDICATED BY DIMENSIONS ON PLANS
-FIRST - FLOOR - PLAN-
- COCOANUT GROVE -
-BOSTON MASS.-
-MEASURED & DRAWN DECEMBER 6-14 1942-
AFTER FIRE OF NOVEMBER 28, 1942
-BY-
-STEVENS, CURTIN MASON & RILEY, ARCHITECTS-
-BOSTON-

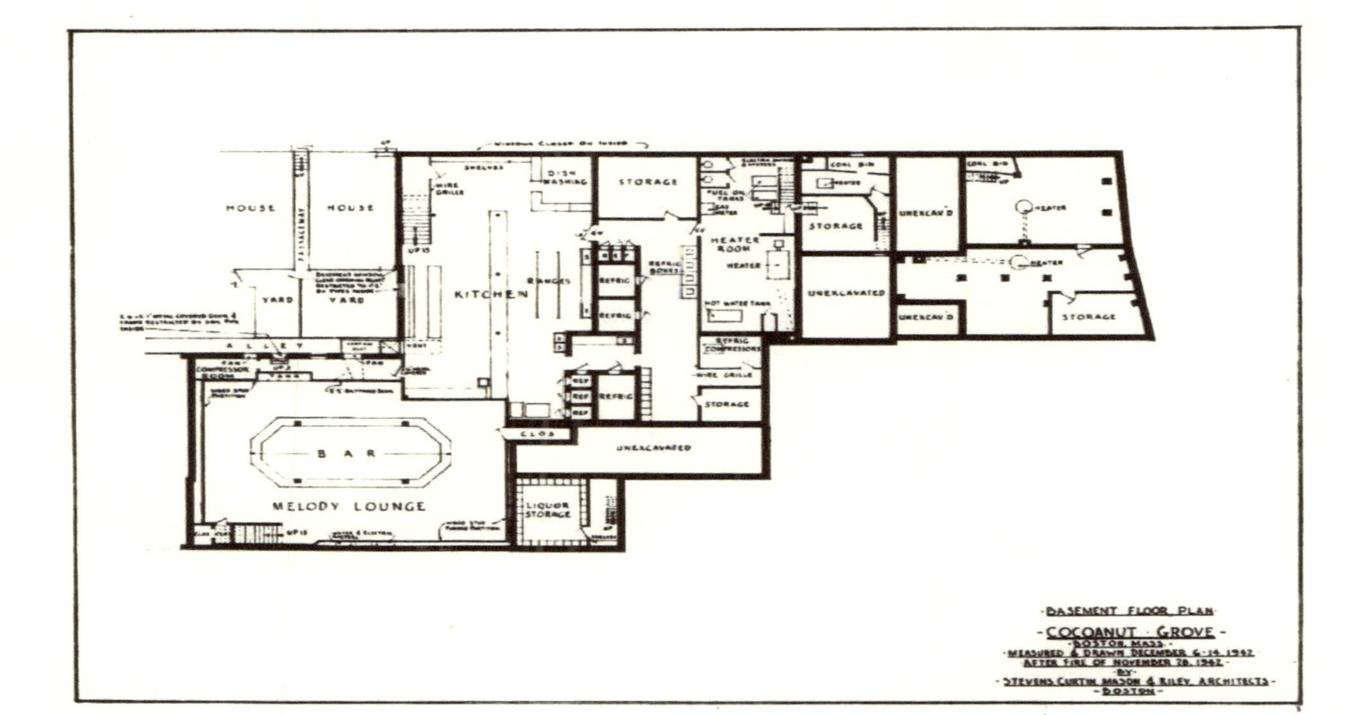
HOUSE
HOUSE
PASSAGEWAY
YARD
YARD
ALLEY
KITCHEN
RANGES
SHELVES
WIRE GRILLE
DISH WASHING
STORAGE
REFRIG
REFRIG BOXES
HEATER ROOM
HEATER
HOT WATER TANK
FUEL OIL TANKS
REFRIG COMPRESSORS
WIRE GRILLE
STORAGE
UNEXCAVATED
CLOS
BAR
MELODY LOUNGE
LIQUOR STORAGE
COMPRESSOR ROOM
UP 15
COAL BIN
STORAGE
UNEXCAV'D
UNEXCAVATED
HEATER
UNEXCAV'D
STORAGE
·BASEMENT FLOOR PLAN·
- COCOANUT GROVE -
- BOSTON, MASS. -
· MEASURED & DRAWN DECEMBER 6-14, 1942
· AFTER FIRE OF NOVEMBER 28, 1942 ·
· BY ·
· STEVENS CURTIN MASON & RILEY, ARCHITECTS ·
· BOSTON ·

CHAPTER ONE

Danny McGuire hid in the shadowed alcove of a vacant store, watching for his prey to make a move. The recessed doorway was the perfect vantage point for the job he had come to do.

Diagonally across the street, Sal Russo stood like a sentry before one of the three archways to the entrance of the swankiest nightclub in Boston. Perched on its roof, an unlit, vertical neon sign prominently displayed the name "COCOANUT GROVE." Because it had once been a well-known speakeasy that had been expanded, it was now an odd, mismatched, L-shaped series of connected buildings dressed up by a stylish concrete façade. On any given night, people stood in line along the sidewalk in front of 17 Piedmont waiting to get in. But this being Saturday morning, the area was practically deserted and appeared a bit seedy in the stark light of day.

Sunlight glinted off Sal's diamond pinky ring as he lit a cigar and tossed the match into the gutter of the dirty, narrow, cobblestone street. He puffed on the cigar and admired his brand spanking new '42 Cadillac parked at the corner of the building.

In a black cashmere topcoat and classic fedora, the Grove's cocky strong-arm almost seemed refined. Almost. That impression was dashed the minute anyone heard him speak. Having grown up in the Roxbury section of Boston, he had adopted the street talk of the toughest guys in his neighborhood. As a result, he sounded less than dignified, always dropping the "g" from words ending in "ing" and often saying "yous" when speaking to more than one person.

Danny wished things would get rolling, so he could be done with it. The cold November weather wasn't doing him any favors. It numbed his fingers and made his bum leg ache like hell. There was no time to worry about that now. Someone was coming.

A well-dressed, middle-aged man strolled along the brick sidewalk toward the Cocoanut Grove. An air of confidence shone in his polished smile. As he approached, Sal was quick to shake his hand, eager to do business. They engaged in friendly conversation, punctuated with laughter. Eyes gleaming, the man withdrew a document from his coat pocket and handed it to Sal in exchange for a wad of cash.

This was it. The moment had come. Danny prepared himself to take the shot. "Say cheese, you son of a bitch," he spat under his breath then covertly captured the incriminating exchange.

Sal instinctively looked toward Danny.

Danny ducked back into the shadows.

Grinning, the man stuffed the money in his pocket. He shook Sal's hand and nonchalantly strolled away.

Sal smugly tucked the document into his breast pocket.

Danny had to admit that Jim was right. Getting that shot brought back a little bit of the old excitement. But the last time Jim had an idea to advance their careers it hadn't turned out so well. It hadn't turned out well at all.

A short way up the street, Jim Reed was slouched down in a '36 Packard. From beneath the brim of his dressy fedora, he kept an eye on Sal in the rearview mirror. It was getting pretty cold in the car now that the engine had been off for a while. He turned up the collar of his herringbone topcoat and worried about poor Danny standing outside in that doorway. It seemed like he was always worrying about Danny nowadays. And yet things seemed to be going along well, that is until he spotted Ginger Logan coming out of the club from the corner door. His whole body tensed as he waited to see Danny's reaction to this. He sure hoped Danny wouldn't blow their cover.

Danny's heart wrenched when he saw the girl he had once planned to marry. It was the first time he'd laid eyes on her since he'd gotten back. He felt as if a hot spike had been driven through his chest. She was lovely even in a warm wool coat, especially with those strawberry blonde curls peeking out from under her soft-brimmed hat. She had a natural beauty that radiated from within and always exuded a sweet kind of confidence. Just the sight of her made him fall head-over-heels all over again.

Rita Russo scooted out after Ginger. Her stylish dress coat hugged her body in all the right places. Rita was a spicy dame who craved attention. She worked a little too hard at it for Danny's money, getting all dolled up with dramatic makeup and clothes that showed off every curve. Yet, he found her vivacious and funny in an innocent kind of way.

Sal disappeared through an archway while Ginger and Rita waited for him by his Cadillac. He ensured that the club's brass-trimmed revolving door entrance was locked. The plate glass door beside it, with no visible handle, gave the appearance of only being a window covered on the inside by a red velvet drape. Sal checked to see that this door was locked as well.

As Danny watched Sal strut to the corner door, bile rose from his gut. He loathed Sal. It infuriated him that the bastard had risked exposing Ginger to his dirty dealings. Of all the guys Ginger could have gone with, and there were plenty, it still floored Danny that she had chosen to get involved with Sal Russo. Sal was nothing but a two-bit thug. Her "boyfriend"—that thought almost made his breakfast come up—was as crooked as they came. Danny couldn't help but wonder if Ginger had lost all self-respect.

"Come on, Salvi!" Rita whined.

Sal locked the corner door and pocketed his keys. "Hey, heads would roll if Mr. Welansky found them doors weren't locked," he told Rita as he swaggered over. He patted the hood of his car and boasted, "I do a good job around here. That's how I could afford this Caddy. It's one of the last off the line, you know, now that the war's on."

Rita flashed her big brother an adoring smile. She draped a vibrant fall scarf over the crown of her dark hair and twisted it artfully about her neck. She checked her reflection in the mirror of her compact and began to touch up her scarlet lipstick.

"Rita, get in the back," Sal commanded.

She obediently got in and struggled to close the door.

Sal opened the front door on the passenger side for Ginger. He teasingly demanded, "Baby doll, give us a kiss."

Danny felt his heart drop like a runaway elevator and land in the pit of his stomach when he saw her kiss Sal's lips.

Once Ginger was seated, Sal got behind the wheel. The Cadillac purred as he started it up, and they drove away.

Watching that kiss left a sour taste in Danny's mouth. He yanked out the used sheet film holder on which he had captured the payoff and deposited it into his camera satchel. With a heavy sigh, he closed his prized Graflex Speed Graphic press camera and packed it away.

Danny stepped out from the shadows to the sidewalk, hampered by a metal brace clamped around his right leg over rumpled trousers. His well-worn leather bomber jacket hung a little too loosely from his broad shoulders, but he wouldn't give it up. It fit who he used to be. A press pass was stuck in the band of his ordinary brown fedora. He wore the hat tilted low on his forehead. He liked it that way. Others couldn't see the pain in his steel blue eyes.

Now that the coast was clear, Jim started the engine. He threw the Packard in reverse and careened down the street. The car screeched to a halt right in front of Danny. Jim flung open the passenger door.

Danny cringed. "Geez, Jim! Take it easy with my baby!"

Jim grinned sheepishly. He knew he shouldn't have been so reckless with Danny's beloved Packard. He would have been jealous if the shoe was on the other foot. Not being able to drive anymore must be killing Danny. But when Jim had come out of the house this morning, he had found that his own car had a flat. He'd have to go to the shop and see about getting a patch kit next chance he got. There'd be no getting a replacement tire now that the Japs had conquered the rubber producing nations. Desperate, he'd had to beg Danny to let him use *his* car today. They had to catch Sal at his game. Everything was riding on it!

Jim asked, "Did you get anything we can use?"

Danny nodded. "For all the good it will do."

Danny didn't exactly share Jim's enthusiasm, but they'd been best friends since they were pipsqueaks exploring the backyard of the Roxbury three-decker they'd grown up in. He'd always admired how smart and self-assured Jim was. When Jim had gotten a tip that Sal would be up to his old tricks paying off officials, the tenacious reporter had asked Danny to be ready and waiting. Danny knew Jim was hell-bent on blowing the lid off the shady practices at the Grove. It was the kind of big story that could drive their careers at the *Boston City Press* from the sports section to the front page. Danny didn't care so much about all that, although he sure wouldn't mind taking Sal down.

Jim said, "Good God, that gutter rat is slick from his Brylcreemed hair to his shiny Italian shoes. Can you believe the S.O.B. greased that city official's palm right in broad daylight?"

"That's Sal for you. He thinks he's bulletproof," Danny grumbled. He leaned in, placed his satchel on the front seat, and eased himself into the car.

"You doing okay, buddy?"

Danny let out a frustrated sigh. "I got it." He pulled his braced leg in with his hands, reached out, and yanked the door shut.

Jim knew not to press him further. Instead, he shifted the car into drive and pulled away.

"I still can't believe she's with Sal Russo, of all people."

"Well, you did let her go, Danny," Jim gingerly reminded him.

"I know it," Danny retorted through gritted teeth.

They were headed across town to Fenway Park to cover the most anticipated football game of the season. It was the big Thanksgiving weekend game between their much-favored-to-win alma mater Boston College and its rival, Holy Cross.

Jim was really looking forward to being there. Danny, on the other hand, stared out the window in a sullen mood. He was dreading it. Jim knew it. As he turned the car onto Charles Street, he took a stab at lifting Danny's spirits. "*Flying Tigers* is playing at the Paramount. Want to go and see it tomorrow night?"

"Nope. Take one of your sweeties."

"Come on. It's John Wayne," Jim coaxed.

Danny shook his head.

"Why not?"

"I've already seen more war than I ever wanted to."

"Oh, Danny, it'll be more love and glory than blood and guts."

"If those Hollywood big shots got a taste of the real thing, they wouldn't think it was so glorious."

Jim chuckled. "You're probably right about that. But you've got to admit, it gets guys to join up. So, I'm sorry to say, I think they'll be making war pictures for a long time to come."

Sal sped through a yellow light. The tires squealed as he took a sharp turn at the next corner, cutting off another driver.

Ginger gasped. The other car seemed to be coming straight at her.

Rita slid across the backseat and slammed up against the door. Annoyed, she griped, "Geez, Salvi!"

The irritated driver of the other car leaned on his

horn.

Sal put the fingers of one hand beneath his chin and whipped them out in a vulgar Italian gesture. "Eh, back off! I got here first!"

Ginger closed her eyes and resigned herself to Sal's rude behavior.

Rita sat back up and neatened her scarf. Leaning forward, she rested her chin on her hands atop the front seat to chat with Ginger. "Andy is so handsome. I can't wait to watch him play today. I'll bet anything he gets a touchdown!"

Ginger smiled at Rita. "I sure hope so!"

Sal rolled his eyes. He couldn't fathom Rita's infatuation with Ginger's stupid kid brother.

"Serenade in Blue," by big band leader Glenn Miller, came on the radio. It caught Ginger off-guard. That song always made her think of Danny. Worried Sal might be able to read what she was feeling, Ginger turned her head and gazed out the passenger window, memories flooding her mind.

Traffic slowed to a crawl by the Boston Public Garden. Jim turned on the radio. "Serenade in Blue" was playing. The lyrics made Danny melancholy. It was true. It *had* felt like being in another world when he'd been alone with Ginger. Now, he was merely trying to cope with the hand he'd been dealt and lead a quiet life without her, though constant reminders of her made it pretty darn hard.

Danny gazed out the window at the park. The trees were almost leafless, the gardens bloomless. Visitors braced themselves against crisp autumn winds as they crossed a footbridge over an icy pond. Danny's mind spun back to a day in June.

The park was in full bloom. He strolled hand-in-hand with Ginger along the footbridge while swan-shaped boats filled with passengers glided beneath. Radiant in a fluttery, blue summer dress, she took his breath away. He drew her close. She smiled up at him dreamily. They were so in love.

The singer on the radio crooning "forevermore" dredged up what Danny had been fighting to keep buried with every fiber of his being. Yet the memory, like a geyser, shot to the surface.

His hand clutched the box in his pocket. He hoped she would like the diamond ring he'd worked so hard to afford. Down on one knee, he took her hand and pledged his love. He asked her to be by his side "forevermore" as his wife. Ginger didn't hesitate to accept. He saw her eyes dance with excitement as he slipped the engagement ring on her finger. He was so thrilled that he lifted her off her feet and kissed her right in public. She was more than willing.

The memory of that smoldering kiss was the sweetest kind of pain. Yeah, that had been his life *before* the brace. Now their love, once in full bloom, was as withered as those gardens.

A lump formed in Danny's throat as he listened to the final lyrics and relived the heartbreak of letting Ginger go. He was so lost in thought that he didn't even notice Jim monitoring him.

Sal caught Ginger pinching back tears as "Serenade in Blue" came to an end. He pursed his lips. A nerve in his cheek twitched when the thought hit him that she might be daydreaming about McGuire. It steamed him to think that she'd ever been with that self-righteous showoff.

Ginger was all too aware of being under Sal's scrutiny. She didn't dare let on what that song had brought up for her. It was agonizing to realize just how deep and raw her emotions still were regarding Danny.

She had been frightened to learn that he, along with Jim, had taken a job as a war correspondent on Guadalcanal. She'd worried day and night that Danny would get hurt or worse. The last thing she'd ever expected was that he would fall for the nurse who tended to him while he was recuperating from malaria. Although Jim had assured her it was true, deep in her heart Ginger hadn't believed it. But, when a couple of months had passed and Danny still hadn't come home, she was forced to accept what she had been told.

Ginger's whole world had come crashing down. She hadn't been able to eat or sleep. Her eyes had been swollen from constant crying. The pain in her heart had created such a tightness in her chest that she'd thought she would die. And she hadn't even cared. Life without Danny was no life at all. She would never love another. Not like that.

As the joyous memory of accepting Danny's marriage proposal rushed up in her thoughts, the physical pain in her chest returned. Her eyes stung from the tears she held back. She struggled to keep her breathing calm. Feeling more and more uncomfortable in Sal's presence, Ginger wondered how her life could have changed so much in just a few months.

CHAPTER TWO

Danny's melancholy walk down memory lane abruptly ended when the flow of traffic resumed at the Boston Public Garden. Jim attempted to lighten the mood. "Did you hear Buck Jones is in town?"

Danny looked over at him, interested to hear about the cowboy movie star.

Jim continued, "He was at Children's Hospital this morning visiting the sick kids, and, now, he's at the Garden for the war bonds rally."

"Busy guy," Danny quipped.

"That's the price of fame." As they waited at a red light, Jim rambled on. "His day doesn't end there. The mayor invited him to the game along with a bunch of bigwigs that are helping him promote his new picture. And you don't say no to the mayor."

"How's he going to have time for that?" Danny wondered out loud.

"He's probably just doing a few lasso tricks. He'll be done with the rally in plenty of time. By the way,"

Jim paused to catch Danny's eye, "Eddie wants us to get something on him at the game, too."

Danny rolled his eyes. "That's Eddie for you. Two stories for the price of one."

Jim chuckled.

"Pull over, Jim. I need some smokes."

Jim lucked out and snagged a parking space close by a Rexall Drug Store. "Hey, did you know this is Mr. Marshall's new store?"

"Our old neighborhood druggist?"

Jim nodded.

Danny let out a heavy sigh. "What time are we looking at?"

Jim glanced at his wristwatch. "It's quarter past twelve, so you better make it snappy."

Danny shot him a dirty look.

"What?" Jim teased. "Do you want me to go in and get them for you?"

"No! I can do it," Danny fired back. He opened the car door.

Jim gave him a mischievous smile and said, "Pick me up a Sky Bar."

Jim could be exasperating, but Danny couldn't keep from laughing.

Jim watched Danny labor to get out of the car and limp along the store-lined avenue. He pounded his fists on the steering wheel in frustration. He loved Danny like a brother and couldn't stand to see him struggling even though he knew it was in the guy's best interest to do things on his own. He couldn't help feeling it was all his fault that Danny was in this mess.

He owed his life to Danny, and he knew it.

Danny noticed a display in the window of an upscale ladies' clothing store. A mannequin wore a smart skirt suit priced at $22.95. Another flaunted a luxurious fur coat for $79.50 and a fancy hat for $2.49. He shook his head in disbelief at the exorbitant prices. He continued on and entered the Rexall.

Mr. Marshall, the middle-aged druggist, was behind a glass partition counting out pills to fill a prescription. He called out, "Be right with you!"

Danny scanned the shop while he waited. He was impressed by the size of it, the beauty of the tin ceiling, and the richness of the wood trim and marble counters.

Mr. Marshall, dressed in a neat white lab coat and a bow tie, came out from behind the partition and greeted him with a smile. "Hello, Danny."

"Hello, Mr. Marshall. This is quite an upgrade."

"It's a lot bigger than the one I had on the corner of your street." Mr. Marshall beamed with pride. He glanced down at Danny's brace. "Jim told me about your situation, Danny. You look like you're getting around okay, now, though. How are you feeling?"

Danny shrugged. "The brace takes some getting used to."

"I understand," Mr. Marshall said with compassion. "What can I get for you?"

"Just a pack of Luckys."

Mr. Marshall retrieved the package of cigarettes and joked, "A sale's a sale, right?"

Danny smiled back politely. Remembering Jim's request, he took a Sky Bar from a candy rack. He placed it on the counter adding, "And this."

The cash register dinged as Mr. Marshall rang up the sale. "That will be thirty cents."

Danny handed him a dollar bill. While he waited for his change, he glanced at the stack of *Boston Daily Globe* newspapers on the counter with the headline "EAGLES 4–1 FAVORITES TO DEFEAT HOLY CROSS BEFORE 41,300 TODAY."

"You back to work covering the big game?"

"Yup," Danny answered.

"With the way B.C.'s been winning, it ought to be a real massacre," Mr. Marshall declared, his eyes sparkling.

"That's for sure!" Danny agreed as he accepted his change.

Sal drove onto a side street beside Fenway Park. Throngs of people were walking down the street toward the entrance. He tooted and gestured for them to get out of his way. At a vacant space blocked by two metal barrels, he blared his horn.

A few feet away, a chain-link fence surrounded the park's private lot where team busses were parked. A rugged, grey-haired security guard came out through the gate when he heard Sal's horn and hurried to remove the barrels.

Sal parked in the spot. He handed the security

guard a few bucks and said, "Thanks, Joe."

Joe winked. "Anytime, Mr. Russo."

Sal spied four teenage boys climbing the fence behind Joe's back. "Hey, Joe, looks like you got yourself some moochers."

One boy got his sweater caught on the fence trying to jump over it into the lot. He wriggled free and fell to the ground. The seasoned security guard nabbed him. He rounded up the rest of the boys and had no trouble kicking them all out.

"Serves those punks right for trying to sneak in," Sal said and snickered to Joe. Still smirking, he helped Ginger and Rita out of his car. He draped an arm around each of them and herded the women toward the crowded public entrance of the stadium.

A few minutes later, Jim turned the Packard onto the same busy side street at Fenway Park.

"Oh, swell!" Danny groaned when he saw Sal's Cadillac.

Jim sighed, empathizing. "And doesn't it just figure? The son of a bitch got the best parking spot!"

Danny shook his head in disgust, thinking how he might have to deal with Sal on top of everything else. And he certainly didn't want to run into Ginger. His heart pounded at the thought of having to talk to her.

Jim stopped the car beside the chain-link fence. He took a deep breath and launched in, "This is the moment of truth, buddy."

Danny swallowed hard.

"How are you going to explain that?" Jim asked, pointing to the brace.

Danny stared down at it and shrugged.

"It's good you came out of hiding, but everybody's going to wonder what the hell happened. It might have been better if I'd told the truth," Jim reasoned.

"Not to Ginger!" Danny snapped. He put an end to that conversation by getting out of the car.

Jim sighed. He wasn't going to argue with Danny. The poor guy had enough on his plate. Jim tore open the Sky Bar and held it out to him. "Here. Have a piece. It'll make you feel better."

Danny scrutinized the four sections of the chocolate bar. He broke off an end piece. He bit into it and grinned impishly as caramel oozed out.

"Sure, take my favorite flavor," Jim complained, but his twinkling baby blues showed he was only joking.

Danny laughed, licking caramel from his fingers. Jim handed him the satchel. Danny slung it over his shoulder.

"You all set, buddy?" Jim asked one last time.

Danny gave him a nod and shut the car door. Jim drove away in search of a place to park.

Joe, the security guard, saw Danny limping to the gate of the chain-link fence. He had known Danny for years, first as a football player and then as a sports photographer. Though he had heard the young man had gone overseas to cover the war, he was shocked to see him in a leg brace. He wondered if it had happened over there, but he didn't want to be too nosey and make Danny feel uncomfortable. Instead, he ended up stammering, "Da… Danny McGuire? How are you?"

Hearing the hesitancy in Joe's voice, Danny lowered his eyes self-consciously and murmured, "Good to see you, Joe."

The security guard grinned, yet the sadness in his eyes betrayed him. As he let Danny in, he was quick with a comment to hide his uneasiness. "B.C.'s gonna clobber 'em!"

Danny gave Joe a thumbs-up and headed toward the building. He relished being back. He loved Fenway. He'd had a lot of good times in this park with Jim. They had come every summer since they were kids to watch the Red Sox play baseball, and they would be back every fall for football season. So, when they both were fortunate enough to be accepted to Boston College and make the football team (Danny as a running back and Jim as a quarterback), they were over the moon to actually play at Fenway Park.

Danny wound his way along a corridor beneath the stadium. He paused in a vestibule festooned with memorabilia to look at their team photograph hanging on the wall. He gazed at it fondly. On the day it was taken, he had made the winning touchdown. The thrill of that rushed back into his mind.

He leapt up and snagged Jim's pass. He rushed the length of the field, zigzagging around imposing defensive linemen into the end zone. Touchdown! The crowd erupted. The announcer's voice reverberated over the loudspeaker, "Danny McGuire scores yet another touchdown! What an astounding effort from this terrific young athlete!"

It was hard for Danny to believe that was only a few years ago. He'd had it all then. But that photograph was just a burning reminder of glory days never to be had again.

The noise of fans arriving in the stadium above spurred Danny to get moving. The teams would be ready for the press soon, and he couldn't afford to miss his chance to capture the moment. He joined other local newspaper photographers gathering outside the doors of the locker rooms.

Some of the guys he'd worked with in the past greeted him warmly, but everyone seemed a little bit awkward. When they eyed his brace, it made Danny squirm. He knew they were probably wondering why Jim hadn't tipped them off about it. A locker room door swung open. He was grateful. It took their attention off him. He hurried to get his camera out, insert a sheet film holder, and put in a flashbulb.

The Holy Cross Crusaders, suited up in purple and white, filed out first. These polished sons of affluent parents were serious and edgy. They dutifully lined up and posed for pictures. Flashbulbs went off one after the other. Danny and the rest of the photographers hustled to exchange their used single exposure film holders for fresh ones. They replaced their flashbulbs and got ready for the next shot.

The unruly B.C. Eagles, wearing maroon and gold, burst out from their locker room. These boisterous everyday Joes from white middle-class families mugged for the cameras.

Andy Logan's jovial mood faded fast once Danny lowered his camera. The strapping B.C. player with boy-next-door good looks locked eyes on Danny.

Danny could feel Andy's emotions rising in defense of his sister. Here it comes, torpedoes loaded, full steam ahead! Danny sucked in a breath and tried to prepare himself for the inescapable confrontation with Ginger's brother.

But Andy spotted the brace and stood down. It floored him that the football star he had idolized was now disabled. Confused, he whispered, "Geez, Danny."

Danny couldn't look him in the eye. He wasn't ready to explain himself yet.

The Crusaders were shepherded together by their coaches and sent jogging down the corridor to the opening to the field. The Eagles followed suit with the photographers hot on their heels. Andy hung back, hoping Danny would fill him in, but Danny waved him on. Disappointed, Andy took off after his team.

Danny was relieved. He had dodged a bullet. He bent down and rubbed his aching leg; a habitual, subconscious effort to alleviate the pain in his heart. He took a few deep breaths to rally himself. At the opening to the field, daylight flooded in. He could feel the excitement as he stepped out.

The park was brimming with anticipation amidst the usual hoopla of college bands and cheerleaders warming up. The aroma of hotdogs and hot roasted peanuts wafted through the air. Thousands of spectators packed the stands. Servicemen, home on their first leave since the war began, wore their uniforms proudly. Loyal fans waved pennants displaying the colors of either Boston College or Holy

Cross.

On the field, photographers were flocking around the teams. Danny caught up with them and got a shot of the B.C. co-captains posing together for pictures. He scouted around for Jim and saw him with other reporters interviewing an enthusiastic B.C. coach.

Jim spotted Danny and jogged over to him. He studied Danny to see how he was coping. Danny sensed Jim's unanswered question and grumbled, "I just saw Andy."

"Well, that was inevitable. What did you say to him?"

Danny didn't answer, and Jim didn't press him. He patted Danny on the shoulder. "It's lousy you had to cover a B.C. game your first day back. Don't let it get to you."

A robust Catholic priest with shocking white hair led the B.C. football players in prayer. Jim nudged Danny and noted, "Father Mike's praying for the win, just like he did when we played."

"As if God cares who wins," Danny quipped.

A young Holy Cross priest was praying with his own team. Amused at the irony, Jim pointed this out to Danny and told him, "Yeah, especially when both teams are praying."

A commotion in the stands drew Danny and Jim's attention. They crossed the field to check it out. Buck Jones, the tall, well-built movie star, had arrived and was being thronged by his adoring fans. Wearing a white cowboy hat, he was still good-looking at fifty years old. Movie moguls flanked him. Mayor Maurice

Tobin and his chum Fire Commissioner William Reilly welcomed him and his entourage into their section of box seats.

Ambitious newspapermen rushed off the field and swarmed Buck. Jim and Danny jockeyed with them to get an interview and photographs.

A couple of sections away, Sal, Ginger, and Rita also sat in box seats. Sal pointed out the mayor's box and bragged, "Look how close yous are to Buck Jones and Mayor Tobin, eh?"

Rita's eyes widened with excitement. "Buck Jones? The cowboy movie star? Here?" Ginger and Rita craned their necks to get a better look. "Oh, Salvi!" Rita squealed. "Ginger, is my brother something or what?"

Sal puffed up proudly. "I take care of my girls."

Ginger gave Sal a sweet smile. "These are great seats. Thank you, Sal."

The fact that Ginger was impressed filled Sal with bravado. He figured if he continued to play his cards right, he just might get lucky. But she was no longer paying any attention to him. She was riveted to the hubbub around Buck Jones.

Ginger was glad to see that Jim was among the crowd of newspapermen vying for an interview with Buck. She knew he was good at his job and deserved a chance at a hot story. She shifted her gaze to his accompanying photographer and couldn't believe her eyes. She felt as if she'd been punched in the stomach. Ginger stared numbly at Danny.

Jim finally got his turn. Danny took a group shot of the affable movie star with the fire commissioner and Boston's handsome mayor.

Rita was busy chatting with Sal. She tried to include Ginger in the conversation. When she couldn't break Ginger's focus, she informed Sal with a giggle, "See, Salvi. She's starstruck."

Ginger's intense concentration aroused Sal's suspicion. He followed her gaze and spied Danny. His blood pressure rose. He knew he had to nip this in the bud, but he didn't want to give himself away. He spoke in an even tone, informing the girls, "I'll be right back."

Sal stood up, bringing Ginger back to reality.

"Where you going, Salvi?" Rita asked.

Sal left without a response and headed toward the mayor's box.

Rita naively concluded, "I bet he's gonna get us an autograph."

But Ginger could see that Sal was making a beeline straight for Danny. Her heart raced. She hated that Sal had such a jealous streak. It scared her. Sal could be vicious. With years of animosity between Sal and Danny, something was bound to happen.

After thanking Buck and the mayor, Jim and Danny started down the crowded stairs. People were flowing, single file, in both directions. Danny hobbled along close behind Jim until two rambunctious kids cut in between them.

Ginger watched and waited on pins and needles as Sal drew nearer to Danny. She was surprised by the awkwardness in Danny's gait. She strained to get a better look at him through the foot traffic and was so stunned by what she saw she almost fainted.

Jim was unaware that Danny had been separated from him. When Sal passed by on his way up the stairs, Jim snickered to himself. Exposing Sal in his article was going to be fun.

Sal noticed that Danny was limping. He zeroed in on the brace. Waiting until they were on the same step, he deliberately knocked into Danny, throwing him off balance, and taunted, "Big man on campus has come down a few pegs."

Ginger could barely breathe. She prayed this wouldn't escalate.

Danny's brace had gotten hung up on the arm of a seat. He swallowed his pride and refused to give Sal the satisfaction of getting into a fight with him. Sal smirked and continued on.

Jim turned around to check on Danny and realized he was no longer with him. Danny was struggling to free his brace. Jim pushed past the two kids behind him. He went back up to offer his help but stopped when he saw Danny's face flush with humiliation.

Ginger's mind reeled. Danny was crippled? What possible reason could Jim have had for not telling her? It was all she could do to keep from crying. But it wouldn't be wise to let Rita catch on to what she was feeling because if Rita knew, Sal would know. And if he thought that she was still carrying a torch for Danny, God only knew what Sal would do.

CHAPTER THREE

Sal stepped into Mayor Tobin's box like he owned the place. The movie moguls watched him with suspicion as he moved in behind Buck's seat. With a salesman's demeanor, he rested a hand on the movie star's shoulder and boasted, "You're gonna enjoy yourself tonight at the Cocoanut Grove. We got you the best seat in the house."

Buck smiled pleasantly.

Sal leaned over to the movie moguls and warned, "Make sure he gets to the Grove. You don't wanna disappoint Mr. Welansky."

Before any of the affronted movie moguls could respond, Buck offered, "I'll try, but I've got a bit of a cold coming on."

Sal turned venomous. He told Buck, "Take a couple of aspirins. You'll feel better."

Buck chafed under Sal's pressure. He warily observed Mayor Tobin and Commissioner Reilly exchange a knowing look.

Sal also noticed it and chuckled. With a broad smile, he reached an arm over the seats and shook hands with the two city officials. "Mayor. Commissioner. I hope you'll stop by to see the new lounge. You know the drinks are always on the house for you boys."

The mayor and the fire commissioner grinned back at Sal sheepishly.

Over in Sal's box seats, Rita's attention was glued to the B.C. players gathering in front of her on the sideline. She nudged Ginger, who was fixated on Danny. "There's Andy!" Rita announced. She jumped up, waved her arms, and yelled, "Andy! Andy, over here!"

Andy waved back at them.

Ginger called out, "Go get 'em, Andy!"

At the sound of Ginger's voice, Danny froze. He glanced around, wondering where she was. He caught sight of her watching the players. He hoped she hadn't seen him. Danny immediately turned away. He was quick to merge in with other newspapermen who were entering the press box situated along the field. He squeezed by them, sunk down next to Jim, and stored his camera. Thinking he'd dodged another bullet, he lit a cigarette and sighed in relief.

Ginger covertly scanned the press box. She spied Danny and was satisfied that she would be able to keep an eye on him.

Sal returned to their box. Rita looked to him with anticipation, eager to receive Buck Jones' autograph. Sal was oblivious, basking in his own glory. He had just strong-armed the mayor of Boston. How many people could lay claim to that? Smirking, he checked the time on his wristwatch and took his seat.

Ginger noticed Rita pouting like a little girl and felt sorry for her. But, at the first sign that the game was about to begin, Rita's mood brightened.

The Holy Cross players headed out on the field as their band played the Crusaders' fight song, "Chu, Chu, Rah, Rah." Their fans stood up, shouted encouragement, and waved purple and white pennants.

Boston College fans hooted and hollered and gave a rousing applause as their team took the field. The Boston College band launched into "For Boston," the Eagles' fight song.

The cheerleaders of each college performed energetic routines, shaking pom-poms as they cheered their teams on.

At the kickoff, the roar of the crowd was deafening.

Katherine, the Cocoanut Grove's head cashier, peered out the club's corner door. Dressed smartly in a dove grey skirt suit, the heavyset, middle-aged woman fretted, wondering what was keeping the electrician.

A beat-up sedan rattled toward the club and

stopped in front of the entrance. Two hulking guys dressed in woolen jackets and faded trousers got out. The driver retrieved an old toolbox from the trunk, and both men approached Katherine. In a polite gesture, the driver lifted his cap revealing his thick, dark hair. He flashed a smile that was a combination of charm and smarm and said, "Good afternoon, ma'am."

"Hello, Dominic." Katherine eyed his companion. "Who's this with you? Mr. Russo didn't tell me anyone else was coming."

"Don't worry. This here's Gino, another cousin of Sal's," Dominic explained, indicating the younger lookalike beside him. "He's just learning the trade, so I brought him along as my helper."

"Oh, all right." Katherine stepped aside and let them in.

Nothing remarkable happened until halfway through the first quarter of the football game. Crusaders fullback Bobby Sullivan caught a long pass. As he zigzagged around B.C. players determined to take him down, fans screamed for him to keep going. The Holy Cross cheerleaders enthusiastically rooted for him. Sullivan sped forty-eight yards before being tackled. The energy in the park was electrifying.

Danny and Jim were amazed at what they had just witnessed. Jim jotted the play down. Even though

Sullivan was on the opposing team, Jim couldn't help marveling at his incredible feat. "Geez, Danny. He moves like you used to."

For a split second, Danny was filled with pride. Then he frowned down at his leg brace and grumbled, "Yeah. Used to."

Play resumed. Sullivan scored a touchdown. Resounding cheers emanated from the stands. The Holy Cross band struck up a triumphant tune sparking their fans to display even more exuberance.

Ginger and Rita frowned. Sal wiped a devious grin from his face. The announcer's voice reverberated across Fenway Park from the public address system, "It's a touchdown for Bobby Sullivan, putting Holy Cross on the board first!"

On a large, green, rectangular scoreboard next to the letters "H.C.," the number six was added. Disappointed B.C. fans grumbled. A Crusader kicked the ball, and it sailed through the goal posts. Cheers erupted from Holy Cross fans. The announcer affirmed, "And they get the extra point!" The score on the board changed to seven.

As the game went on, both teams missed opportunities to score. When Andy caught the ball, he rushed down the field spurred on by Eagles fans and cheerleaders. Ginger and Rita jumped up and shouted in unison, "Go, Andy, go!" Sal snickered, amused by them. Their joy was short-lived, however. Andy was tackled by two Crusaders. Ginger and Rita grimaced, but Sal wore a sly smile.

"Damn it!" Danny pounded his fist on his thigh,

frustrated. "That T-formation isn't working for them today!"

Jim shook his head and groaned, "We just can't get around these guys! B.C.'s not going to win this way!"

Danny gaped at him in mock surprise. "I thought reporters were supposed to be unbiased," he chided.

"Yeah," Jim retorted with a chuckle. "In the paper."

An Eagles receiver fumbled a pass. The ball was intercepted by a Crusader. Jim threw his hands up in the air and yelled, "Come on, butterfingers!" He turned to Danny and declared, "That would be the day you'd have missed a pass like that from me!"

Danny nodded. "You know it!"

The Crusader started to run with the ball. Two Eagles pounced on him. A referee blew his whistle.

When the Holy Cross quarterback threw the ball, Andy leapt in front of the receiver and snatched it out of the air. Ginger and Rita jumped up and screamed with joy. Danny and Jim were ecstatic. B.C. fans were on the edge of their seats. They cheered Andy on as he sped to the end zone for a touchdown.

B.C. fans went wild. The Eagles' band played a victory song. Andy's teammates patted him on the back while his coaches applauded him. Grateful, B.C. priest Father Mike glanced up to the heavens and blessed himself.

Danny pumped the air with his fist and shouted, "All right! About time!"

Jim backhanded Danny's arm triumphantly and proclaimed, "That's what I'm talking about!"

Ginger and Rita were thrilled for Andy. Ginger beamed as the announcer bellowed, "Andy Logan has put the Boston College Eagles on the scoreboard!"

Ginger shouted out, "Atta boy, Andy!"

"Isn't he wonderful?" Rita gushed.

Sal rolled his eyes.

An Eagle kicked the football for the extra point. It went wide and missed the goal. Fans heckled him. The B.C. fans' excitement deflated with a collective groan.

"The score stands Holy Cross seven, Boston College six," the announcer reported.

Storm clouds rolled in as the game progressed. Despite the change in the weather, Holy Cross fans were euphoric because their team continued to dominate. It seemed the more depressed Boston College fans became the darker the sky got. They were frustrated that the mediocre Crusaders were leading thirteen to six in the second quarter. The Eagles had been undefeated all season. Something didn't feel right. It didn't make sense.

Sal kept checking his watch. He was about to break it to the girls that he needed to get back to the club when he spotted a sailor eyeing Ginger. Sal rose slowly. He aimed a piercing stare at the sailor and shouted a warning, "Listen up, pal! Don't get any ideas. She's taken!"

Ginger was mortified. She closed her eyes, wishing she could disappear. The sailor just shrugged and looked away. Sal sneered at him, satisfied that he'd made his point. He withdrew a wad of cash, peeled off a few bills, and handed some to each of the women.

Rita and Ginger stared at him, puzzled. "It's dough for a cab ride home so you don't have to take the streetcar," he explained. "I gotta get back to the Grove."

"Aw, Salvi," Rita whined.

"You're leaving?" Ginger asked, surprised that Sal never intended to stay until the end of the game. Though put off by this, her heart skipped a beat as it dawned on her that she might now get the chance to talk to Danny.

"It's business. I gotta do what I gotta do."

Rita pouted. Sal gave her a peck on the cheek and planted a kiss on Ginger. He told them, "Behave yourselves, and go right home after the game. Get yourselves all dolled up, and I'll see you two at the club tonight."

Sal left the box and trotted down the stairs out of sight. Once he was gone, Ginger could no longer hide her disdain. Rita mistook Ginger's mood for disappointment.

"Don't worry, honey, he's just busy," Rita offered. "It's gonna be a big night at the club. Lots of fellas are gonna be spending their last night on the town before they get shipped out." Rita stood up, looked around impishly, and loudly announced, "Don't forget B.C.'s victory party at the Cocoanut Grove tonight!"

Boston College fans sitting nearby hooted and applauded their approval. Their mood soon waned, however, when Holy Cross scored yet another touchdown.

In a shrill voice, Rita complained, "Aw, come on,

boys! You're breaking my heart! This isn't what we came to see!"

Ginger was also disheartened by the game, but she was more interested in keeping her eye on Danny and Jim.

Jim scribbled down the last play. He stuffed his notepad and pencil in his pocket. He leaned toward Danny and griped, "What a goddamn beating we're taking! Twenty-one to six? I'm heading below to beat the halftime crowd. Let me know if I miss anything." Jim tossed his cigarette down and made his way out of the box.

Ginger spotted Jim leaving and stood up. She started for the stairs, hoping to get some answers.

"Where you going?" Rita asked, bewildered.

"To powder my nose," Ginger answered, praying Rita wouldn't tag along.

"Now? Well, I'm not going with you. I wanna watch the game."

Relieved, Ginger descended the stairs in search of Jim. She scanned the lines of people waiting to buy refreshments at the indoor concession area. She took notice of each man who came out of the men's room. She spotted Jim exiting and cornered him.

Jim was caught off-guard. "Ginger. How you doing?"

Ginger landed on him like a ton of bricks. "How do you think I'm doing, Jimmy? For crying out loud, why didn't you tell me Danny's crippled?"

Jim felt like a bug trapped under glass and knew he had to come clean. He heaved a sigh. "Because *he* didn't want me to."

Ginger's heart sank. She knew right away that this was the truth. But she wasn't going to let Jim off the hook. She was determined to get the whole story this time. "What the hell happened to him?"

Jim removed his hat and nervously smoothed his dark, wavy hair. He put a finger to a jagged scar along his temple. "Remember how I told you I got this covering the fighting at Guadalcanal? And I told you that Danny got sick with malaria? Well, the truth is Danny got hit..." Jim explained, choking up, "...saving my life." He turned away, fighting tears.

Ginger shuddered. "Oh, Jimmy," she whispered, reaching out and gently touching his arm.

Jim went on. "At first, the doc thought he might never walk again."

Ginger gasped, horrified.

"When we got stateside, he could barely stand. He sunk deep. He didn't feel like a whole man, you know? So, before I left for home, he made me promise to make up a line to tell you." Jim looked away. "To let you down easy."

Ginger's eyes flashed with indignation. "Easy? I cried my heart out! We were going to get married and have kids! How could you tell me he was in love with another girl? Why didn't you tell me he was hurt? What the hell, Jimmy?"

Jim squirmed. Regretting what he'd put her through, he offered a weak defense. "Well, I knew you'd never let him go unless you thought he was with someone else."

Now that it was halftime, fans flooded into the concession area. Danny joined the line waiting for the restrooms. He stood behind a young soldier who was snuggling with his girl. When the couple separated to enter their respective restrooms, Danny saw Ginger with Jim and froze. Because he didn't move forward, the people waiting behind him pushed past.

Jim awkwardly tried to smooth things over with Ginger. "I'm sorry. It wasn't my call to make. He's my best friend, for Christ's sake."

"I thought I was your friend, too!" Ginger snapped.

Smarting, Jim assured her, "You are my friend, Ginger." He cleared his throat and put his hat back on. "Even though Danny got feeling back in the lower half of his body, he'll have to wear that leg brace for the rest of his life. And he doesn't want you saddled with a gimp."

"Jimmy!" Ginger scolded. She was appalled that he would ever call his best friend such a thing.

Jim caught sight of Danny watching them and seized the opportunity to slip out of this uncomfortable situation. He pointed Danny out to Ginger and said, "His word, not mine."

Ginger melted when she saw Danny. She waited expectantly, but Danny avoided her gaze.

Jim moved to Danny. "You're on your own now, buddy." He patted Danny's arm and walked away.

Danny could not bring himself to look at Ginger and those beautiful, pleading eyes. The longer he resisted, the more frustrated she became. People pushed past them in both directions. Ginger moved closer to face off with him.

"Will you please talk to me!" she insisted.

"I've got nothing to say," Danny said flatly.

Ginger was baffled by his reaction. "Nothing to say?"

"The game's about to start again," he muttered. "I've got to get back."

She stood her ground. "What you've got to do, mister, is look me in the eye and tell me the truth!"

Danny brushed past her, starting for the men's room. Ginger grabbed his sleeve. He looked at her, tormented. Ginger's eyes filled with tears as she pressed for answers. "Why would you think your injury would make a difference?"

"Because it does!" Danny spat back bitterly.

"Not to me!" Ginger insisted.

"Well, it does to me!"

Ginger's heart broke for him. She could not imagine the depth of emotional pain he must be in to believe his disability would ever keep her from loving him. She would not be daunted by his bitterness or accept this pretense that he no longer loved her. Ginger loosened her grip on his sleeve and reminded him, "You used to say we could weather anything as long as we had our love. When did you stop believing that?"

Danny knew she was right, but he'd be damned if he'd put her through a life of living with half a man. Though it hurt like hell and he hated what he was about to do, it was for her own good. He lifted a hand to her face and wiped a tear from her cheek. He drew in a breath to steel himself. Then he pulled back on his bow and let the arrow fly. "When I saw you kissing Sal Russo."

His words had met their mark. Devastated, Ginger stood there trembling.

Danny abruptly moved off to enter the men's room.

Rita pressed her way through the concession area toward Ginger. She saw Danny hobbling away and scrunched up her nose in disgust. Sensing Ginger's distress, Rita wrapped a comforting arm around her and said, "Well, it looks like that two-timer got what's coming to him. Don't worry, honey, you wouldn't want to be with a crippled fella anyway. He can't ever give you the kind of life my brother can. Come on. Let's go get an orangeade."

CHAPTER FOUR

It was just after three-thirty when Sal parked his Cadillac in the V.I.P. section of a garage a block away from the Cocoanut Grove. He hoped it would make a good impression if he came in early and checked to see that everything was ready for the big night.

Sal was in a pretty good mood until he found the club's corner door unlocked. Furious, he charged in. He slammed the door and locked it with his key. Despite the fact that the door had a glowing exit sign right above it, he pushed on its panic bar to satisfy himself that it would not open. He stormed down the dimly lit corridor past the stairway that led to the Melody Lounge, the nightclub's basement bar.

Katherine was busy counting out money in the club's office. The precise cashier had stacked bills neatly on the ostentatious walnut desk. Sal bristled in. The bills fluttered up into the air and down onto the floor. She scurried to collect them.

While the room was not big on space, no corners

were cut on the décor. Three matching hobnailed, oxblood leather upholstered chairs gave it the feel of a high-profile lawyer's office. A bottle of aged scotch and several fine whiskey tumblers sat atop a tall, wooden filing cabinet.

Sal's eyes narrowed. Without warning, he slammed his keys down on the desk, startling Katherine. He launched into a tirade, bellowing, "What's the big idea leaving the corner door unlocked? And you're in here counting out dough, Katherine? What if Mr. Welansky got wind of this? You'd be canned! And me, right along with ya! You're responsible for all that money, you know. If something happened to it, you'd have to pay it back!"

His assault made Katherine quiver. "I'm so sorry, Mr. Russo. I let your cousins into the Broadway Lounge and forgot to lock up. It won't happen again. I promise."

"Damn right it won't!" Sal sneered.

Sal shrugged off his topcoat. He draped it around a sturdy wooden hanger and hung it, along with his hat, on a coatrack. Retrieving the ill-gotten permit from the inner pocket of his topcoat, he smirked at his coup. He neatened his well-tailored black suit, thinking how it had really paid off to make friends with a city official on the take. He fished out some tacks from the desk drawer, grabbed his keys, and growled at Katherine, "Don't forget to lock up this office when you leave."

Without a second look, Sal strode out. He nonchalantly posted the latest permit for electrical wiring on the wall outside the office. It was already covered with permits and licenses—some legit, some not.

As the third quarter of the game commenced at Fenway Park, Danny returned to the press box and plunked down next to Jim. His hands shook as he lit a cigarette.

Jim waited impatiently, but Danny wasn't forthcoming. Irritated, Jim griped, "I felt like a nickel with Ginger."

Danny ignored him. He focused on the game, trying to keep his emotions in check.

Not wanting to draw attention to them, Jim kept his voice low. "You drive me wacky! Anybody would think you took the hit to the head instead of me. A dame like Ginger? The girl's a knockout, and it's obvious she's still crazy about you! She thinks you hung the moon, for Christ's sake!"

Danny just shook his head.

"Jesus, Danny, I always thought you had more guts than this. Why are you letting that brace stop you? Smarten up, will you!"

"My leg's not the only part of me that doesn't work anymore, Jim!" Danny sniped back bitterly.

Jim was stunned. For once, he had no comeback.

Sal strutted into the Cocoanut Grove's arched foyer and crossed the carpeted floor to the main entrance. The prominent revolving door was not operational until they were open for business. He pulled back the velvet drapery that kept the single plate glass door beside it cleverly hidden. He checked to be sure the door was locked and then straightened the drape to conceal it again. He turned to head toward the main room but paused to glance across the foyer at the unattended coat checkroom.

Sal recalled how he had done whatever he had to do to sneak a peek at Ginger when she worked behind that coat check counter. He had come up with every excuse in the book to go to the office or the Melody Lounge just so he could walk through the foyer. Sal chuckled to himself thinking about how he'd pretended to make calls in one of the two phone booths there.

He had always wished she'd get moved somewhere he could see her better but *not* to cigarette girl. That would have driven him crazy. He would never have been able to stand seeing guys putting their paws all over her. So, instead, he had finagled to have her made a cashier selling drink tickets across from the maître d's podium.

Katherine hadn't wanted to give up that prime spot. Though she'd squawked at first, he'd laid it on thick. He'd managed to convince her that the customers who spent time in the Melody Lounge were heavier drinkers than the upstairs crowd, and he trusted her more than the new gal to handle the dough in that dim lighting. He'd also told her it was necessary to have someone with her experience to keep up with the pace. To tip the scales, he'd added that he'd see to it she got made head cashier. It had worked like a charm.

Now he had Ginger right where he wanted her. He could keep an eye on her from any angle in the main room all night long. Besides, it was a step up for Ginger. She was happy to be making more dough, and the customers loved her. He felt as if he'd hit the trifecta! It was good for her, good for the club, and great for him. If he could have patted himself on the back, he would have.

Sal moved on through a wide archway to the ritzy main room, passing the maître d's podium to his left and the cashier's station to his right. Frank, the tuxedoed maître d', was on the phone. He stood behind the podium before a shimmering drapery backdrop and confirmed, "Daley. Party of four. Seven o'clock," as he logged it in the reservation book.

Sal turned by the Caricature Bar, so named because it was adorned with drawings and photographs of celebrities and noteworthy patrons. This prestigious, forty-eight-foot, elliptical bar was the jewel of the main room. Perched on a raised platform surrounded by a railing, it offered a bird's eye view of the dance floor and the stage. Below it, on the main floor, were dining tables partially covered by a colorful Spanish tile canopy. Both the bar and the stationary stools encircling it were awash in richly padded crimson leatherette. A grand liquor bottle display dominated its center island, and small star-shaped mirrors dotted the paneled ceiling.

Behind the Caricature Bar, a smaller bar was tucked in an alcove on the Piedmont Street side of the club. Plush red settees lined the wall. Little tables accompanied them.

Sal sauntered into the glamorous dining and dancing area. It featured six artificial palm trees bordering the vast dance floor and offered the illusion of attending an elegant party under the stars. In the summertime, the ceiling was rolled back to allow a view of natural starlight. Billowy, dark blue satin covered the ceiling in the colder months to simulate a night sky. To complete the tropical effect, the walls were graced with wrought-iron lanterns and lined with porthole-shaped mirrors mimicking the windows of a cruise ship.

The Terrace, an elevated area made to resemble a Spanish-styled courtyard, overlooked the dance floor and provided the best view of the stage. An ornate wrought-iron railing bordered it on three sides. A short set of stairs at its center led to dining tables. Via a stairway beneath the Terrace, waiters were bringing up dinnerware from the kitchen.

Sal eyed the stage as he crossed the dance floor. Before a luxurious drapery backdrop that concealed the performers' entrance, musicians' podiums monogrammed "M A," a free-standing microphone, a full set of drums, and several conga drums awaited the orchestra.

He maneuvered past waiters setting linen-covered tables beneath another Spanish tile canopy on the opposite side of the room from the Caricature Bar. Below an illuminated exit sign, Sal opened two Venetian doors that created a façade hiding double doors to Shawmut Street. He ensured that the actual exit doors were locked, as well as the bolt at the top of one of them, before covering them up again.

Sal acted like he owned the joint the way he stalked around giving the place a once-over to assure everything was getting done. He figured making himself indispensable would cinch him a spot on the boss' radar. He was proud to be associated with the Grove. After all, it *was* the classiest nightclub in Boston, and he kind of liked that it had a bit of a scandalous past. During the days of Prohibition, notorious mobster Charles "King" Solomon ran it as a speakeasy. When he was gunned down in 1933, his lawyer, Barnett Welansky, took it over. "Barney" turned it into a very profitable, legitimate business that drew big name performers. Barney Welansky was someone Sal could respect.

Barney's brother James, filling in as manager of the club, swaggered into the dining area smoking a cigar. Though only in his forties, his bald head and stocky build made the shrewd businessman look older. He carried himself with an air of entitlement in his expensive double-breasted suit. He called out, "Sal!

Come here a minute!"

Sal adjusted his tie and hastened to respond. He was honored that a guy like Jimmy Welansky even remembered his name.

Welansky, having an ulterior motive, uncharacteristically doled out a little praise to Sal. "Barney would be happy to see you're checking them doors."

Sal's ego inflated, but he chose to stay as cool as a cucumber. "We wouldn't want anybody skipping out without paying their tab, right? By the way, Mr. Welansky, I ran into the mayor and the fire commissioner at the game. I figured you'd want them to stop by to see the new lounge, so I extended a personal invitation."

"Good. Too bad Barney couldn't be here to show it off."

"How's the boss doing?"

"Not so good. He's still in the hospital. It's too bad his ticker gave out on Thanksgiving, eh? Sal, you've got to help me out. I've got my own business to run, so I need you to take charge of things around here while Barney's out of commission."

Sal was on cloud nine. He'd been waiting for an opportunity like this his whole life. "Don't worry, Mr. Welansky. You can count on me to do whatever you need."

"Barney said I could." Welansky slapped Sal on the back. "There'll be something in it for you. We take care of our own. You're going to go places with us, kid."

Sal puffed up with self-importance. If he stayed in the Welanskys' good graces, he could finally buy his mother a big house. No more living in a lousy tenement flat for him and Rita! And maybe he could get one with an attached garage for his Caddy.

Welansky studied Sal. Something about him seemed familiar. "You're Vinny Russo's kid, aren't you?"

Sal was caught off-guard. Unsure where Welansky was going with this, he nodded hesitantly.

"It's a shame he was such a schmuck, slipping up and landing in the joint. There's no room for mistakes in this business, Sal."

The words stung. Sal winced. He hoped his old man's screwup wouldn't get in his way.

Welansky patted his shoulder. "Now go and see if those electricians are done adding that exit sign. We wouldn't want my brother getting pinched for forgetting something so stupid. If they did a good job, reward them with a little something extra from our private stash."

Sal nodded. He headed across the room, passed the Caricature Bar, and went through a doorway with an "Employees Only" sign posted above it. He wound his way along a shadowy corridor and strode into the Broadway Lounge. Sal watched Dominic and Gino finish connecting the exit sign over the lounge's public entrance. Dominic flipped a switch, and the new sign lit up. Sal gave his cousins a big smile, and said, "That oughtta do it. Nobody can squawk now."

"This is a pretty snazzy watering hole," Gino

remarked.

Sal nodded, admiring the room. It was encircled by round mirrors and a border of stars. Two side-by-side glass block windows and a multitude of chrome-rimmed tables offered a contemporary feel. Sal slid his hand along the sleek, curvy bar and appreciated its well-stocked, striking liquor bottle display. He straightened one of the tall leather stools that lined the bar. He left his cousins to finish up their work and reentered the main room.

At the Caricature Bar, Arthur, the debonair head bartender, was setting up for the evening while listening to the game on a portable radio. With a touch of grey at his temples, he looked elegant in a crisp white shirt, a black bow tie, and black trousers. He twisted open a bottle of liquor, breaking the paper tax seal. He inserted a pouring spout and added the bottle to the elaborate display. He panned the club and heaved a melancholy sigh. Seeing Sal approaching, he busied himself preparing garnishes for cocktails.

Sal stopped to listen to the radio for an update on the game. When he heard that Holy Cross was leading by a wide margin, he snickered, arousing Arthur's suspicion.

Sal removed his suit coat, exposing a handgun tucked in a leather shoulder holster. He draped the coat over a barstool. His white silk shirt clung to his muscular physique. He retrieved a metal stepladder from a small utility closet nearby and set it up behind the bar. Arthur watched him climb the ladder and slide back a ceiling panel to reveal a trapdoor. Sal pushed the trapdoor open and reached up inside. Arthur asked him coyly, "Mr. Welansky know you're getting into his private stock?"

Sal immediately got defensive. "What's it to ya?"

"You know his motto, 'Trust no one'," Arthur reminded him.

Eyeing Arthur warily, Sal handed down two bottles of whiskey to him. He pulled the trapdoor shut then slid the ceiling panel back again before descending the ladder.

Arthur placed the bottles on the bar and examined them. Something didn't look right. He studied them and realized they had no tax seals. As he thought about just how many cases of liquor King Solomon had left behind up there, a shrewd smile came to his face. He now knew they were all illegal. And he knew the Welansky brothers knew it, too.

Sal slipped out through the end of the bar near the entrance to the Broadway Lounge. Dominic and Gino appeared in the doorway as he put his suit coat back on and buttoned it up. "All set?" Sal asked.

"Yup. There shouldn't be any problems now," Dominic assured him.

Sal took out his wad of cash, peeled off some bills, and paid each of them. He grabbed the bottles of whiskey off the bar. "Compliments of Mr. 'W'," he said, handing one to each of them. "Dom, he really appreciates you coming back and getting it done before tonight."

His cousins beamed and eagerly accepted the bottles. "Thanks!" Dominic and Gino said in unison.

Dominic added, "I appreciate you getting me the work, Sal. There aren't a lot of people willing to hire unlicen—"

Sal cut him off, "Ah, don't worry about it. We're family, right?"

Arthur, never one to miss a trick, tucked that information away.

"What a day for the Crusaders!" the radio announcer proclaimed. "With less than three minutes to play, has all hope for the Eagles flown away?"

Dominic and Gino looked to one another, surprised. "You really think they could lose?" Gino asked the others.

"There doesn't appear to be any way out of this one," Arthur lamented.

"Gonna be a big payday for somebody," Sal snidely piped in with a sly grin.

Arthur didn't have to think too hard to figure out who that "somebody" might be.

"Arthur! Get rid of that ladder," Sal ordered.

Arthur bristled but complied.

Sal beckoned his cousins. "Come on, boys. I'll let yous out."

Cradling their booty, Dominic and Gino dutifully followed Sal.

Arthur opened the utility closet, shoved the stepladder inside, and slammed the door shut.

Sal escorted his cousins to the foyer. He stopped at the podium and demanded to know from Frank where the usual maître d' was.

Frank was a little put off by Sal's tone. However,

having overheard that Sal was in charge for the time being, he curtly informed him, "Mr. Lippi's out sick. I'm covering."

"*Gesù Cristo!*" This was a big weekend. It irritated Sal that he wouldn't have the experienced maître d' to lean on. Needing to know, though almost hesitant to find out, he asked, "How's it looking for tonight?"

Frank didn't hold back from giving it to him straight. "Reservations for over three hundred already, and it's only five o'clock."

Sal felt the nerve in his cheek twitch. He grumbled to Frank, "I better warn the kitchen."

Frank watched as Sal led the two men into the foyer. He was gleeful that Sal was chafing under the weight of his responsibilities. But he also knew with somebody like Sal running the show, it was going to be a long night.

Sal shook hands with Dominic and Gino in the corridor by the office and gave each one a thankful pat on the back. He let them out the corner door, locked it behind them, and headed down to the Melody Lounge. Its narrow stairway felt claustrophobic with all the fish netting hanging from the walls and billowy material covering the ceiling.

In the tropically themed lounge, Sal squeezed by tables and chairs that crowded every available space. Dim light emitted from small bulbs in faux palm trees situated in each corner. Zebra-striped leatherette settees lined the perimeter. Driftwood, fish netting, and rattan adorned the fabric and leatherette covered walls. Like the main room above, its canopied, dark blue satin ceiling gave the impression of a night sky.

Sal skirted around the large octagonal bar that showcased within it an upright piano on an elevated platform. He opened a door camouflaged in the wall and stepped into a short corridor. He moved through it and entered the bustling kitchen, where the staff was busy prepping food for that evening. Sal shouted out to the tall, mustached head chef, "It's gonna be a full house!"

CHAPTER FIVE

At dusk, a cold mist settled over Fenway Park. It reflected the dismal mood of Boston College fans. A horn blew, signaling the end of the football game. B.C. fans were stunned. Holy Cross fans, though surprised as well, were jubilant. The Crusaders had beaten the Eagles 55–12. The newspapermen in the press box muttered amongst themselves about the incredible upset.

"No going to the Sugar Bowl now," Jim griped.

"That game had to be fixed! They haven't lost all season! I'll bet Russo had something to do with it," Danny bellyached.

"They could have just had a bad day, I suppose. Still, it does seem fishy," Jim agreed. "I wouldn't put it past that arrogant son of a bitch."

"It wouldn't be the first time," Danny reminded him. "Remember how his old man fixed that game when we were in school? Imagine what Sal would make off this game with four-to-one odds?"

Jim raised his eyebrows as he calculated. He whistled long and low.

Danny shook his head in disgust. "It's all about the almighty buck. He's just like his old man. Running a racket. People don't matter. He has no respect for the game or all the hard work the guys put into it. And if not him, there's always another two-bit hood around every corner."

Ginger and Rita paced outside the bus lot's chain-link fence, trying to keep warm while they waited. The football players sporadically exited the building and boarded their team buses. No longer in uniform, many wore letterman jackets. Rita's eyes lit up when she saw Andy come out. She nudged Ginger, and they both called to him.

Andy moped to the fence, head hanging and hands stuffed in his pockets. He murmured, "Hey, Sis."

Rita smiled coyly and piped in, "Hi, Andy."

Andy gave Rita a weak smile. "Hey, Rita." He kicked at a stone in the parking lot. "I can't believe we lost," he groaned.

Seeing how disappointed Andy was, Rita frowned.

"But *you* played great," Ginger said.

"Didn't help much," he grumbled.

Rita attempted to cheer him up. "That's okay,

Andy. You can dance your troubles away tonight at the Grove. With me."

"Yeah. I'll be there, too. It'll be fun," Ginger added.

Andy heaved a sigh. "I don't think I'm going."

Rita moaned, crestfallen.

"Coach canceled our party at the Grove," Andy griped.

"Oh, no!" Rita gasped, thinking how much this would upset Sal.

"Yeah. Instead, he's making us go to the mayor's stinking Holy Cross party at the Parker House," he said and then added sarcastically, "to show our good sportsmanship."

"You should come see the Grove's new bar afterwards! It's really something!" Rita said.

Andy shrugged. "I don't know. None of the guys are in the mood now." He didn't realize he was breaking Rita's heart. He turned to Ginger. "Hey, Sis. Um... I've got something to tell you. Danny's back! And he's in a leg brace!"

Rita scowled and watched for Ginger's reaction. Ginger avoided her gaze and quietly told him, "I know."

Andy was bewildered. He wanted to ask her how she knew. But the bus engines revved up, alerting him that he had to go. He rushed off yelling back to Ginger, "See you at home, Sis."

Rita pouted when Andy boarded the bus without even saying goodbye to her.

The *Boston City Press* newsroom was alive with ringing telephones, competing voices, and the clacking keys and dinging carriages of typewriters. Seated side-by-side in rows of desks, reporters scrambled to get their stories in on time.

Jim typed rapidly, sleeves rolled up, a cigarette dangling from his lips. Danny maneuvered through the crowded room and dropped his developed photographs on Jim's desk. Jim leafed through them. Before he could make a comment, their boss barreled over.

Eddie Eisner was stout and balding. Despite his gruff demeanor, he held a soft spot for Danny and Jim. He had been an editor for more than fifteen years and could always spot raw talent. He chomped on an unlit cigar and growled, "How was your first day back, McGuire?"

"Okay, Eddie," Danny answered, trying to sound confident.

"Reed, what have we got?"

Jim held up the photograph of the B.C. co-captains, wearing the numbers "55" and "12," and said, "The Crusaders beat the Eagles fifty-five to twelve. Eerie coincidence, huh?"

Always impressed by Jim's clever angles on stories, Eddie's eyes gleamed. "I like it! We'll work that into the headline."

Jim grinned.

Eddie continued, "I'm still sending Flynn and Ross to cover the winning team, only now they'll be going to the Parker House. After all, they're familiar with all the Holy Cross kids' pedigrees."

Jim looked to Danny behind Eddie's back and rolled his eyes but turned back to Eddie and nodded in agreement. Danny coughed to hide a laugh.

Eddie suppressed a smile. He knew that sending his ace reporters, Flynn and Ross, instead of his sports guys would rankle Jim and Danny. He picked up Danny's photographs and shuffled through them. He was intrigued by the one of Sal and a notable city official outside the Cocoanut Grove. "What's going on here?"

Danny and Jim had been caught red-handed. They sought a cue from one another on the best way to answer. Although Jim was the one who had insisted on getting a picture, Danny knew he had to accept responsibility for taking it on the company's dime. He wanted to be truthful and hoped Eddie would go easy on him since it was his first day back. "Jim got a tip that a bribe was going down, so I went to see what I could get."

Eddie paused for a long time, thinking about what he could offer Jim and Danny after all their hard work. He eyed them shrewdly. Jim was ready for a tongue-lashing. But, instead, Eddie told them, "I want you two to go to the Grove. See what people are saying about the game's outcome and get a comment from Buck Jones. And sniff out what else is going on there."

Jim was thrilled that Eddie thought enough of them to give them the Grove assignment. He checked Danny for his reaction. Danny's face gave nothing away, and he remained quiet. Jim raised an eyebrow as Eddie strode back to his office. Once their boss was out of earshot, Jim asked Danny, "Did he just give us his blessing?"

"Sounds like it." Danny raked a hand through his sandy blond hair. "So, we're going to the Grove. That's just great. So much for getting steaks at Durgin Park. I guess it's sandwiches for us now."

Ignoring Danny's annoyance, Jim opened a desk drawer. He fingered through file folders, paused on one labeled "GUADALCANAL," and lamented, "It's lousy that we got nicked before our coverage paid off."

Danny's jaw tightened. "We sure sacrificed an awful lot for nothing. Not to mention all the horrible shit we saw. I hope I never have to cover anything like that again."

"I realize you hated it, but people need to see the truth, Danny. And a battlefield isn't the only place where bad shit happens," Jim countered.

Danny shrugged off his comment.

Jim withdrew a folder labeled "COCOANUT GROVE" from his drawer. It contained his notes and typewritten pages, newspaper clippings, and additional photographs. He slipped the picture of Sal and the city official into the folder triumphantly and boasted, "When we expose what those gangsters have been up to and all the contractors, inspectors, cops, lawyers, and crooked politicians in cahoots with them, it will finally be our ticket out of the sports pages."

Danny was skeptical. "You really think it'll make a difference?"

"If we get enough proof, it will."

Danny was so tired of this topic. It was all Jim was interested in lately. Having heard enough, Danny asked, "What time is it?"

Jim glanced at his watch. "It's almost seven." He filed the folder away and took out a fresh notepad.

Danny made an appeal to Jim, "Let's just get what we need at the Grove and get the hell out of there."

"Aw, Danny," Jim whined. "It's Saturday night, and it's the hottest spot in town! We can have a few drinks and catch the show. Let's have a good time."

"Sure. And I'll take a few spins on the dance floor while I'm at it," Danny quipped. A nightclub was the last place he wanted to be, especially one where Ginger worked.

Jim frowned. Then it dawned on him. "If you're worried about running into Ginger, don't. She doesn't work on Saturday nights anymore."

"Well, I'll tell you, if she was there, I'd make damn sure she wised up about running around with that thug."

"What do you care?"

Danny's eyes flashed.

Jim tried to smooth Danny's ruffled feathers. "Come on. We can snoop around and see if we can find that brand new wiring permit. Maybe get a picture of it." Jim could see that he'd sparked Danny's interest, so he laid it on a little thicker. "And we've got to say so long to Arthur."

Danny sighed. "Yeah, I do want to see Arthur." From a coatrack where his bomber jacket and a grey wool topcoat were hanging, he retrieved a dark blue suit.

Jim spied an ugly necktie dangling from the hanger. "I hope you're not planning on wearing *that* tie! Come here." Jim opened another desk drawer to reveal several tasteful neckties folded on top of neatly stacked dress shirts. He chose a stylish blue and silver tie, held it up to Danny's suit, and said, "Ah, much better." He hung the tie around Danny's neck. He grabbed Danny's ugly tie off the hanger and quipped, "I wouldn't even put this on a snowman!"

Danny laughed self-consciously as Jim chucked it into a wastebasket.

Ginger sat in the cozy kitchen of her family's home. Fresh from a bath and bundled up in a pink chenille robe, she sipped a hot cup of tea. The Logans lived on an urban street in a modest house that her father had been able to afford without difficulty before the Great Depression. She absently traced a finger along an intricate vine of roses her mother had expertly embroidered on the tablecloth. Tempting homemade cookies were within reach, yet Ginger ignored them. She just drank her tea and dwelled on her thoughts.

Her mind sifted through memories of Danny from her schoolgirl crush on him, to their eventual first date, to the thrill of their first kiss. Though she had a smile on her lips, there were tears in her eyes.

Ginger heard Andy bustle into the house. She knew he would stop in the parlor to chat with their parents. She used to be able to hear their father's voice loud and strong throughout the house, but now it seemed so soft and feeble. He'd been unwell for years. For the last couple of months, he wasn't able to work at all. Financial stress had taken its toll. He was so weak it scared her. She knew her father had made an effort to listen to each and every play of the game on the radio and that he would praise Andy for the contribution of his touchdown. But their mother, seeing the sadness on Andy's face because the Eagles had lost the big game, would start to cry and hug him like he was a six-year-old who had skinned his knee. Ginger also knew Andy would try to escape this as fast as possible.

Andy clamored into the kitchen, poured a tumbler of ice-cold milk, and guzzled a third of it before noticing Ginger. After grabbing a cookie and devouring it, he asked, "So, what's up with Danny?"

Andy gobbled down two more cookies while Ginger filled him in on all that Jim had told her. Andy had his mouth full and almost choked when she said the doctor's first thought was that Danny might never walk again. Brushing cookie crumbs from his lips with the back of his hand, Andy mumbled, "Holy moly!"

Ginger placed her teacup down and buried her

face in her hands.

Not knowing what else to do, Andy stroked the back of her head. When she looked up, he said, "So Jimmy told you a lie."

"Yeah. A whopper!"

Andy polished off his milk and put his glass in the sink. He leaned back against the counter. "What are you going to do, Sis?"

Ginger took another sip of tea before answering, "I don't know. Danny doesn't want anything to do with me now."

"What? Really?"

Ginger nodded. "He's so angry that I've been seeing Sal. But he made Jimmy convince me that he didn't want me anymore. What was I supposed to do? Sit around and never go on another date?"

Andy closed his eyes and scrunched up his face. "No. But Sal? Did you have to pick Sal? Danny hates that guy!"

"I know. When I agreed to go out with him, I thought it would only be a couple dates. I never expected him to stick with me. Now I don't know how to get out of it." She groaned. "I should've known Danny would never have fallen for another girl. And even if he did, he would have told me himself. How could I have been so stupid?"

Andy sighed. "I still can't believe Danny's crippled."

Ginger swiped at the tears trickling down her face. "He only did what he did to spare me. But did he think I'd never find out what really happened to him? It's not fair! He's put me in a real pickle."

CHAPTER SIX

Despite freezing drizzle, scores of patrons waited on the sidewalk outside the Cocoanut Grove. Cars filled its small parking lot and lined the length of Piedmont Street. It was a sharp contrast to how deserted it had been nine hours earlier. There was a long line to pass through the center archway to the entrance where everyone had to make their way in, one at a time, via the revolving door.

The line was moving at a snail's pace. Impatient to get inside, Jim shook his head and complained, "You'd think they'd have more than one way into this joint besides that useless revolving door!"

Danny chuckled. He gazed up at the Grove's vertical neon sign. It glowed seductively. His pulse quickened as he recalled how often he and Ginger had danced the night away here. It had always filled him with excitement to have the chance to hold Ginger close. But that was never going to happen again.

"I'm surprised they still keep that sign lit. No one

can even have Christmas lights this year," Danny noted.

Jim added irreverently, "You never know when that Luftwaffe might fly over."

While those who had overheard Jim shuddered and looked up to the sky, Jim and Danny moved forward and entered the club.

The joint was jumping. The popular Glenn Miller tune "In the Mood" was filtering into the foyer live from the main room. The peppy music prompted spirited patrons to move their feet to the rhythm. As Jim brushed water droplets from his shoulders in time to the music, he feigned a few dance steps of his own. Danny rolled his eyes at him.

Marilyn, a tall, voluptuous, young redhead working the coat check counter, spied Jim's antics. She appreciated his sense of humor. He was her definition of tall, dark, and handsome, and he always looked refined. His suits fit him like he had a personal tailor, and every hair on his head stayed in place as though they dared not disobey. He carried himself with an air of self-assurance. He wasn't conceited; it was just that he was usually happy with himself and what he was doing, and it showed.

Since Danny hadn't been around in a while, she hadn't expected to see him with Jim. Those two could always light up a room. In the past, Danny had appeared larger than life, a man who shone with star quality. Now he seemed lost, uncomfortable in his own skin, a shadow of the man who'd come in often with the world on a string and Ginger on his arm. There was no longer a bounce in his step. When she saw the brace, she realized how much that must have changed his life.

Danny and Jim joined the long line at the coat checkroom. They removed their topcoats, shook the moisture from their hats, and then transferred their press passes from their hats to their suit coats. Danny resituated the satchel on his shoulder.

At the counter, Jim handed his coat and hat to Marilyn. Danny waited to check his coat with either Vera, a demure black girl, or Rosie, a cute brunette.

Ever the charismatic charmer, Jim smoothed his hair and made sure his tie was straight before giving Marilyn a wink. "What's cookin', good-lookin'?"

Marilyn smiled coyly.

"How was your Thanksgiving?" Jim asked.

"Great. How was yours?"

Jim patted his flat belly. "Ate too much, as usual."

Marilyn laughed.

"Kind of busy in here tonight," Jim observed.

"Yeah. Being a holiday weekend, it's already madness." Marilyn handed him his claim check.

As soon as Danny's turn came, he walked up to the counter with a big smile. "Hi, Rosie."

Rosie's eyes twinkled warmly. "Danny? Sure is good to see you!"

"Nice to see you, too." Danny gave her his coat and hat. He took his claim check and followed Jim toward the main room.

Rosie spotted Danny's brace and her heart sank. She nudged Marilyn to draw her attention to it. "Poor guy. I wonder if Ginger knows."

"After what he's put her through, I wonder if it would make any difference," Marilyn speculated.

A scary thought crossed Rosie's mind. "Do you think Sal knows he's back?"

Danny and Jim navigated around a group of customers waiting to be seated in the dining area, which was filling up fast. Frank, the maître d', stepped out from behind the podium and stopped two black soldiers from entering.

Jim leaned into Danny's ear and said, "For crying out loud. Someone like Vera is allowed to work here, but she couldn't order a drink any more than these two poor guys who are willing to fight for their country."

Danny shook his head in disgust. "I know. It's just ridiculous."

Danny and Jim bought drink tickets from a pleasant female cashier who deftly kept the line moving, then they joined people flooding to the Caricature Bar.

The Grove's patrons were dressed to the nines. Distinguished men strutted about with glamorous women. Friends and relatives greeted each other warmly as they met up. Many military men on leave, sporting crisp dress uniforms, were embraced with great joy by those who had missed them.

Bandleader Mickey Alpert led his formally dressed orchestra as couples danced to the music in the main room. In his late thirties and dapper in a white dinner jacket, he commanded the stage.

Arthur and several other bartenders, also dressed in classic white dinner jackets, masterfully handled the crowd at the Caricature Bar. Danny mounted its platform's stairs by easing his lame leg up one step at a time. He and Jim maneuvered past clusters of people at the busy, smoky bar. They made their way to the far end by the employees' entrance to the Broadway Lounge and took seats near a group of rowdy soldiers. Danny stored his satchel beneath his bar stool.

A gung-ho soldier raised his glass to his companions and proclaimed, "Those Jerries aren't gonna know what hit 'em when we get over there!"

The other soldiers whooped in agreement. They clinked their glasses and toasted one another.

Danny leaned into Jim and said, "Poor bastards don't know what they're in for."

Jim cleared his throat. He was hesitant to lower the boom, but it was now or never. "By the way, I've been meaning to tell you something." He looked Danny in the eye. "I'm going to sign up." He waited for Danny's response.

Danny knew this news was inevitable. Still, it felt like a punch to his stomach. Although he had no desire to witness any more bloodshed, it bothered him that he would be unable to do his part. His injury would keep him from the warfront.

Since they were little, they'd faced every challenge in life together. Now Jim would be going without him. The fact that Jim could die over there scared the hell out of him.

To smooth over the awkward moment, Jim made light of his decision. "Well, I figure guys like them," gesturing toward the soldiers, "are going to need somebody to show them the ropes."

Danny wasn't about to let on that he was afraid for Jim, so he teased, "Don't you think you're tempting fate going without me?"

Jim's eyes twinkled. "Maybe. You've gotten me out of plenty of scrapes. And it *will* be my first adventure without you. I'm going to feel like Laurel without Hardy!"

"Or Crosby without Hope," Danny quipped, giving him a wry smile.

"Oh, yeah. Me without hope. Ha. Ha. Ha." Jim was relieved that Danny had taken the news so well.

Arthur delivered a martini to a waiter holding a tray of drinks at the end of the bar. The debonair bartender spotted Jim. He went over with a welcoming smile. He and Jim shook hands. Delighted to see Danny, he clasped his hand and shook it, too.

"King Arthur! I've missed you," Danny told him.

"I've missed you, as well," Arthur said sincerely. "Quite a crushing defeat for B.C. today."

Danny and Jim groaned.

The bartender grinned. "Oh, enough about that. What can I get you two fine gentlemen?"

Danny answered promptly, "This gentleman will have a Dewars."

"That martini you just made looked pretty good. Can you make me one of those?" Jim asked.

"I can, and I shall." Arthur moved off to prepare the drinks.

Danny snickered. Jim pretended to be offended. "What?"

"Who do you think you are, Cary Grant?"

"What's wrong with being sophisticated?"

"Nothing," Danny scoffed. "But you can be classy without looking like a sissy."

"Hey, if it's good enough for F.D.R., it's good enough for me."

As a fan of the president, Danny had to agree with this point.

"And for your information, mister smart guy, there's more booze in a martini than in your scotch."

Arthur smiled and nodded in agreement with Jim as he placed down their drinks with panache. Danny laughed and shook his head, unconvinced. "I've got this one," he told Jim. He thanked Arthur and handed him drink tickets and a tip.

Arthur took a bow. Danny and Jim chuckled. Jim motioned Arthur nearer and boasted, "We got Sal paying off that city official."

Arthur leaned in close. Jim and Danny were all ears as Arthur snidely informed them, "And, as if that wasn't bad enough, Sal brought in his unlicensed cousin Dominic again to do the work."

Danny groaned. Jim grumbled, "That figures." He took a sip of his martini. "I appreciate you giving me the heads-up about that permit, Arthur."

"It was the least I could do after Sal kindly invited me to leave," the bartender said with a wily grin.

Danny lamented to Arthur, "I couldn't believe it when Jim told me this was your last night. You've been a fixture here for years!"

Arthur's mood dimmed. "Too many years,

according to Sal."

"You going to be okay, Arthur?" Danny asked.

"Oh, don't worry about me. I will find something else," he assured him. When a couple of sailors beckoned, Arthur left to wait on them.

A glamorous brunette across the bar gave Danny a seductive smile. Jim noticed and nudged him. "Say, she's got eyes for you."

"Sure. She can't see the brace," Danny muttered cynically.

Jim ignored Danny's pessimism. He was too focused on the stunning blonde in an elegant, black cocktail dress heading his way. She carried a tray before her that was secured by a ribbon around her neck. It displayed cigars, cigarettes, and Cocoanut Grove matchbooks. As she approached, Jim flashed her a charming smile and beckoned her closer. "Hellooo, Mary! Come on over here. How've you been?"

Mary cozied up to him. "Missing you, handsome."

"Well, you don't have to miss me anymore," Jim purred.

Danny was amused by Jim's shameless flirting.

Jim, with his eyes still focused on Mary, tapped Danny's arm. "Meet Mary, the new cigarette girl. Mary, this here's my partner in crime, Danny McGuire."

Danny lifted his glass to her.

Mary waved back at him. She leaned in closer to Jim. They put their heads together, laughing and chatting in hushed tones.

Danny savored his scotch as he took in the club through the smoky haze. Waiters, outfitted in neat white jackets and black bow ties, moved about the dining area serving meals and bringing drinks. Couples flocked to the dance floor to take advantage of the orchestra's latest set.

Danny looked toward the foyer. People continued to pour into the club. His heart stopped. Ginger was in line with Rita at the coat checkroom. Hoping to escape being seen by her, he considered ducking into the Broadway Lounge until he noticed the "Employees Only" sign. He prodded Jim, who was busy admiring the view of Mary as she sashayed away into the Broadway Lounge corridor. Danny pointed to the sign above its entrance and griped, "Don't tell me they're making people go outside and walk all the way around to get into the new lounge?"

Jim gave him a mischievous grin. "What do you mean? We'll just follow Mary."

Danny slugged down his drink and grabbed his satchel. Jim was happy that Danny was showing an interest. He guzzled the rest of his martini before heading for the platform stairs. Danny hobbled down them behind him.

Watching, Arthur reflected on how Danny and Jim had seemed to change roles. Danny had always been the more outgoing personality, while Jim had been his quiet, good-looking sidekick. Now Jim was taking the lead, while Danny, less sure of himself, hung back.

Sal strode in from the Broadway Lounge and nearly collided with Danny and Jim. "Get outta my way, you stupid micks," Sal growled. He skirted around them and continued on toward the foyer.

Danny shook it off. But Jim, still irritated by Sal's earlier stunt at the ballpark to embarrass Danny, muttered, "Damn greaseball!"

At the coat checkroom, Ginger and Rita shed their coats as they waited in line. Ginger was dazzling in a chic, sapphire blue dress, silver ankle strap high heels, and matching silver evening bag. Her hair was fashioned in a flattering updo. Rita was sultry in a slinky red dress and sexy high heels. The two women attracted the attention of men around them, much to Rita's pleasure.

Rita was admiring Ginger's shoes. She suddenly scowled. "You still have a pair of silk stockings?"

Ginger frowned. "They're my last pair."

"Stupid Japs!"

Ginger laughed at Rita's snappy comment then lamented, "It stinks that they stopped selling us silk. And now all *our* silk has to go to the war effort to make parachutes for our boys."

"I know," Rita said, dejected. She whispered, "I used face makeup to cover my legs and my eyebrow pencil to draw on a seam." She lifted her dress a little and stuck out her leg to show Ginger. A couple of sailors behind them whistled.

Ginger elbowed her and whispered back, "Well, it seems to be working." She and Rita giggled to one another.

Rita moved up to the counter. While Vera hung up her coat, Rita looked toward the maître d's podium for

Mr. Lippi and was surprised to see Frank there. He seemed flustered by the backlog of patrons waiting to be seated. She beamed with pride when Sal showed up to save the day.

Beside the podium, Sal unlocked a closet beneath the Terrace. He flagged over Henry and Tony, two brawny teenage busboys, who hauled out chairs and small tables. Waiters scurried to set them up on the edge of the dance floor and anywhere else they would fit. It was clear by the way the employees responded to Sal that they all knew Welansky had put him in charge.

"Squeeze in everybody you can!" Sal barked at Frank.

Rita plucked her claim check from Vera's hand and headed over to Sal. She gave him a peck on the cheek and said, "Oh, Salvi, I was so worried you'd lose business when I heard the B.C. party got canceled."

He shrugged it off. "Eh. This place is never hurting for business."

Marilyn took Ginger's coat and asked, "How's working weeknights?"

"Good. And I enjoy working for Katherine. How do you like my old job?"

"It sure beats getting pawed over for cigarettes. And you were right. The tips are great," Marilyn answered. She glanced past Ginger at the mass of waiting customers. She heaved an exaggerated sigh and joked, "If I'm alive after tonight to spend them!"

Ginger was amused.

Between customers, Rosie butted into the conversation and blurted out, "We just saw Danny!"

Ginger was stunned. "Here?"

Rosie and Marilyn nodded in unison. Rosie was about to go on, but Sal, wearing a broad grin, strutted up with Rita.

"There's my baby doll," Sal broadcasted in a booming voice.

Ginger tensed as he grasped her arms and drew her toward him. Making a big show of it, he brazenly planted a kiss on Ginger's lips. Rita giggled. When Rosie and Marilyn covertly grimaced to one another, Vera stifled a laugh.

As Sal guided Ginger and Rita into the main room, he bragged, "I got you girls the best table in the house. Mr. Welansky's!"

Rita gasped, impressed. But Ginger, distracted, barely heard him. She was on the lookout for Danny. They followed Sal to a table at the edge of the dance floor with a choice view of the stage. Two floral boxes, each containing a gardenia, awaited them. Sal seated Ginger.

"Thank you, Sal," Ginger said with a polite smile. "This is really nice."

"Yeah! This is great, Salvi! Thanks!" Rita gushed. She gazed at Sal adoringly. He glowed.

Lenny, a cocky young waiter, rushed over and pulled out a chair for Rita. It irked him that she barely acknowledged him.

Rita removed the gardenia from her box and inhaled its scent with pleasure. Ginger had already fastened hers in her hair. Rita pinned hers in her own hair with Ginger's assistance.

"You two look like a million bucks." Sal whistled his approval, drawing looks from people seated nearby. Rita beamed while Ginger blushed and wished she could hide under the table.

Sal turned to Lenny and ordered, "Bring 'em a bottle of champagne on me and whatever else they want."

"Will do, Mr. Russo," Lenny replied.

"Nothing but the best for my gals," Sal said. He informed the women, "Listen, I gotta take care of some business in the new lounge. I'll be back later. Enjoy yourselves." Sal gave both Ginger and Rita a peck on the cheek before heading off.

Rita leaned over to Ginger. "Salvi is so thoughtful. You're a lucky girl, Ginger."

Rita's unwavering worship of Sal never ceased to amaze Ginger. Rita took out a cigarette. Lenny snatched up a matchbook from the ashtray on the table. Hoping to impress her, he smiled and gallantly lit her cigarette. She puffed on it absently as he offered her a menu. With a glare, he shoved a menu at Ginger and muttered, "Must be nice to be the boss' girl. I'll be right back with your champagne."

Ginger was relieved when Lenny left. She brushed off his petty jealousy. She surveyed the club, hopeful, yet a little fearful, that she might spot Danny.

CHAPTER SEVEN

Danny and Jim nonchalantly snuck into the classy, new Broadway Lounge. They couldn't believe their luck. They were able to snag up two seats at the crowded bar right where they'd entered.

Jim scanned the room for Mary. When his eyes landed on her, he watched her fondly as she made the rounds with her cigarette tray. Danny waved over the cheerful, heavyset, young bartender and ordered a couple of drinks. He had to speak loudly to be heard above the din of chattering patrons. "Tiny, you look good behind this swanky new bar. Congratulations."

Tiny's eyes shone with pride as he fixed their drinks. "Holy Cross must've had angels on their shoulders today, huh, guys?" He roared with laughter. "How else would Sullivan get away with forty-eight yards?"

Danny winced. "All through the game, I kept hoping I was dreaming. Then the horn sounded."

"Yeah, it was a real nightmare," Jim added,

playing off Danny's words. He beat Danny to the punch and gave Tiny tickets and a tip in exchange for their drinks.

Tiny chuckled. "Even when everything's been going your way, you never really know, do you?"

As Tiny moved off to wait on another customer, Danny muttered, "You can say that again."

James Welansky was entertaining Assistant District Attorney Garrett Byrne at a table near the bar. With a cunning grin, Welansky puffed on a cigar. He refilled their glasses from a bottle of Johnnie Walker Black Label.

Jim noted, "Hmm ... Jimmy Welansky and the Assistant D.A.? Now there's a pair to beat a full house."

"And here comes Buccigross." Danny pointed out the well-known police captain.

Capt. Joseph Buccigross was entering via the inward opening door beneath the lit, newly-installed exit sign. Dressed in a fine tweed suit, he deposited his overcoat at the small, recessed coat checkroom. He paused to admire the lounge. With commanding presence, he approached Welansky's table. Buccigross shook Welansky's hand. "The place is looking good, Jimmy!"

"Captain! Sit down. Take a load off," Welansky said. He flagged Tiny for another bottle and an additional glass.

Buccigross shook hands with Byrne. He removed a cigarette from a silver case and lit it before taking a seat.

Nearly everyone in the room was smoking. Jim took a drag of his cigarette as he wrote down the names of the men meeting with Welansky.

Danny covertly asked Jim, "What do you suppose that's about?"

Jim's eyes narrowed. "They're probably in cahoots over some crooked deal. Sleazeballs."

"Speaking of sleazeballs...," Danny griped.

Jim groaned as Sal swaggered past. "Now that they've got a fourth, they can play bridge," Jim joked.

Danny cracked up, and this made Jim laugh, too. But Danny was antsy to get the job done and get out of there. And knowing Ginger was in the club made him even more impatient. He tapped his wrist. "What time is it getting to be?"

Jim lifted his arm dramatically to check the time, exaggerating his exasperation to Danny. "Time for you to get a watch." Danny chuckled. Jim let him know it was half past eight.

Danny was itching for Jim to finish his drink. "Buck Jones should be here by now. He's probably in the celebrity section on the Terrace." The second Jim swallowed the last drop, Danny stood up. "It's been a hell of a day. Let's just get what we came for and hit the road."

Jim sighed heavily. He had wanted Danny to have a good time, but his hopes had been dashed by Sal. As soon as Jim had risen, Clifford Johnson, a young coastguardsman, made a move for their barstools. He was grateful that he was finally able to provide his date with a seat.

Danny and Jim slipped back to the main room via the employees' entrance. They were amazed at how much busier it had become. They were forced to weave through throngs of patrons. Every table in the dining area was taken. Waiters hustled to offer timely service. A couple of young women gave Danny and Jim the eye, hoping to attract their attention. Jim winked back, but Danny ignored them and pressed on toward the Terrace.

Across the room, Ginger was enjoying her Filet of Sole Florentine. All the food was cooked to perfection, yet Rita glumly picked at her Lobster Newburg. Ginger wondered what had brought on this change in Rita's mood. "Rita, you seem sad. What's the matter?"

"I really wanted Andy to be here," Rita whined. "I bought a new dress and everything. Stupid Crusaders!"

Ginger suppressed a laugh. She tried to sound hopeful. "He might come later."

Rita perked up. "You really think so?"

Ginger shrugged and gave Rita an encouraging smile. "Maybe."

"Do you think he likes me?"

"Of course, he likes you."

"No. I mean *likes* me likes me."

Ginger was careful not to hurt her feelings. "Well, I guess. I don't know. You know how guys are. They don't tell you what they're feeling."

"Gee, I really like him. He's a dreamboat. And he's a college man. Imagine me married to a college man!"

Ginger coughed on a mouthful of champagne.

"Married? Rita, you haven't even gone on a date with Andy."

Rita pouted.

Ginger was quick to add, "Yet."

"But wouldn't it be swell if I married your brother and you married mine? Then we'd really be sisters!"

Ginger smiled, yet the thought of marrying Sal could not have been further from her mind.

Over on the Terrace, Buck Jones was dining at a front row table along with the movie moguls and their wives. Buck was inundated by autograph hounds.

Danny and Jim waited in line on the Terrace stairs for an opportunity with Buck. They attempted to watch the floorshow but were constantly jostled by waiters brushing past with large trays loaded down with dinners.

Jim panned the club. It gave him a start to see Ginger and Rita at a table on the main floor. He nudged Danny. "I know what I said at the paper, but I've got to break it to you. Ginger's here."

Danny grumbled, "Yeah. I know."

"You know? Danny!"

In order to avoid the issue, Danny focused on preparing his camera.

Mickey Alpert stood on the stage before the microphone and announced, "And now for your listening pleasure, Mr. Billy Payne singing 'I'll Never Smile Again'."

Charismatic tenor Billy Payne came to the microphone to rousing applause. Mickey tapped his baton, and the orchestra began to play. Billy's velvet voice was mesmerizing.

The song lyrics tore at Danny's heart. Swept up by his emotions, he glanced over at Ginger. It didn't go unnoticed by Jim. He knew Danny's heart must be aching. But what could he do? He'd tried everything he could think of. Danny just wouldn't listen. The guy's mind was made up, and he wasn't going to budge. When it came to Ginger, Danny was his own worst enemy.

At the end of the number, Billy took a bow. The audience applauded. All eyes turned to three trumpeters as they came out from behind their podiums performing a jazzy intro to "Anchors Aweigh." As the orchestra got into full swing, Sammy, Ray, and Pete marched back and forth along the stage playing their trumpets and bobbing their heads in time with the music.

The audience laughed at the comical trumpeters. Navy men cheered the patriotic tune. Men whistled and hooted as chorus girls in sexy sailor costumes came out tap dancing, led by long-legged, blonde bombshell Kicky.

Jim was so entranced by the shapely dancers that Danny had to smack his arm to get his attention when their turn to interview Buck Jones finally came. Jim wasn't happy about the timing, but he dutifully refocused and approached the cowboy movie star. He flashed his press pass, introduced himself, and inquired, "How did you like that game today, Mr. Jones?"

"It was very exciting. Although, from what I

understand, it was a surprising outcome," Buck replied, noticeably congested.

Three athletically-built men in their early twenties waited in line behind Danny and Jim to meet Buck. Agitated by Buck's remark, one said loudly, "I'll say! I still can't believe the crappy Crusaders took down the Eagles today."

Danny nodded in agreement to the outspoken fan.

Jim chuckled at the comment but continued his conversation with Buck. "Yes, it was very surprising. If you don't mind me saying so, it sounds like you've caught a cold."

Buck coughed to clear his throat. "I almost didn't make it tonight. I'm afraid this raw New England weather hasn't helped it any."

Jim smiled, empathizing, before asking, "What can you tell me about your new picture, Mr. Jones?"

Buck filled Jim in on the details of his latest project. Danny took a photograph of the movie star.

The outspoken B.C. fan was growing impatient. As his two pals lamented about the game, he noticed a young man wearing a Holy Cross letterman sweater sitting with his family at a table near Buck's. Irritated, the B.C. fan shouted, "Damn it all! We should have been celebrating with the Eagles here tonight!"

The father of the family took offense. He rose and told him, "Young man, watch your language. There are ladies present. Don't be such a sore loser. Holy Cross won simply because they played better."

Once the man sat back down, the B.C. fan and his pals mimicked him behind his back. The well-mannered patriarch, becoming aware of their antics, urged his family to ignore them.

Jim wound up his interview and thanked Buck. Before he and Danny departed, Jim turned to the movie moguls and teased, "Boys, don't keep our star out too late. He needs his rest."

The Grove's resident caricature artist stood nearby capturing Buck's likeness on his sketchpad. Danny and Jim had to squeeze past him to get to the stairs. Jim stopped to take another look at Ginger and Rita. This allowed Danny time to better observe Ginger.

Danny still found Ginger irresistible. He remembered the first time he had seen her all dressed up. It was the night of her senior prom. The pretty little girl he had grown up with had transformed into a glamorous young woman who took his breath away. And every time they went out on the town since, she had looked gorgeous. His heart twisted, knowing she was now dressing up like that for Sal.

"Ginger's looking sweet tonight," Jim remarked appreciatively. "And that Rita! Va-va-va-voom! She's sizzling. She looks like she's ready to give it away."

"Have a little class, will you?" Danny scolded.

Jim was amused and a little surprised by Danny's reaction. "When did you become such a boy scout? I have class. I have eyes, too."

"Well, stick them back in your head."

Jim brushed it off and headed straight for the Caricature Bar. Danny followed begrudgingly.

Sal, on his way to the Terrace, couldn't believe he was crossing paths with them again. His eyes blazed when he caught Danny glancing back wistfully at Ginger. He shoved Danny, knocking him right into Jim. Before Danny could react, Sal warned, "She's not yours anymore, McGuire. So mind your goddamn business, or I'll mind it for ya!"

Sal glared at Danny to drive his point home. With a sneer, he abruptly moved on. Danny just smirked and shook his head. Jim, on the other hand, smacked his fist into his palm and declared, "Just once, I'd like to pop that S.O.B. right in the kisser!"

At the foot of the Terrace stairs, Sal pulled Lenny aside. He stuffed a bill in the breast pocket of Lenny's dinner jacket. Sal patted it and told him, "If anybody comes sniffing around Ginger, you let me know." Using the streetwise signal, Sal tapped the side of his nose. Lenny tapped the side of his own nose to affirm he understood that it should stay confidential. Sal started up the steps, satisfied that he'd secured a stool pigeon.

Lenny inspected the money. His eyes widened. It was a ten spot! He puffed up with self-importance.

Sal was able to climb the stairs unhindered. The number of clamoring fans had diminished. He swaggered over to Buck's table. "How's your lobsters? They always taste better on the house, eh? We'll top it all off with some Baked Alaska."

After assuring that all the V.I.P.s on the Terrace were satisfied, Sal trotted down the stairs and went to check on Ginger and Rita. He had to work to get their attention because they were so engrossed in the floorshow. "Hey, girls!" With a glint in his eye, he pointed to the Terrace and boasted, "Buck Jones is sitting up there."

Rita turned around, spotted Buck, and squealed, "Oh my God! Twice in one day?"

Sal laughed at her excitement. "Are you girls having a good time?"

"It's a swell show, Salvi, but we need some dance partners," Rita whined.

"I know. In a little while. I gotta say hello to my friend, Public Safety Director Walsh." Sal kissed Rita's cheek. He turned to Ginger and studied her. He tried to detect if she knew McGuire was in the club. "How come you're so quiet?"

Ginger put on a smile. "Just enjoying myself."

Sal bought her explanation and gave her a peck on the cheek.

Jim, standing with Danny at Arthur's end of the Caricature Bar, followed Danny's icy stare in time to catch Sal giving Ginger a possessive squeeze. Jim challenged Danny. "How can you let that son of a bitch of a greaseball put his hands on Ginger?"

Danny banged his fist on the bar.

"Well, do something about it!" Jim urged.

Danny shut his eyes tight and did nothing. Jim threw his hands up in the air. Danny ignored him and packed his camera away in his satchel.

The same soldiers who had toasted each other earlier were still there at the bar. They were now enjoying the attention of flirtatious young women. Jim was amused by their interaction but kept his eye on Sal.

Sal sauntered over to a table of distinguished businessmen and glad-handed them all. He made sure to spend extra time with Walsh, who seemed very pleased with the well-positioned table Sal had reserved for him.

The B.C. fan and his pals gathered within earshot of Danny and Jim. As they continued to complain loudly about being reprimanded on the Terrace, Jim rolled his eyes. Danny just shook his head.

Arthur delivered another Dewars and a martini to Danny and Jim. As Danny withdrew drink tickets from his wallet, a well-worn photograph of Ginger fell out onto the bar. Jim snickered. This proved his point. Jim knew Danny was all talk. And, no matter how much he professed that it was over, he'd never actually let her go.

Arthur picked up the picture and smiled. Handing it back to Danny, he said, "I wasn't fooled. I knew you would never cheat on Ginger."

"Yeah. Though she's having no trouble lapping up what Sal gives her now," Danny said.

Arthur was quick to rebuke him. "Danny. You need to give that young lady a break. Are you aware that her father can no longer work? She quit nursing school to help put her brother through college."

Danny was shocked. He turned on Jim. "Did you know about that?"

Jim nodded.

"Why the hell didn't you tell me?"

Jim shrugged. He uttered in a low voice, "I figured you'd just feel worse."

Danny took a minute to digest this news about Ginger. He came to the conclusion that Jim was right. It did make him feel worse. Sal passed by on his way to the Broadway Lounge. Danny bristled and asked Arthur, "How the hell did Sal get in the picture?"

An intoxicated patron vied for Arthur's attention. "Hey, barkeep! I need another drink!"

Arthur eyed the man shrewdly. "It would appear you've had one too many already, sir." Arthur returned his focus to Danny and answered, "You know Sal, ever the opportunist. He always had his eye on her."

Danny sighed in disgust.

Arthur went on, "Ginger was feeling pretty badly when you ended it with her. Still, she would not give Sal the time of day. But when he learned of her situation at home, he'd found his angle. He got her a new position with better hours and a raise."

"Doesn't mean she had to go out with him," Danny snarled.

"No, but he knew full well she'd feel indebted to him. It was not hard for him to convince her after that. Devil's bargain, if you ask me."

Danny couldn't believe Ginger had allowed Sal to manipulate her like that.

"No doubt she's having trouble shaking him off now. You know how possessive Sal can be. Maybe you can give her a hand with that," Arthur advised. Before moving off to tend to other customers, he added, "You know she still loves you, Danny."

Danny contemplated Arthur's words.

Mary, minus her cigarette tray, approached Jim with a hopeful look in her eye. "I'm on my break now."

"Want to dance?" Jim grinned and didn't wait for an answer. He grabbed her hand. As an afterthought, he glanced back at Danny.

Danny waved him on. He lit a cigarette and watched enviously as Jim led Mary to the crowded dance floor.

CHAPTER EIGHT

Drums beat out the tribal rhythm to the opening of "Sing, Sing, Sing." Rita and Ginger, on their way to the ladies' room, navigated past enthusiastic couples converging on the dance floor. The horn section blared as the fun, fast-paced song got underway.

Ginger, trailing behind Rita, caught sight of Jim and Mary dancing wildly. She instinctively scanned the club for Danny and got butterflies when she found him watching her from the Caricature Bar. She stared back at him longingly.

Even from that distance, Danny could feel the love Ginger had for him. He thought he'd done everything possible to discourage her, even to the point of being cruel. He could not understand why she still cared. But as much as he wanted to hide from her, it frustrated him when couples dancing blocked his view.

Ginger was forced to duck the elbow of a man spinning his partner. Laughing in surprise, Ginger decided to take a safer route. In order to catch up to

Rita, she squeezed behind tables that waiters had set up along the dance floor.

Rita had stopped below the Terrace and was gazing up at Buck. Emboldened, she blew him a kiss. He smiled back. She grabbed Ginger's arm and gushed, "Did you see that? He smiled at me!" They giggled with excitement and continued on toward the foyer.

As they neared the maître d's podium, Ginger and Rita heard a commotion between Frank and a customer. A man with an air of entitlement criticized, "Who are you? Maître d' Lippi would never make us wait this long! He knows who Mr. Welansky's friends are."

Frank was quick to appease him. "I'm sorry, sir. Your table is ready now." He signaled a waiter to usher the arrogant man and his fashionably dressed wife to their table. Other customers, still waiting to be seated, bemoaned the special treatment.

Ginger felt sorry for Frank. She paused by the podium. "Oh, Frank. What a crazy night!"

Nerves fraying, Frank rubbed his temples. "How does Mr. Lippi do this? I don't know where to put everybody!"

Having no helpful advice for him, she shook her head in sympathy.

Danny spied Ginger entering the foyer and made up his mind. It was time to heed Arthur's words and talk to her about Sal. He left his empty glass on the bar, picked up his satchel, and descended the platform stairs.

Jim escorted Mary off the dance floor. They stopped to catch their breath on the walkway between the tables and the Caricature Bar. Jim asked, "Can I get you a drink, gorgeous?"

"No thanks. I need to fix my hair and makeup before I go back on the job," Mary replied, smoothing her hair into place.

He grinned. "You look fine to me."

Mary was charmed. "See you later," she said as she started to move away.

Jim pulled her back and whispered mischievously, "Next time, we'll make it a slow dance."

Mary beamed at him before slipping into the crowd.

Danny tapped Jim's shoulder, startling him, and suggested, "Let's check for that phony permit."

Jim was pleased that Danny seemed motivated and nodded conspiratorially.

A steady stream of patrons continued to enter the club from the revolving door. Throngs waited at the busy coat checkroom. Groups clustered in front of the phone booths. Waves of people pressed toward the Melody Lounge past others struggling to get to the maître d's podium and to buy drink tickets from the cashier. It was chaos.

Ginger and Rita headed toward the corridor off the foyer that led to the ladies' room. They had to push past newcomers flooding to the main room. Rita groaned, "*Madonne!* We're packed in here like sardines!"

"Imagine how much busier it would have been if

B.C. hadn't canceled their party?" Ginger speculated.

"Did you have to remind me?" Rita pined.

Ginger suppressed a laugh.

Danny and Jim struggled to move through the crowd. Danny was impatient. "Come on, Jim! Let's check the wall outside the office."

Jim noticed Ginger and Rita ahead of them. "Yeah. And maybe if we hurry, you can get a minute with Ginger, too."

Danny grinned, but his mood deflated when he saw Ginger and Rita disappear into the corridor to the restrooms. He had missed his chance.

Jim chuckled at Danny's bad timing and coaxed him on to the corridor to the Melody Lounge.

Back at the Caricature Bar, the B.C. fan and his pals knocked back their drinks. They headed to the Terrace, fueled by liquid courage. They stomped up the stairs and approached the family of the Holy Cross letterman. The B.C. fan got in the patriarch's face and shouted, "Hey, jackass!"

The man was appalled. His family was shocked by the B.C. fan's behavior. The ruckus drew the attention of patrons at nearby tables, including Buck and the movie moguls, and distracted Henry from refreshing water goblets.

The drunken B.C. fan slurred, "What the hell are you talking about? Holy Cross plays better? The Crusaders just got lucky. The Eagles won every game this season!"

The patriarch sprang to his feet. He grabbed the disruptive B.C. fan and ushered him away from the table. The B.C. fan's pals stepped in to help their friend. A few male diners rose to thwart the troublemakers. Henry signaled to Lenny below.

Like a man on a mission, Lenny scrambled past tightly packed tables in the main room and into the Broadway Lounge. Once inside, he scoured the room for Sal.

Sal sat puffing on his cigar like a big shot as he listened to the conversation of the others at Welansky's table. When he saw Lenny heading his way, his jaw tightened. If McGuire had so much as tried to talk to Ginger, he would flatten him. He instinctively clenched his fist against his thigh.

Lenny rushed up to him and whispered in his ear. Sal was relieved. It wasn't about Ginger. He stood up and announced, "Excuse me, gentlemen, I got a fire to put out in the other room." Leaving his cigar smoldering in an ashtray, Sal followed Lenny out. Welansky and his cronies could not have cared less.

Lenny directed Sal to the skirmish on the Terrace. Sal marched up the stairs. The patriarch kept a hold on the B.C. fan while Henry and several male diners subdued his pals. Sal was formidable. The B.C. fan panicked. He broke free and vaulted over the railing, stunning everyone. Sal bolted down the stairs in hot pursuit.

The B.C. fan scurried past Frank at the podium. Sal charged after him. The fan quickly realized he couldn't escape through the mob at the revolving door, so he bulldozed through the crowd in the foyer. He nearly knocked an elderly couple, Fred and Gladys, to the floor. Sal didn't bother to stop to see if they were okay. He dogged the B.C. fan toward the corridor to the Melody Lounge.

In the busy corridor, Jim scanned the documents posted on the wall near the office door. Danny got his camera ready. Jim broke into a broad smile and yanked on Danny's camera strap. "Found it!" Jim eyeballed the permit for the electrical wiring Sal had paid for that morning. He scoffed, "I don't see Dominic Russo's name on here."

Danny laughed as he popped a flashbulb into his camera. He took a photograph of the permit.

Jim examined other documents. "Get a load of this fire inspection certificate. It only authorizes four hundred and sixty people. There's got to be twice that number in this joint tonight." He whipped out his pad and made a note of that.

Danny had no sooner gotten a picture of the fire inspection certificate and was lowering his camera when all hell broke loose. The B.C. fan plowed down the corridor shoving people left and right. Sal came barreling after him. Jim looked at Danny, eyes wide, knowing it had been a close call. Danny stashed his camera in his bag. He feigned wiping his brow. He stuck out his tongue and mimed hanging from a noose. Jim cracked up.

The B.C. fan slammed on the exit door's panic bar but was frustrated to find it locked.

"Where do you think you're going?" Sal yelled. He grabbed the guy by the collar, spun him around, and pinned him up against the door. He fished in the B.C.

fan's pockets and yanked out his wallet.

"What are you doing?" the B.C. fan complained.

"You're not getting outta here without paying!"

"I bought drink tickets, and I didn't eat anything!" the B.C. fan whined.

"Well, we'll just make sure you leave a good tip, eh?" Sal ripped cash from the wallet. He unlocked the door, pushed the B.C. fan outside, and tossed his wallet out after him. Sal pulled the door shut and locked it again. He started back to the foyer and was irked to find Danny and Jim scrutinizing him. He bellowed, "What are you two looking at?"

"Not much," Jim answered smugly. He chuckled and nudged Danny.

"Gee, Jim, Sal sure has come a long way since the days when he used to steal our lunch money," Danny announced for all to hear.

Danny's mischief filled Jim with glee. He was more than happy to follow Danny's lead. "Oh, yeah! I hear the mob pays plenty for those skills. Not everybody can be a 'born bastard'."

Sal bristled at their taunts. He lurched toward them, but the corridor was too crowded for him to pounce on them effectively. Sal shouted at Danny and Jim, "You want a piece of me? 'Cause I promise ya, I'll give ya a piece!"

Danny and Jim loved getting to him. In a mocking tone, Jim said, "Oh, Sal, why don't you take that money you just extorted and go buy yourself a drink. You earned it."

Sal squared his shoulders and straightened his tie.

Strutting away with a cocky grin, he said, "I think I will."

As Sal reentered the foyer, Marilyn beckoned him over to the coat checkroom. He muscled his way to the counter and asked, "What's up, doll?"

"We're out of hangers."

"There's five hundred of 'em!" he griped.

"We used them up a long time ago," Rosie piped in.

"Quit your squawking and hang 'em double!"

"We already have, Mr. Russo," Vera explained. "We can barely move in here." She showed him how overstuffed the coatroom had become, forcing them to pile coats on the floor.

"*Gesù Cristo!* I'll get the coatrack!" Sal stormed to the closet next to the maître d's podium. He jerked out a rolling coatrack so hard, it set the hangers swinging. He shoved it forward parting a sea of annoyed patrons.

Danny and Jim, returning to the foyer, paused to watch Sal's antics. Sal ensured that the exit beside the revolving door was still locked. He neatened the velvet drapery that concealed it and left the coatrack blocking the door. Jim backhanded Danny's arm. "Did you see that? There's another door behind that curtain! Sal keeps it locked, of course, leaving everybody out in the rain."

Jim took a chance and moved off toward the Caricature Bar. He wasn't ready to leave just yet, and he didn't want to give Danny a shot at calling it a night. Besides, things were starting to get interesting. The lughead had finally come around and wanted to talk to Ginger.

Danny had a pretty good idea of what Jim was up to. He decided to humor him and have another drink. It might give him enough time to finagle another opportunity to get to Ginger.

Ginger and Rita returned to the main room. They weaved through the compact dining area in an effort to get back to their table but had to stop. Elegantly dressed house photographer Lynn Andrews was taking pictures of a wedding party sitting beneath the colorful canopy on the Shawmut Street side of the club. The bride wore a fancy corsage on the jacket of her lavender skirt suit. The groom, handsome in a dark suit, sat close beside her. The beaming young couple kissed. Their party applauded. Lynn lowered her camera and said, "I'll have these ready by eleven. Congratulations, you two."

Lynn departed, opening the way for Rita to press on. Ginger followed. She glanced at the finger where Danny's engagement ring should be then looked back wistfully at the newlyweds.

Danny and Jim stepped up to the bar. Jim beckoned Arthur. Danny noticed Sal greeting a smartly dressed man on the walkway in front of the bar. He alerted Jim. Both were fully aware of the man's identity.

Arthur was curious to see who had drawn Danny and Jim's attention. Peering through the smoky haze, he stated in disgust, "Well, if it isn't Sharps, Sal's bookie."

The three of them watched Sal accept a thick

envelope from Sharps and, with a broad grin, stash it inside his suit coat. Danny and Jim exchanged knowing looks. Arthur noted, "It would seem by the size of Sal's smile that he must have bet on Holy Cross."

Danny fumed. "What did I tell you, Jim? That game probably *was* fixed!"

His declaration drew looks from patrons close by. They started to buzz about what they'd overheard.

Sal, noticing a change in the energy, wondered what was up. He panned the bar where he caught Arthur fraternizing with Danny and Jim. He directed Sharps to wait for him in the Broadway Lounge.

Squaring his shoulders, Sal strode up beside Danny and Jim. He slapped the bar hard and growled, "Arthur!" Danny and Jim tensed up ready to jump to their friend's defense. Arthur eyed Sal coldly. Sal warned him, "If I catch you giving these two saps any free drinks, you're gonna pay for it!"

Without so much as a look at Danny and Jim, Sal turned on his heel and stalked off toward the Broadway Lounge. Danny was steamed. Jim spat, "What an asshole."

Arthur grinned at their reactions. "Two drinks? On the house?"

Danny and Jim burst out laughing. With a wink, Arthur went to prepare their drinks.

The resident caricature artist came up onto the platform of the Caricature Bar. He tacked up his latest drawings near Danny and Jim. Admiring his work, Jim commented, "Wow, you're really good. You sure captured Buck Jones."

"Nice touch adding the lasso," Danny chimed in.

"Thanks for noticing." The artist grinned and then headed off in search of his next subject.

Arthur returned with their drinks. Danny and Jim tried to outdo each other's extra big tip for him. Arthur chuckled over their good-natured gesture. He was humbled when they forced him to take their money.

Jim artfully changed the focus. "By the way, Arthur, we saw Welansky boozing it up with Byrne and Buccigross in the new lounge earlier."

"Like his brother, he grafts people in high places to ensure that the law keeps their dirty little secrets," Arthur said matter-of-factly.

Jim took a sip of his martini. "They're always hiding something."

Arthur leaned in. "Speaking of hiding something...."

Jim alerted Danny with a nudge.

Arthur continued, "I was planning to keep this under my hat until was I out of here." He glanced up at the ceiling. They both followed Arthur's gaze as he explained, "See that panel with three stars? It conceals King Solomon's old speakeasy hideaway. The Welanskys have held onto a few thousand cases of liquor with no revenue tax seals and consider it their own private stash."

Jim's eyes lit up. This was the break he needed before he went overseas! A big story like this would secure him a position at the paper when he got back. And he'd be able to leave knowing Danny had a chance at a better paying position as a news photographer. Jim wrote down all the details Arthur had shared. He let out a long whistle. "That's big-time tax evasion! It's the kind of evidence we've been waiting for! Arthur, you're a prince."

"That's what put Capone in the slammer! Prince? Heck, he's the king!" Danny corrected.

Jim and Danny raised their glasses and toasted Arthur.

Arthur smiled with great satisfaction.

CHAPTER NINE

A flame shot up from a petite Baked Alaska. Amused, Ginger gasped and sat back in her chair. Rita squealed and clapped her hands in delight as Lenny lit hers. Lenny smiled at her excitement, believing he'd finally made an impression. He waited for a word of praise, but Rita was more interested in the dessert than in him. He backed away from the table muttering, "Enjoy your dessert."

Next, Lenny checked on the wedding party. He picked up a bottle of champagne chilling in an ice bucket on the table, popped it open, and refreshed their glasses. The jovial father of the bride ordered another bottle. As Lenny walked away, the best man led a toast to the bride and groom for what seemed to the waiter like the umpteenth time.

On his way to the Caricature Bar, Lenny encountered Henry coming down the Terrace stairs with several empty water pitchers. He noticed Henry chuckling to himself and asked, "What's so funny?"

"See that party at the table over there in the corner?" Henry nodded in their direction and blurted out, "It's a whole family of undertakers!"

"Ha! They must have been *dying* to get in here!" Lenny said with a snicker.

Henry cracked up, nearly dropping his pitchers.

Ginger took one last bite of her dessert, followed by a sip of coffee. Rita tapped her fork against her plate in time with the music. She turned to Ginger and complained, "Gee, I really wanna dance. I'm sick of waiting for Andy. I'm gonna dance with the first fella that asks me. You should, too, Ginger. It wouldn't hurt to show Salvi that he shouldn't be leaving you alone all night." Ginger was a little surprised that Rita would encourage this.

Rita began scouring the nearby tables for prospects. She zeroed in on two good-looking young soldiers. One winked at her. She gave him a coy smile and winked back. Ginger laughed at Rita's unabashed flirtation.

It wasn't long before the men came over and invited them to dance. Rita sprang up, eager to accept her admirer's hand. Ginger remembered Sal's reaction to the harmless interest of the sailor at Fenway Park and hesitated. She shook her head, but the handsome army private pleaded, "Aw, come on. Please, miss. I'm shipping out tomorrow."

Ginger gave in and allowed the tall, blond soldier to escort her to the dance floor. He expertly led her in a foxtrot to the romantic hit song "Moonlight Serenade." She closed her eyes. In a moment of stolen pleasure, she pretended she was dancing with Danny again. Those nights had been so magical. Pain pierced her heart as she realized this was something he could no longer do. She felt a pang of guilt knowing how frustrated he must be.

Danny finished his complimentary scotch. He checked to see if Ginger had returned to her table. It was still empty. He scanned the room. He saw Rita on the dance floor and wondered if Ginger was also dancing. He looked from couple to couple. His heart sank when he spotted Ginger with a soldier. Seeing her in the arms of another man filled him with regret and envy.

Jim watched Danny watching Ginger. He handed him another Dewars. "I figure we're staying awhile."

"Thanks, buddy." Danny was grateful that Jim understood and that he had refrained from needling him.

Lenny brushed past Danny and Jim at the bar. While waiting to request a fresh bottle of champagne, he spied Rita and was crushed. He'd done everything he could to get Rita to notice him, and yet she wouldn't even give him the time of day. But it didn't surprise him to see her having a good time with a hero. He knew an everyday waiter wouldn't be good enough for her.

Then he caught Ginger with a soldier and smiled with smug satisfaction. Lenny could feel that ten spot burning a hole in his pocket. Maybe there'd be more where that came from now that he had something juicy to report. He made a beeline to the Broadway Lounge, plowing past Kicky. She was hovering in the entryway between the main room and the lounge. The lead chorus girl with legs that went on forever sighed in disgust at his rudeness.

Kicky peered into the main room. She was amazed to find Ginger dancing with someone other than Sal, especially with Rita so close by. When the song came to an end, she beckoned Ginger over. Ginger thanked her partner and broke away.

The orchestra slid into another number. Rita was thrilled that her soldier drew her in to dance again. He was cute, even with red hair and freckles. Not as cute as Andy, but at least he was paying attention to her.

Ginger and Kicky gave each other a warm hug. Kicky teased, "Sorry to call you away from that handsome soldier boy, kiddo, but I'm on break now. Want to go down to the Melody Lounge with me for a drink? I've got big news!"

"You do?"

Seeing that Ginger's curiosity was piqued, Kicky flashed a wicked smile before announcing, "I dumped Mr. Good-for-nothing!"

Ginger was proud of her. She had been telling Kicky for months that she deserved better and was glad to hear she had finally ended it with that freeloader. Now, anxious to share her own news, Ginger clasped Kicky's hands and whispered in her ear, "Danny's back!"

Kicky was intrigued by Ginger's unexpected excitement. "Ooo! What does that mean? What did he have to say for himself?"

Ginger filled her in on her encounter with Danny at Fenway Park. Kicky was shocked to learn the truth. But she hoped it meant Danny would eventually come around, and they'd get back together.

In the Broadway Lounge, Sal concentrated on how Welansky handled Capt. Buccigross and A.D.A. Byrne. He admired Welansky's finesse. Sal was distracted when Lenny entered and caught his eye. The scrappy waiter tapped the side of his nose to indicate he had information that Sal would want to know. Sal grew tense. He immediately excused himself from the table to join Lenny, who couldn't wait to tell him about Ginger and the soldier. The news threw Sal for a loop. Even though he knew Ginger was a beautiful dame and any guy would die to make time with her, he had not expected that. He returned to the table, muttered to Welansky about needing to see to something, and quickly left the room.

Danny was secretly happy that Ginger was no longer dancing with the good-looking soldier, though he'd rather the soldier than Sal. He needed to get Ginger away from Sal for her own good. With Rita busy dancing and Ginger in deep conversation with

Kicky, this was the opportunity he'd been waiting for. He downed his scotch for courage and turned to Jim. "Keep an eye on my camera."

Jim grinned. "Go get her, buddy."

Danny hobbled down the platform steps of the Caricature Bar as fast as he could. Beneath the colorful Spanish tile canopy, he awkwardly tried to squeeze past tables.

Ginger saw that Danny was on his way over. She couldn't keep from quivering. Her eyes darted back to Kicky imploring her to act nonchalant.

In his haste, Danny's braced leg banged hard into the chair of a woman in a feathered hat, causing her drink to splash. Jim saw it happen and winced. The woman began to sop up the spill on the table, saying nothing. Her husband, a naval officer in dress uniform, leapt to his feet and bellowed, "Watch it, buster!"

Danny was flushed with embarrassment and quick to apologize. Cursing his own clumsiness, he leaned over and self-consciously rubbed his braced leg. The naval officer, now aware of Danny's disability, softened and sat back down. The mishap prevented Danny from seeing Sal storm in from the Broadway Lounge with Lenny at his heels.

Sal was steaming. He had to set Ginger straight. To avoid Kicky's interference, he clutched Ginger's arm and forced her onto the dance floor. Ginger was mortified. His intensity scared her. She didn't dare make a scene.

Lenny smirked at her reaction. He sauntered back up to the Caricature Bar for the wedding party's next bottle of champagne.

Kicky, furious at Sal for his callous treatment of Ginger, decided to stick around out of concern for her friend. She wished Danny would put that bastard in his place. She glanced over at Danny and realized he was tending to his crippled leg. Kicky's annoyance melted into compassion. The thought of what it must be like to have to live locked in that brace sent shivers up her spine. Her legs were her livelihood.

Danny had not witnessed Sal abusing Ginger. Jim hadn't seen it either. He had been distracted by Mary, who was on another break. And Rita was having so much fun dancing with the soldier, she wasn't even aware Sal had come into the room.

Danny finally looked up and was distressed to find Ginger was no longer with Kicky. He had blown his chance again. He was crestfallen to find she was now dancing with Sal.

Sal held Ginger rigidly in a vice grip. With a menacing smile, he grilled her, "So, tell me, Ginger, did you enjoy yourself with that soldier?"

Ginger tried to appease him. "I was just being nice. He's shipping out tomorrow."

"Where's he now?" Sal snapped as he sized up every soldier around them. "He's gonna have more than Hitler to worry about."

"It was only one dance, Sal."

He glared at her and told her in no uncertain terms, "I'm your only dance partner. *Capisce?*"

She had grown so tired of Sal's threats. He acted like he owned her. But Sal was dangerous. If he was this jealous over a dance with a random soldier, she could only imagine what he would do if he thought she wanted to get back together with Danny.

Ginger looked away. She spotted Fred and Gladys dancing cheek to cheek, the way she and Danny often had. She had gotten to know them when she had waited on them every week at the coat checkroom and was touched that the elderly couple still adored one another. Then she saw the loving groom gazing at his new bride as they danced. She choked back tears. That should have been her and Danny.

Ginger caught sight of Danny standing at the edge of the dance floor watching her. He seemed heartbroken. At least that's what she would like to believe. A lump formed in her throat as she became aware that Sal was focused on Danny, too.

Sal's anger swelled. He dragged Ginger off the dance floor and abruptly let go of her arm, leaving her alone and embarrassed. He swaggered over to a bristling Danny.

Ginger was alarmed. She knew Sal meant business. Her blood ran cold. Kicky rushed to her side.

Sal shoved Danny and growled, "Listen up, McGuire. Ginger's my girl now, and I give her everything she needs."

"Everything but respect," Danny spat.

"I'll teach you about respect," Sal snarled. He unbuttoned his suit coat to expose his handgun as a warning.

Danny didn't flinch. "What are you afraid of, Sal?"

"Not a gimp, that's for sure."

Danny found it hard not to laugh. Sal hadn't changed a bit. He still argued like a little kid and acted like the schoolyard bully.

Sal wanted to wipe that smug grin off McGuire's face and pound him into the ground. But too many people were watching. It occurred to him that it wouldn't be good for the club to let customers see him beating up on a cripple. So, he decided to let it drop for now. With a sneer, he re-buttoned his suit coat and returned to Ginger.

Danny stood there baffled by Sal's sudden reversal and continued to observe his every move.

Kicky hovered over Ginger in an effort to protect her.

Sal ignored Kicky and moved his face in close enough to Ginger's that she could feel the heat of his breath against her skin as he threatened, "You better watch your step!" He shot one last look of warning at Danny before heading back into the Broadway Lounge.

Rattled, Ginger broke away from Kicky and attempted to flee to the foyer through a sea of people. Kicky started to go after her but saw that Danny had beaten her to the punch and knew Ginger would be in good hands.

Danny wasn't about to let that bastard, Sal, disrespect Ginger anymore. He pressed through the crowd and called out her name. She stopped but didn't turn to face him. He caught up to her. Trying not to sound too harsh, he asked, "Why do you let him treat you like that?"

Ginger reeled around. "What do you care?"

"I care." Danny took her hand and asked gently, "Can we talk?"

"Oh, so now you want to talk," she snapped and swiped away tears.

"Come on. Let me buy you a drink."

Although she was still angry with him, she was curious about what he had to say. So there was no way she was going to refuse.

Danny assumed she was apprehensive when she glanced at the Broadway Lounge entryway. "Don't worry about him."

Ginger allowed Danny to guide her through hordes of people to the Caricature Bar. He squeezed her into a spot at Arthur's end of the bar and stood close behind her.

Jim and Arthur were chatting. They were thrilled to see Danny with Ginger. Grinning, Jim gave Danny a thumbs-up and winked at Ginger. It warmed Arthur's heart to know that Danny had taken his advice. Sporting a big smile, he went over to wait on them. "Danny. Ginger. What's your pleasure?"

"The lady will have a…" Danny looked to Ginger for confirmation and asked, "…pink lady?"

Ginger nodded. Her eyes twinkled.

Danny blushed. He turned to Arthur and added, "And I'll have another Dewars."

"Coming right up."

It felt natural to Danny to be standing there with Ginger, almost as if nothing had changed. Everything about her felt so familiar, so right. He breathed in the scent of the gardenia in her hair. It's what he'd always bought for her. The fact that Sal had bought this one made him jealous. But he was too caught up in the moment to dwell on that.

"You look so beautiful tonight. You always did look great in blue." The words tumbled out of Danny's mouth before he could stop them. Feeling awkward, Danny was grateful when Arthur delivered their drinks. Arthur refused Danny's payment with a wink and moved off.

Ginger was flattered by Danny's words but kept her emotions in check. After a glance toward the Broadway Lounge entryway, she picked up her cocktail and turned around to face Danny. She sipped on it as she studied him.

Danny took a gulp of his scotch. His defenses crumbled under her watchful eye. "I'm sorry I didn't tell you the truth. It wasn't right. Or fair."

"No. It wasn't."

"You have every right to be sore. I didn't want to hurt you but—"

"You did hurt me! You hurt me a lot, Danny! Why didn't you trust me to understand?"

"I did trust you to understand. That's the problem. I can't give you the life we planned. You deserve that life, Ginger." He thought about how Sal had treated Ginger, and it made him angry all over again. "And you're not going to get it with Sal Russo!"

Ginger closed her eyes and fought back tears. Danny hated himself for causing her pain. He leaned in and gently kissed the top of her head. He whispered tearfully, "I'm sorry."

Ginger stared down at her drink. "Your mother must have been beside herself when she found out you were injured. If she'd known all this time, there's no way she wouldn't have told me."

"Yeah. I wasn't ready to tell *her* either," Danny confessed sheepishly.

Ginger shook her head, astounded that he went to such lengths to keep his injury a secret. Knowing him so well, she could just imagine how hard it must have hit him to learn that his leg would be permanently lame. And he never was good at accepting help. She wanted to hold him, comfort him, and assure him that all would be well. But he would be too proud to let her. Frustrated, she wondered how he had ended up in the line of fire. "I thought you were only going over there to take pictures."

"Yeah. Funny thing about that. Those Japs don't make a distinction between enlisted men and correspondents," he said cynically. "And there was no place to hide."

"Oh, Danny. I never wanted you to go."

"I know. And now look at me." He backhanded his braced leg, resentful. "Ginger, you deserve better than half a man."

Ginger looked him in the eye, exasperated. She couldn't believe how hard he was being on himself.

Danny took another gulp of his drink. "You know, when I saw you out there on the dance floor with that soldier ... and then with Sal..." he choked up and looked away before admitting, "...I was wishing it was me out there with you."

Ginger's heart broke for him. He was still the same man to her, but she didn't know how to make him see that.

The orchestra began to play one of Danny and Ginger's favorites, the romantic number "The Nearness of You." Ginger got an idea. Though she wasn't sure how Danny would react, she was willing to give it a try. She put her drink on the bar. She reached for his scotch and placed his glass next to her own. She boldly took his hand, positioned it on her waist, and moved them into a dance pose.

Danny couldn't understand what she was thinking. He figured she must be in denial if she thought he could still dance. He knew he should nip this in the bud. To touch her and hold her again like this was unbearable. It was killing him.

Ginger felt Danny's resistance, but she wasn't going to stop now. Heart pounding, she met his gaze and implored him to give in to her. He was hypnotized by her sparkling green eyes. And once she rested her head against him, he couldn't fight it anymore. He reveled in being this close to her. Before he knew it, they were "dancing," swaying to the music, lost in time.

CHAPTER TEN

Rita, still dancing with the young soldier, began to wonder if Andy had arrived yet. She looked over at her table and was surprised to see no one there. She scanned the club and was stunned to find Ginger with Danny at the Caricature Bar. She couldn't understand what Ginger was doing with that *mamaluke!* Much to the soldier's disappointment, Rita quickly excused herself from him. She was determined to talk some sense into Ginger. She had almost reached them when Jim stepped in beside them. Instead, she positioned herself close enough to eavesdrop.

Danny was gazing at Ginger, unwilling to let her go. Her smile was filled with love. Jim tapped the face of his watch and interjected, "I hate to break up this reunion, kids." He flashed a smile at Ginger and said, "Hi there." Turning to Danny, he informed him, "It's quarter of ten. We've got to get back to the paper before they print the next edition."

Danny shot Jim a look of total frustration. He

couldn't believe he had to leave Ginger now. He'd gotten to a point with her that he'd thought would never be possible again. He was starting to think maybe Jim was right; maybe he could have a life with Ginger after all.

Jim saw the desperation on Danny's face. He offered to go get their coats to give Danny a few more minutes alone with Ginger. Grateful, Danny handed Jim his claim check. Jim gave him back his satchel and headed off.

Danny turned his focus back to Ginger. "I wish I didn't have to leave, but he's right. Eddie will be champing at the bit."

Ginger told him she understood and that she was supposed to meet Kicky in the Melody Lounge anyway. She glanced nervously toward the Broadway Lounge entryway again.

Danny whispered in her ear, "Don't let Sal ruin your plans." He took her hand and led her to the overflowing foyer.

Rita covertly followed.

The Grove was now filled beyond capacity. Revelers entering the nightclub had nowhere to go. At the bustling coat checkroom, Jim waved to catch Marilyn's eye. He pointed to his watch. She flagged him over to the counter, much to the annoyance of people who were waiting their turn. He gave her the claim checks with a substantial tip. She passed him the coats and hats. He winked. Her eyes gleamed, and she blew him a kiss.

Rosie nudged Marilyn to take notice of Ginger

walking hand-in-hand with Danny toward the revolving door. With a glint in her eye, Marilyn quipped, "Well, I guess Ginger *does* know Danny's back."

Rita pushed past intoxicated patrons to stay close to Danny and Ginger and listened in as Danny asked Ginger, "Can I see you later?"

Danny silently pleaded with Ginger. She was hesitant to give him an answer. While she longed to be with him, she feared Sal's reaction. "I really should explain things to Sal first, don't you think? I owe him that much."

"You don't owe him a damn thing. Why don't you let *me* take care of Sal?" Danny offered protectively.

Not wanting Danny to tangle with Sal, she insisted, "No, Danny. I'll talk to him. It's the right thing to do."

Danny didn't feel comfortable that she would be dealing with Sal on her own, but he relented. "Okay. I'll be back later anyway."

Rita was furious. Sal was aces. And Ginger was going to break up with him? Her poor brother! She had to let him know. She headed straight for the Broadway Lounge.

Jim brought Danny his things. They donned their coats and refastened their press passes to their fedoras. Jim gestured to the revolving door and lamented, "What a madhouse! Look at that mob! We'll never get out of here!"

Ginger giggled. Jim hugged her goodbye. Danny pulled her in close and kissed the top of her head. They gazed deep into each other's eyes one last time before he turned to follow Jim, who was squeezing through the crowd to the exit. The door rotated with a herky-jerky motion as it was pushed forward by people continually entering it and then slowed by people exiting it one section at a time. Ginger stifled a laugh as she watched Danny and Jim impatiently waiting their turn.

She began her own slow process of pressing through the packed foyer to the corridor leading to the Melody Lounge. Following others down the narrow stairway to the more intimate bar, Ginger had to contend with a number of intoxicated revelers heading up.

A couple of airmen tried hard to clear a path for Ginger. They made an interesting pair. One was tall and muscular. The other was short and wiry. The muscular one kept smiling back at her while the wiry one yelled out, "Clear the way for the beautiful girl!" Laughing, Ginger thanked them as they all entered the smoky, noisy, jam-packed lounge.

Ginger spotted Stanley, a sixteen-year-old busboy, clearing a table. He gave her a shy smile when she waved to him. She noticed Katherine across the room selling drink tickets. Ginger made her way toward the bar where Kicky was chatting with charming, young barman Daniel "Weissy" Weiss, the nephew of Barney and Jimmy Welansky.

Kicky took the last sip of her Manhattan. She was glad to see Ginger approaching. She wondered how it had gone between Ginger and Danny and was anxious to get the lowdown.

Ginger couldn't contain her excitement. Her apology came out in a gush. "Sorry, Kicky. I was with Danny!"

Kicky wore a Cheshire grin. "I know."

"He wants to see me later!"

Kicky locked eyes with Ginger and spoke to her soul. "Kiddo, you two belong together." Ginger nodded in agreement. Kicky sang Danny's praises, recalling what a great guy he had always been. Ginger beamed. But when Kicky pointed out how he still had guts, standing up to Sal, she sensed that Ginger had become uneasy. She empathized with her. "Yeah. We both know what a short fuse Sal has." She paused, letting it sink in before she went on. "He's bad news, and you know it. I saw what he did to you upstairs."

Ginger flushed with shame.

"You need to ditch Sal and fast," Kicky advised.

"I know. I will." The thought of having to confront Sal put Ginger's stomach in knots. She wished she was as brave as Danny.

"You can do it." Kicky gave her hand a reassuring squeeze. "But listen, I've got to scram and get ready for the next show. We're doing 'Ragtime Cowboy Joe' for Buck Jones! So let's talk later, honey." She touched her cheek to Ginger's.

Kicky looked over to fellow chorus girl Dot. The shapely, raven-haired beauty was having a drink at a table with an enamored sailor. Kicky called out to her, "Dot! Time to shake a leg!"

Dot stood up. She leaned over and gave the sailor

a seductive smile. Trailing a finger under his chin, she said, "Come on up and catch the show, good-lookin'." She winked and wriggled away to join Kicky. He followed Dot like a puppy dog through the crowd and up the stairs.

Ginger was in no hurry to return to Rita. She knew she couldn't hide the truth from her. She decided to stay for the show and enjoy a few minutes to herself.

While she waited, she began to worry. What was she going to say to Sal? No matter how she put it, he was bound to think she was ungrateful. He would be furious. Would she lose her job? Was Danny worth that? Of course he was! But her family counted on her income. She'd just have to cross that bridge when she came to it. Kicky was right, though. Sal had such a temper. Would he actually harm her? Worse yet, would he go gunning for Danny? The thought made her shudder. She tried to calm herself and was thankful the show was starting.

"Good evening, folks! I'm Goody Goodelle," announced a bawdy, buxom blonde in a flaming red dress. She was greeted with hoots and hollers and rousing applause. The two airmen gave her provocative whistles.

Goody sat down at the piano on the raised platform that turned slowly within the bar and shouted out, "Let's sing one for all the sailor boys out there!" She played and belted out a raucous rendition of "Bell Bottom Trousers." Rowdy drunken patrons sang along. Fun-loving Marines, airmen, and soldiers teased sailors and heckled their song.

Ginger found it all amusing and clapped in time with the music. A strong hand suddenly gripped her shoulder. Her eyes darted to it. Her heart skipped a beat when she recognized Sal's diamond pinky ring.

"What are you doing down here?" he asked. Ginger could feel the threat behind Sal's words. She shrank from him. He dug his fingers deeper into her shoulder and growled, "I asked you a question."

Ginger turned to face him. Rita was right there by his side. Under his interrogation, Ginger found herself empathizing with the many customers she'd seen Sal intimidate.

"Rita says she saw you with McGuire."

Ginger didn't deny his accusation. His eyes blazed. Rita stood there wearing a cold, I-told-you-so expression. Sal was incredulous. "But he's a goddamn cripple now!"

Ginger's anger flared in defense of Danny. Emboldened, she snapped, "You just shut your mouth!"

Rita was shocked. Ginger had never spoken to Sal that way.

Sal wanted to smack Ginger. He couldn't believe she'd turn on him like this, especially in front of all these people. The ungrateful bitch! She wasn't going to make a fool out of him. But she was the best dame he had ever gone around with, and he didn't want to lose her. In an effort to compose himself before he did anything rash, he gazed across the room.

Sal zeroed in on a soldier unscrewing a lightbulb from a palm tree in a corner. Frustrated, he shouted to

Stanley, "Hey! Kid! Get over there and screw that bulb back in the tree!"

Stanley, who was wiping off a table, hesitated. He saw the soldier and a girl kissing on the settee in the shadows beneath the palm tree. He was uncomfortable having to disturb them.

Rita sighed in disgust at Stanley's lack of confidence.

"Get over there, and do what I said!" Sal demanded.

Ginger eyed Sal with disdain.

"You got something to say about it?" he shot back at Ginger with venom. He grabbed her arm and was about to backhand her but checked himself. Instead, he leaned in close and snarled, "You're some piece of work. I'll deal with you later." Sal abruptly let go of Ginger's arm, leaving her shaken. He pushed past gawking customers and shoved his way up the stairs.

Rita watched after him with concern. She felt sorry for her brother. It seemed to her that he always got a raw deal when it came to women. She'd thought Ginger was different. Disappointed, Rita pounced on her. "How could you do this to Salvi? He's been nothing but good to you. I've never seen him so mad!"

Ginger blinked back tears.

Rita, not giving Ginger a chance to reply, started for the stairs to catch up with Sal. Noticing Stanley hadn't replaced the bulb yet, she gave him daggers.

Stanley withered under her disapproving stare. He saw an opportunity to redeem himself when a customer stood up to leave. He grabbed the empty chair and squeezed it in beside the soldier who was still smooching with his girl. Stanley stepped up onto the chair to screw the lightbulb back into the coconut shell on the faux palm tree.

The soldier looked up at Stanley and pleaded, "Aw, come on! We just want a little privacy."

Stanley tried to be polite. "I'm sorry, sir. It's rather dark in here. The few lights we have help to keep everybody safe."

Ginger heard some customers booing Stanley. The two airmen couldn't keep from laughing. She frowned at the disrespectful behavior. After all, she thought, the poor kid was just doing his job.

Satisfied that Stanley was obeying Sal's orders now, Rita made her way to the stairs.

Tipsy customers staggered out of the Grove onto Piedmont Street. Jim and Danny exited the revolving door. Jim, frustrated by the ridiculous amount of time it had taken them to make their way out, complained, "Christ Almighty! If this joint closed right now, it wouldn't empty out till midnight!"

Danny shook his head, amused. They buttoned up their topcoats and braced themselves against the frigid night air as they walked to the parking lot beside the club. Danny rubbed his hands together vigorously. "Man, it's cold out here!"

Jim gave Danny a wise-guy grin. "Especially

compared to the heat between you and Ginger."

Danny smiled back slyly. He wasn't about to disagree with him. "I'll say. I wouldn't have believed it, Jim, but when I was holding Ginger, I found out my third leg isn't dead after all."

Jim gaped in exaggerated awe. "You dog, you!" He roared with laughter. Feeling his liquor, he put Danny in a headlock and noogied his fedora.

Danny erupted into unrestrained laughter. He was positively euphoric. The floodgates had opened after months of holding in his emotions. Not to mention, he'd put away a few more Dewars than expected. It was so good to feel alive again.

Danny broke free of Jim's grip. "By the way, your timing stinks!" he said. "I was just getting somewhere with her."

"I'm sorry, buddy."

"You've got to bring me back here when we're done at the paper," Danny insisted.

"I've got no problem with that."

Danny relaxed, grateful. He shifted gears. "I'm sure you don't. I figure you want to get back to Mary, too," he said with a twinkle in his eye. "She's a looker. I'll give you that."

"Yes, she is. She's a sweet kid, too."

Danny found Jim's response surprisingly sincere.

Jim deflected the conversation back onto Danny. "So, you want Ginger back after all."

Danny shrugged but couldn't hide his joy.

"Good. Rip Van Winkle finally woke up," Jim ribbed him self-righteously. He flicked at the knot of the necktie he'd loaned Danny and professed, "I'm telling you, the tie worked. I bet she's thinking you've got some class now, and she should go back to you."

Danny rolled his eyes and batted Jim's hand away but couldn't help chuckling.

A fire alarm blared across the city, jarring them out of their reverie. Sirens wailed throughout the neighborhood. Flashing red lights reflected in the sky nearby.

Jim's face lit up. "Sounds like they stopped a couple of blocks away. Want to check it out?"

Danny sighed heavily. This was going to take more time than he wanted to spend.

Jim checked his watch. "It's only quarter past ten. We've got a couple of minutes."

"Oh, sure. *Now* we've got a couple of minutes," Danny teased.

Jim laughed and shrugged.

Kicky and Dot hastened up the stairs and into the chorus girls' dressing room. It was alive with chatter. Most of the other dancers were starting to put on their outfits for the next show. A few gals, already wearing flashy cowgirl costumes, vied for the mirror to touch up their makeup.

As Kicky and Dot got changed, Dot told Kicky, "That sailor was nice."

Kicky was amused. "You think all the sailors are

nice."

"But he was! He even bought me a drink. And he was cute, don't you think?" She fished a piece of paper out of her cleavage and showed it to Kicky. "Look. He wrote out his whole name and put down the name of his ship, too. He asked for my address and said he'd write to me."

"Well, that's sweet. I hope it turns into something good," Kicky said sincerely.

"Me, too." Dot winked.

Sal, still fuming from his encounter with Ginger, strode up to the bar in the Broadway Lounge. He muscled in between young Coast Guardsman Johnson and his date and bellowed to the bartender, "Gimme a shot of Johnnie Walker!"

Tiny hustled to pour the shot. Sal swigged it. He banged the glass down on the bar, startling Johnson and his girl. Sal took a deep breath. He straightened his tie, put on a smile, and returned to Welansky's table.

Rita struggled to squeeze past people cavorting with one another on the mobbed Melody Lounge stairway. She was anxious to find her brother and make sure he was all right.

Downstairs, Goody began to play "White Christmas." Fans, recognizing Bing Crosby's recent chart-topping hit, cheered and sang along with Goody.

Ginger saw that Stanley was having trouble in the dim light locating the bulb that had been loosened. She hoped the amorous soldier and the hecklers would leave him alone to finish his task.

Stanley lit a match, found the darkened bulb in the palm tree, and tightened it until it glowed. He blew out the flame, jumped down from the chair, and stepped on the match to be certain it was extinguished. Nearby patrons, including the two airmen, mocked him with a round of applause. Stanley just ignored them and went back to clearing tables.

Ginger was glad Stanley didn't let their childish behavior bother him. She was about to turn her attention back to Goody's show when something caught her eye—a bright blue flash high in the palm tree.

CHAPTER ELEVEN

A flame flickering in the palm tree in the Melody Lounge ignited silver-tipped fronds. Flames shot up reaching close to the hanging ceiling fabric. Ginger jumped into action. She grabbed Stanley's arm and made him aware of the dangerous situation. He rushed over and tugged hard on the tree to keep it away from the ceiling.

Ginger also alerted Weissy. He ran to Stanley with a pitcher of water. A bartender followed with a tank of seltzer. The men did their best to douse the flames, but it wasn't enough. Stanley yelled for the staff to bring more water.

It was so noisy in the lounge that most people were oblivious to the potential threat and kept singing along with Goody. Meanwhile, bartenders, barmen, and busboys dashed back and forth, water sloshing in their pitchers. Every time they managed to extinguish one flame another would spring up in a different spot. Customers sitting nearby remained unconcerned and even amused. To them, it all seemed like the madcap antics of a circus clown act. But this was no laughing matter.

The treetop quickly became a torch. A barman ran over and sprayed the entire contents of a fire extinguisher at it. Yet the flames were relentless. They rose up and set the ceiling fabric on fire.

Bits of sizzling satin rained down on Stanley and the other men standing below. Frightened by the sparks landing on their hair and clothes, they were quick to pat them out.

Ginger watched her coworkers with growing anxiety.

Weissy, seeking to stop the fire from spreading, tore a section of burning material away from an untouched portion of the ceiling. He yelped as it disintegrated into cinders in his hands. Despite his efforts, fire consumed more of the ceiling satin while a smoldering black hole grew deeper and wider above the tree.

A strapping bartender yanked with all his might to unmoor the tree. Even though his hands were blistered by the hot trunk and his face was seared by flaming fronds dropping down upon him, he continued to tug at the tree.

Tongues of hungry blue and orange flames licked at the ornamentation mounted on the wall nearby. Imitation bamboo and decorations caught like kindling. Fiery chunks pelted people on the settee below. Howling, they jumped to their feet.

The tree started to topple. Customers screamed as

they were bombarded with glowing embers. Backing away from it, they collided with others behind them.

Ginger was astounded at how fast the situation had gotten out of control. People were getting hurt. She had to get to Frank. He needed to call the fire department. She tried to make her way toward the stairs.

Goody could see the blaze once her piano platform rotated back around. She abruptly stopped performing. Her audience wondered why. Following her stunned gaze, patrons gaped in disbelief.

Katherine became aware of a sense of alarm coming from the crowd. She looked up from her post and was spellbound by the drama unfolding.

Two rows of flames began to make tracks across the ceiling toward where the two airmen were seated. The muscular airman sprang into action. He leapt up onto a table, scattering glasses and an ashtray onto the floor. With his pocket knife, he hacked at the untouched section of ceiling fabric. But the fire persisted.

Some patrons, paralyzed with fear, remained in their seats. Others, waking up from their stupor, broke into a full-fledged panic. Men shouted a warning and led the charge to the stairway. A few punched each other, vying to be first. People cursed and cried out as they shoved each other aside in desperation. Tables and chairs were overturned. The muscular airman and many others were knocked to the floor. The wiry airman was pushed away from his heroic friend and forced along with the crowd.

Ginger got swept up in the tidal wave as everyone tried to flee at once. Flames crackled above. She covered her head with her arms to protect herself from burning bits of satin raining down. She glanced up. The fire was ripping a path to the stairway. Ginger knew she needed to turn back. To divert from the torrent of customers rushing forward, she dropped to her knees and scooted under a table.

All around her, the drive for survival overcame the desire for moral decency. Every thought of civility was lost. Human beings stampeded like a herd of wild animals and trampled over one another.

Four engine trucks, two ladder trucks, and a rescue truck from the Boston Fire Department had responded to a call at the corner of Stuart Street and Broadway a couple of blocks away from the Cocoanut Grove. Well-respected veteran District Fire Chief Daniel Crowley grinned and shook his head. It was only a small fire on the front seat of a parked car.

Jim and Danny arrived just as Arnie, a young fireman, smashed his axe through the driver's side window. The fire quickly fed on newfound oxygen. Flames burst forth. Seasoned hose men, George and Charlie, hustled to extinguish them. Bobby, another young fireman, hacked open the seat to be sure there was nothing left smoldering. The rest of the firemen stood by in case they were needed.

Chief Louis Stickel ambled up to them. The accomplished deputy fire chief, one of Boston's two division chiefs, had been concerned when the call came in from such a populated area. He was conscientious about every fire and was always proud when his men got the job done in record time. He appraised their work with a satisfied nod.

The firemen began putting their equipment away. Jim was surprised to see so many trucks for such an inconsequential fire and listed all of them on his notepad.

Danny hobbled over to photograph the burnt-out car. Once he got a good shot, he packed the camera into his satchel. He was glad to be done taking pictures for the day.

Chief Stickel took note of the photographer's disability. He wondered, knowing the toll war took on young men, if he had seen action or if he had been afflicted with polio like many unfortunate souls, including President Roosevelt. No matter the cause, Stickel had a lot of respect for him. He was holding down a good job instead of shutting himself away.

Jim approached Chief Stickel, notepad at the ready. He introduced himself and inquired, "It seems like you brought an awful lot of equipment, Chief. Was there anything noteworthy?"

The deputy fire chief answered in an unhurried and sociable manner, "Nah, just a car fire. But you never know. This is a busy neighborhood."

Chief Stickel saw Danny coming over to join them

and welcomed him into the conversation. "Sorry, fellas. Nothing for the front page tonight. But I've got to tell you, superstitious firemen are always a little spooked when they get a run at exactly ten-fifteen."

Jim was curious. "Yeah? How come?"

"Because we use the code number ten-fifteen when a fireman dies," Chief Stickel informed them.

This was the kind of fact Jim found fascinating. Naturally, he recorded it on his notepad.

In the Cocoanut Grove's dining and dancing area, patrons were totally unaware of the calamity in the Melody Lounge. The restless audience clapped in rhythm in hopes of getting the next floorshow to begin. Singer Billy Payne approached Mickey Alpert on the stage and asked, "What's keeping the girls?"

The bandleader spread out his sheet music for their nightly tradition of performing "The Star-Spangled Banner." Agitated, Mickey told Billy, "I'm going to have to send somebody up there after them. We have to keep the show on schedule. We've got that live radio broadcast at quarter past eleven!" He noticed a couple of the movie moguls on the Terrace beckoning him over. Exhausted, he swore under his breath and whined, "Oh, Billy, I'm tired."

Billy felt for the poor guy. Mickey had been working night and day.

The temperature in the Melody Lounge was soaring. Thick, acrid smoke from burning satin, rattan, fish netting, and the faux palm tree was filling the place. Everyone was coughing and choking. Overwhelmed, some collapsed. The leatherette covering the walls was melting, curling up like writhing snakes. Toxic vapors were released, heated up, and became superhot gasses creating waves in the air that began to spin into a fiery sphere.

The crowd on the narrow stairway moved at a snail's pace. Rita, finally reaching the top, was startled to hear dreadful screams coming from the lounge below. She looked down and was baffled to see fearful patrons pushing and shoving to get up the stairs. Some passed out and dropped in a tangled heap. Rita was horrified when others recklessly stepped on the fallen to climb their way up.

Downstairs, the wiry airman struggled to go back for his buddy. The surge of the crowd pushing to reach the stairs was making it impossible. The heat was intense. In order to survive, the airman was forced to make the difficult decision to leave his friend behind. Desperate to get past all the people clogging the stairway, he hoisted himself onto the handrail and hauled himself up the length of it.

Rita jumped out of the way when the airman landed right in front of her. To avoid being trampled by the rest of those fleeing the chaos happening in the

Melody Lounge, she had to flatten her back up against the wall of the corridor.

The airman slammed down on the corner door's emergency bar and was exasperated when it did not open. The glowing exit sign above it only served to mock him. The locked door refused to budge. Other men joined him and attempted to force it open. The door remained steadfast.

A blue and yellow ball of flames rocketed up the stairway with a frightening roar. It set fire to the hair of those clambering up and over unconscious patrons. Hot cinders from burning ceiling fabric and fish netting on the walls pelted them. Screaming in agony, they fell down on top of the others on the stairs.

The airman and his helpers abandoned their effort to get the door open and took off down the corridor.

The shock of what Rita was seeing overwhelmed her. Fear for her own life compelled her to run. Panicked survivors drove her on. She bolted ahead of the stampede.

With a loud poof, the fireball shot around the corner from the Melody Lounge stairwell. It blasted in mid-air down the corridor toward Rita. She gasped and ducked as it whooshed past her, singeing people in its path. It zipped into the foyer, created a commotion at the maître d's podium, and tore on toward the Caricature Bar. It moved so swiftly many did not even notice.

Even from the stage, Billy could hear Frank the maître d' yelling and mistook it for the typical disturbance. He elbowed Mickey and pointed it out.

"Hey, there's a fight!"

Mickey sighed wearily and glanced over at the foyer. Frank was diving away from flames racing up the podium's drapery backdrop. Stunned, Mickey shouted, "Good God! It's a fire!"

Rita ran into the foyer and was about to rush out the revolving door with the others who had fled the corridor. Then she thought about her brother. She needed to warn him. Rita pushed through the line at the coat checkroom and cried out to the coat check girls, "Where's Salvi? I gotta find him! There's a fire!"

"What?" Rosie asked. Fearful, she clutched Marilyn's arm.

Panning the foyer from her limited vantage point, Marilyn scoffed, "Where?"

Rita gave up on getting an answer. "Vera! Go warn the people in the bathrooms!" she yelled and then dashed off to search for Sal.

Patrons, having overheard Rita, became alarmed. They clamored for their coats. From inside the coat checkroom, Rosie, Marilyn, and Vera could not see the flames at the maître d's podium. They couldn't tell if there was any real cause for worry or if Rita was just exaggerating. But Vera followed orders and set off for the restrooms. Rosie and Marilyn dutifully continued to tend to their nervous customers.

Rita plowed past a drunken sailor. He gawked at her. She ignored him and hurried toward the main room.

"Where's the fire, honey?" the sailor slurred with a laugh, having no idea how ironic his words were.

Smitten, he staggered after her.

Rita was aghast to see the podium drapery burning up. She had to find Salvi.

Mickey and Billy blanched as the fire spread from the podium to the Terrace in what seemed like an instant. They hurried to get down from the stage and over to the Terrace. They wanted to offer aid to the patrons, but all they could do was watch the blaze in horror.

Henry tried his best to protect the guests on the Terrace. He grabbed a fire extinguisher and shot the stream at the uncontrollable flames until the canister was empty. The busboy realized he'd better get out of there fast. He cast aside the extinguisher and scrambled down the stairs.

The family of Holy Cross Crusader fans and all the other diners seated there were in a mad frenzy to get off the Terrace. Anyone who tripped and fell was trampled. Those in the front row, including some of the movie moguls, leapt off the railing onto people below. Buck Jones was knocked backward in his chair. He crashed to the floor and laid there unconscious.

The gaseous fireball reached the Caricature Bar where Mary had just been peddling cigarettes. Petrified, she fled into the Broadway Lounge. She frantically squeezed by tables to get to Sal. Welansky was busy keeping everyone in his party in a jovial mood. Sharps, the bookie, ogled her. But the men got serious as soon as Mary blurted out that the club was on fire.

"Gesù Cristo!" Sal exclaimed as he and the other

men sprang to their feet. Sal pulled out his keys and started for the main club.

Buccigross wasted no time shifting into police captain mode. He grabbed hold of him and warned, "Sal, don't be a hero. We need to get to a callbox and alert the fire department."

Sal hesitated.

Buccigross shouted at him, "Sal! We've got to get out now!"

Arthur and his fellow bartenders watched in disbelief as the fireball ripped through the air along the Caricature Bar. It shot forward like a blowtorch, felling anyone in its path.

The naval officer who had reprimanded Danny was on his feet. He grabbed his wife's hand. They scurried away from their table and joined others streaming toward the foyer.

Rita was determined to get into the Broadway Lounge to look for Sal. She darted around frightened patrons running in all directions away from the fireball. The drunken sailor, still hot on Rita's trail, jumped aside and dragged her with him as the fireball was sucked into the entryway to the Broadway Lounge. Overcome with dread, Rita screamed, "Salvi!"

CHAPTER TWELVE

Capt. Buccigross shepherded Sal, Welansky, A.D.A. Byrne, and Sharps through the Broadway Lounge's inward opening door, into a vestibule, and out the door to the street. They barely made it out of the building before the blue and yellow fireball blasted into the lounge. It raced along the bar igniting every flammable thing from napkins to wallpaper. Shrieks rose up as anyone unfortunate enough to be in its way suffered its wrath.

A barrage of patrons rushed for the exit. Mary was knocked aside in the chaos. As she fell, the contents of her cigarette tray spilled to the floor.

Coast Guardsman Johnson was anxious to find his date. She had gone to the ladies' room a short time before. The surge swallowed him up. Although he tried to resist, he was shoved outside without her.

Tiny struggled to get out from behind the bar, but the mass of frenzied patrons was blocking the way.

Fearing for her life, Mary ditched the tray and

joined the mob trying to flee. Her eyes filled with tears when she looked back and realized Tiny was hopelessly trapped.

The combined weight of the panicked crowd being pressed up against the inward opening door made it increasingly difficult to keep the door open enough for anyone to get out. Those closest to it shouted at the ones behind them to stop pushing and back up. No one listened.

Ginger, remaining under the table in the Melody Lounge for protection, noticed that the pandemonium around her had quieted down. She coughed and gagged on the smoke and noxious air. She wiped sweat from her face with a trembling hand. Her hair had come undone. Somehow, the gardenia, though wilted, remained pinned in it. Clutching her purse, she crept out on her hands and knees.

An unconscious man lying on the floor was blocking her way. Ginger felt for a pulse but did not find one. Seeing that the man had not sustained any burns, she assumed he must have died from smoke inhalation. She closed her eyes and said a silent prayer for him. Having no other choice, she steeled herself and climbed over the dead body. She stood up and immediately covered her nose and mouth to protect herself from the smoke.

Weissy had taken refuge behind the bar. Aware

that smoke and heat rise, he crouched down low because the air closest to the floor would be easier to breathe.

Stanley, exhausted by his effort to pull down the palm tree, had slumped to the floor before the room had filled with smoke. He slowly got to his feet and immediately started coughing. He surveyed the lounge through the haze. All the flames had diminished, so he hoped the worst was over. But it made him uneasy that he couldn't see many people moving around.

Collecting himself, he shielded his nose and mouth and moved toward the stairway. He was puzzled to see that some of the customers had never left their seats. While upright and seemingly uninjured, they were eerily still.

He crept a little further and could now see a mound of bodies leading to the stairs. The realization that they might all be dead made him shake uncontrollably. He tried to take a deep breath to calm himself, but the smoke triggered another bout of coughing. Tears stung his eyes. He felt helpless. His mind grasped for a different escape route. He suddenly remembered the corridor to the kitchen.

Stanley staggered to the hidden door in the wall. Laboring to breathe, he gestured to it and called out to anyone who might hear him, "Come this way to the kitchen!"

Ginger was grateful that Stanley had found a way out. She saw Katherine hovering over her cash drawer protectively. "Let's go, Katherine!" Ginger croaked, her throat dry and sore.

Katherine whined, "I can't take the drawer. They'll accuse me of stealing!"

Ginger insisted she leave it behind.

Even though she was having trouble breathing, Katherine shook her head and was adamant. "No! I'm responsible for this money!"

"Don't be a fool, Katherine!" Goody yelled, exasperated, as she hiked up her dress and jumped down from the moving platform.

"Katherine, you'll die in here. Please come with us!" Ginger implored.

Everyone was coughing. Ginger checked for signs of life in people lying on the floor between her and Stanley. Her heart sank. She took Goody's hand, and they stepped over the bodies to reach the door. Ginger looked back, pleading with Katherine. The cashier would not budge. With tears trickling down her cheeks, Ginger followed Goody through the doorway.

Stanley glanced around to see if he could get anyone else's attention. Weissy popped his head up from behind the bar. Holding a wet towel to his face, he climbed over the bar and headed toward the door. Stanley could still hear cries, but the only ones who responded were two college boys and their girlfriends. The four of them stumbled through the doorway. Stanley followed them into the cramped corridor. Weissy was the last one through and closed the door behind him.

In the kitchen, the temperamental chef was irritated that waiters had not picked up their orders. Dinners were piling up, and the food was cooling off. There wasn't any space left to put one more plate. But it didn't matter. No new orders had come in. He was about to send a member of his staff upstairs to find out what was going on when the group from the Melody Lounge shuffled in, coughing and gasping. The chef and his staff were shocked to see smoke filtering in with them.

Flames leapt from the Terrace to the billowy blue satin covering the ceiling in the dining and dancing area and rippled across it. Fiery cinders rained onto everything and everyone below. Frank grabbed Lenny and ordered, "Run like hell! Open up that Shawmut Street door!"

Lenny took off like a shot. He shoved furniture aside and pushed distraught people out of his way. He floundered with the Venetian door façade. Angry, he smashed it apart. He thrust on the emergency bar of one of the exit doors behind it and cursed when he found it was stuck. Patrons around him tried it as well. They pounded on the door and kicked at it, but it wouldn't give. They even shouted at it in desperation, hoping they could will it open.

Lenny didn't know what to do. He scanned the burning room and saw Henry heading for the kitchen stairs. Without a word to anyone else, Lenny squeezed through the crowd to the stairs.

He raced down the steps behind Henry only to encounter the people from the kitchen running up. Lenny hollered at them, "Where are you going? There's a fire up here and everybody's going crazy! Get out of the way!"

"Upstairs?" Ginger asked. This news was unexpected and alarming.

Goody turned around and ordered those below her to go back. Everyone hustled down to the kitchen.

Henry darted into the corridor leading from the kitchen to the Melody Lounge, yelling, "We've got to get everybody out!"

Lenny sprinted after him.

Stanley tailed them, shouting, "Can't go that way!"

Lenny ignored the warning and flung open the door anyway. Smoke billowed into the corridor. It made them gag. Lenny and Henry peered into the stillness of the Melody Lounge and were stunned. Lenny gulped. "What the hell? Are all those people dead?"

Stanley pushed the door shut. "Like I said, we can't go that way. That's where the fire started."

Lenny blanched. Henry followed Stanley back to the kitchen with Lenny tagging along behind.

Once the three of them returned, Ginger tried to be the voice of reason. "We all need to stay together and come up with a plan."

When all hell broke loose, Public Safety Director Walsh had wasted no time taking the lead. He had jumped up from his table in the main room and persuaded folks to move away from the Shawmut Street exit and remain calm while he worked to break open the door.

Walsh and another man ran and slammed their shoulders hard into one side of the stuck exit door. Cold air gushed in when it burst open, and they tumbled out. Two more men shoved their shoulders at the other side to make the opening wider, not realizing that it was bolted at the top. It wouldn't budge. And no one was going to wait.

Frank had trouble getting people out through the narrow opening. Billy, who had been separated from Mickey by the crush of the crowd, offered Frank his help. Together, they tried to convince everyone to exit one at a time. But it fell on deaf ears. People stormed the doorway. Cramming to get out, they pressed together, arms jammed against their sides.

The fire was growing in intensity. Billy realized that waiting to evacuate this way would be foolhardy. He climbed onto the stage, charged past rattled musicians, and dove through the curtain. Sammy, Ray, and Pete, trumpets in hand, scrambled to flee the stage, too. In their haste, Sammy and Ray toppled podiums.

Pete tripped over an electrical wire and his foot tore open the bass drum. The rest of the musicians rushed after them, many of them abandoning their instruments. One refused to leave his heavy double bass behind. He barely made it beyond the stage before the curtain erupted in flames.

The fronds of the palm trees sizzled and burned to a crisp as red-hot fabric fell from the ceiling. Fire ravaged the tree trunks. Lightbulbs exploded in the coconut shells, popping like machine gun fire and shooting shrapnel into the air.

Patrons stuck in cramped seating areas tried to force their way out, knocking over tables and chairs. Meals and drinks went flying. Plates and glasses smashed on the floor. Some poor souls, pinned beneath furniture, were left behind.

Under the canopy, the members of the wedding party looked to one another in despair. They were hemmed in at their table by overturned furniture entangled with their own. They made a futile attempt to rise. The tearful bride searched her husband's eyes and saw his fear. He clutched her and held her close. Their mothers gazed at them and wept.

Jittery customers in the foyer were aware of the danger and swarmed the coat checkroom. They were determined to get their coats to protect themselves before fleeing into the frigid night air.

Rosie and Marilyn began to smell smoke. They nervously looked to one another, wondering what to do. Before they could decide, they were inundated by the disorderly crowd.

Upstairs in their dressing room, Kicky, Dot, and the other chorus girls had not yet learned of the horror going on below. They were taken aback when the three trumpeters and some of their bandmates burst in.

"Hey! What do you mean barging in here?" Kicky scolded them. Dot, who was still putting on her costume, reached for her coat.

Sammy, the fatherly one of the trio, averted his eyes and apologized. He turned Ray and Pete's heads away from Dot, as well. Ray batted at Sammy's hand and protested, "What are you doing? There's no time for good manners! There's a fire downstairs!"

The chorus girls shrieked. A few of them dashed out and down the stairs before Sammy could stop them.

Pete, the youngest of the three trumpeters, threw open a window and poked his head out. Sounding hysterical, he announced, "It's all flames and smoke down there! We've got to get to the roof!"

Kicky swallowed hard, eyes wide. "The roof?"

Dark, dense smoke hung in the air at the Caricature Bar. Overcome by noxious fumes, some patrons slumped over the bar, while others slipped from their stools to the floor. Fire consumed all the celebrity caricatures and photos. The likeness of Buck Jones burned to ash.

Arthur was stricken with fear. His only exit, the half door built into the bar, was engulfed in flames. He reached for a fire extinguisher on the wall, but it was so hot that he couldn't touch it. Liquor bottles exploded. Arthur was hit with hot liquid and shards of glass. He held up an arm to shield his face. He began to cough and gasp for breath. Desperate, Arthur climbed up onto the bar to escape but slipped and fell backward. He crashed into the bottle display and was showered with glass.

At the coat checkroom, the arrogant man who had given Frank a hard time about the wait to be seated frantically pushed others aside. Wife in tow, he waved his claim check in Rosie's face and demanded, "Give me my wife's mink right now!"

Rosie shrank off with his claim check to retrieve the coat. Marilyn, feeling overwhelmed, wondered what was keeping Vera.

Screams drew everyone's attention. A woman whose hair was on fire was being shoved across the foyer by those fleeing the corridor from the restrooms.

Marilyn was shocked to see it was Vera! Vera was forced outside via the revolving door.

Hordes of people, driven by sheer terror, flooded into the foyer from the main room. The thunderous pounding of feet mixed with shouts and screams rose to a crescendo. Patrons were instinctively returning to where they had entered the club. As far as they knew, the revolving door was the only way out. They weren't thinking about how long the process would take. Only one or two people at a time could enter each section. They pushed on the door, but it rotated ever so slowly before they could exit.

The naval officer tightened his grip on his wife's hand and led her through the crowd. He was confident they would make it out if they just remained calm. They were almost there. He slipped into the next available section and attempted to take her along with him. But the door jolted forward abruptly. He was thrust ahead against his will, and he lost her.

Rosie brought out the mink coat, looked around at the chaos, and gasped. "What's going on?"

Wide-eyed, Marilyn told Rosie, "We need to get out of here!"

The arrogant man reached over the counter and snatched the mink out of Rosie's hands. He herded his wife to the revolving door. He shoved the naval officer's wife out of the way, pushed his own wife into the next section, and jumped in with her.

The revolving door was overcrowded. Those ready to exit to the street tried to keep it turning. But others, desperate to cram into spaces already occupied, held it back. Only a few more people, including the naval officer, were able to escape.

Once outside, the naval officer looked back through the glass, hoping his wife was in the next section. Undaunted when he did not see her, he gripped the frame of his empty section and tugged on it in an attempt to make the door rotate. Others joined in, but it would not budge.

The naval officer and his helpers watched in disbelief as those still hopelessly trapped inside the door screamed for help. It jerked back and forth. Coats and shoes got caught in its crevices. People struggled to free them. Their hands became wedged in between the partitions. They cried out in agony. Some, squashed within the sections, could no longer bear the escalating heat. They passed out, filling the revolving door with dead weight. It was now jammed shut.

Inside, smoke permeated the air. Everyone in the foyer was coughing. People stormed the revolving door, knocking each other to the floor to get to an exit that was no longer viable. They clawed their way like animals over the fallen, creating a human pile in front of it. Some were crushed beneath the weight of six to eight people layered above them. It was a fierce battle for survival that no one could win.

Many succumbed to the acrid air. Rosie and Marilyn's panic turned to despair when Marilyn started to cough profusely. She choked. Unable to catch her breath, she slumped over the counter. Rosie gasped. She shook Marilyn but could not rouse her. Rosie began to cry. Feeling lost, all sound seemed to fade away from Rosie's consciousness.

Rosie gazed around numbly. Her eyes landed on the overloaded coatrack. With a glimmer of hope, she climbed out over the checkroom counter and made her way through the maze of desperate people to get to it. She shoved the coatrack aside and ripped down the drapery that had been concealing the plate glass door. Though gagging on smoke, she managed to yell, "Somebody help me smash open this door!"

Two Marines came to her aid. They thrust the coatrack at the door. The glass did not break. They attempted it a second time. Still, they had no success. Weakened from taking in smoke while exerting themselves, the Marines passed out.

Rosie banged her fists on the door, whimpering. She slid down it, hands and face pressed against the glass.

In the main room, some waiting to escape through the opening to Shawmut Street began crumpling to the floor. Others scrambled to climb over them but also lost consciousness. Flames shot to the doorway and set it ablaze. Elderly Fred and Gladys watched helplessly from the edge of the dance floor. Fearing this was the end, they clung to one another with the consolation that at least they were together.

The entryway to the Broadway Lounge was blocked by unmoving bodies. The section of the

Caricature Bar leading to it continued to burn. Thick smoke filled the main room.

Rita was becoming woozy from coughing uncontrollably on the noxious air. People were collapsing all around her. She stumbled to the dance floor. She was heartsick to see the redheaded soldier she had danced with lying there unconscious. The smitten, drunken sailor who had saved her from the fireball staggered over. He passed out, knocking her to the floor and pinning her beneath him.

For the nervous group in the kitchen, the options for fleeing the building were becoming limited. Since all exits from the dining room and the Melody Lounge were inaccessible, Ginger and the others considered additional ways they might escape. The quick-thinking chef had a revelation. He shouted out, "The delivery door!"

"Don't bother. It's locked," Billy told them as he stumbled in from an adjoining room, out of breath. Rubbing his sore hands, he added, "So's the stage door. I even tried to bust them open."

Hopes were squashed until Stanley exclaimed, "But there's a key!" He checked a peg on the wall where it was usually hanging but groaned when he found it empty.

Weissy grumbled, "Arthur has the key. There was a late liquor delivery."

Everyone's optimism deflated with a collective sigh. Their anxiety level rose tenfold as the sounds of scuffling feet, crashing furniture, and heavy thuds resounded from above. Anguished shouts and nightmarish screams sent shivers up their spines. Lenny started pacing and cried, "We're going to die down here!"

"Then we'd better give another try to breaking down a door!" Henry challenged.

Lenny nodded to him in agreement, and they both raced into the next room. Ted, the more impulsive of the college boys, elbowed his buddy, Mel. The two of them charged after Lenny and Henry to see if they could help. Ted and Mel's girlfriends, Helen and Susie, clasped hands and rushed to keep up with them. Ginger, Stanley, and everyone else followed close behind.

With the car fire at the corner of Stuart Street and Broadway extinguished and their equipment stowed away, the firemen were ready to depart. Chief Crowley, George, Arnie, Bobby, and Charlie climbed aboard their trucks. The other fire trucks idled nearby. Chief Stickel headed to his car after stopping to chat with Officer Patrick Fitzgerald, a robust beat cop.

"Fitzy" spotted Jim and Danny, whom he held in great affection. He'd known them since they were kids when he was a rookie walking the beat in their neighborhood. As he approached, he greeted them warmly in his strong Irish brogue, "Hello, Mr. Reed and Mr. McGuire. You boys finding trouble again?"

Eyes twinkling, Jim answered, "You know us, Fitzy, always where the action is."

"Oh, don't I know it." Fitzy chuckled. He shook his head, remembering all the times he'd gotten them out of trouble. He spied Danny's brace, grew serious, and noted, "Too much action by the looks of you. Did the Japs get you?"

Danny nodded. Before he could comment, they were distracted by George shouting, "Hey, Arnie, look over there!"

All eyes turned to where George was pointing. A dark column of smoke was rising from a building a block away.

Arnie called, "Chief Crowley! Looks like we've got another one!"

Chief Crowley jumped out of his truck and ran to Chief Stickel's car. He rapped on the window and yelled for Chief Stickel to wait. Stickel got out. He checked where Crowley was indicating and said, "Oh, brother! Not the Cocoanut Grove!"

Chief Stickel got back in his car and sped toward the club. Chief Crowley hopped into his truck and followed. The other trucks pulled out in succession, sirens blaring.

Jim blanched. "Jesus, Danny, they think it's the Grove!"

The blood drained from Danny's face. "Oh my

God, Jim! Ginger's still in there!" Instinctively, he tried to run. Jim kept pace alongside him.

Fitzy's heart skipped a beat upon hearing that Danny's beloved might be in danger. He could only imagine how upset Danny would be if anything bad happened to Ginger. Many lives were likely to be in jeopardy. Without hesitation, he ran toward the club.

Danny was frustrated by his disability. He waved Jim on, pleading, "Go on. Make sure she's all right!"

Jim nodded and bolted away just as a fire alarm rang out.

CHAPTER THIRTEEN

Heavy smoke poured out the double door entrance of the Cocoanut Grove's new Broadway Lounge and billowed upward. Soot blackened the enormous sign that hung corner to corner across this side of the club.

Coast Guardsman Johnson stood outside near the doorway and assisted people out of the building. He was anxious to know if his date was safe and hoped to find her among them. Patrons, who had managed to escape, gathered in small groups along the sidewalk and in the street. Many, having fled without retrieving their coats, shivered in the cold night air. Nervous men hugged crying women.

Sal and Welansky, standing with Byrne and Sharps, shot furtive looks back at the Grove. They were well aware there could be legal problems for keeping most of the doors locked. But Sal talked himself out of taking any action, knowing the staff had keys to the stage and delivery doors.

Capt. Buccigross returned from putting in the call

and made sure people were out of the way of oncoming fire trucks. He saw Chief Stickel pull up to the club and went to fill him in. The deputy fire chief had hoped the issue was concentrated to the new lounge, but, after hearing Buccigross' account, he was instantly unnerved.

Sirens wailed as the trucks that had responded to the earlier call on Stuart Street roared up and screeched to a halt, blocking traffic on Broadway. Chief Crowley leapt from his truck to strategize with Chief Stickel about how to proceed. Stickel put Crowley's team to work on Broadway knowing that Buccigross' call would bring reinforcements he could send to the main entrance on Piedmont.

George hooked up a hose to a hydrant. Arnie, Bobby, Charlie, and the rest of their crew hustled to unload additional equipment. The pulsating red lights of their fire trucks intermittently illuminated frightened faces looking on.

Impatient, Coast Guardsman Johnson pushed his way into the Broadway Lounge. Within seconds, he carried a woman to safety and laid her upon the sidewalk. He dashed back inside and brought out Mary. Her dress was torn, and her face was smudged with soot. He dove back in again before anyone could stop him.

Mary told Chief Stickel, George, and Charlie in a trembling voice, "He's trying to find his date. There are so many people piling up behind the door, it's hard to keep it open! The whole place is on fire! And poor Tiny…." Thinking about him, she broke down.

"Everybody, stay back!" Chief Stickel ordered. He herded people to the street, away from the burning building. Fitzy ran up to the scene. He and Capt. Buccigross held civilians back as George wrangled the hose through the entrance and shot water at the inward opening door to cool it down.

Jim, just arriving, spotted Mary and rushed over to her. He removed his topcoat and drew it around her. She sobbed in his arms.

Bobby and Arnie took turns swinging their axes at one of the lounge's two glass block windows, but it wouldn't break. Chief Crowley beckoned two additional firemen with axes to give Bobby and Arnie a hand. All four whacked at the glass until they smashed through it. Thick smoke poured from the opening. The firemen hastily pried away glass. Their anguished faces conveyed the dire situation.

Everyone watched them with apprehension. Jim took out his pad and scribbled some notes.

A man's charred hands reached out through the jagged hole in the glass. He poked his head out next.

"Get a line on this window!" Chief Crowley shouted. Before hose men could respond, the man went up in flames with a blood-curdling scream. Chief Stickel blanched. He wondered how many more were dying in there. Onlookers cried out in horror. Shudders rippled through the crowd. Jim shielded Mary from the gruesome sight.

Flames roared out, chasing the axe-wielding firemen into the street. Hose men blasted water at the window. Chief Stickel made a decision on the spot given the intensity of the fire and the likelihood of hundreds being trapped within. He told Crowley he was skipping the second level alarm and calling in a third.

Danny was out of breath by the time he got there. He gaped at the flames now rocketing high into the sky. Firemen carried out victims and laid them on the cold, cobblestone street. Danny forced himself to move closer to get a look, not knowing if they were dead or alive. Many were badly burned. He thanked God he didn't see Ginger among them, but it made him even more frantic to find her. He searched the faces of the gathering survivors and spotted Sal. He went straight over to confront him. "Where's Ginger?"

Sal could not believe this cretin was asking him where Ginger was. He didn't know. And even if he did, he wasn't about to tell him.

Danny grew more insistent. "Where is she?"

Sal continued to ignore him. Danny was infuriated by his cavalier attitude. He spun Sal around. Sal tried to brush him off. Danny wouldn't let go of his arm. Sal growled, "I don't know. Last I saw her, she was in the Melody Lounge."

"You left her in there?" Danny yelled, incredulous. "You bastard!" He threw down his satchel, grabbed Sal by the lapels, and slammed him up against the rescue truck. He hauled off and punched Sal right in the kisser, splitting his lip. Before Sal could react, Danny slugged him again.

The commotion drew the attention of both Capt. Buccigross and Fitzy. They ran over to break it up. Jim rushed to Danny's side. Danny let Sal go with a shove. Sal went for his gun. Buccigross took hold of Sal's arm and advised him, "Let it go, Sal. We've got enough to deal with right now."

Sal withdrew a handkerchief. As he dabbed blood from his lip, he glared coldly at Danny. He straightened his clothes and allowed Buccigross to steer him away. Fitzy kept a wary eye on Sal, since he'd never trusted him *or* his father.

"Jesus, Danny, that son of a bitch wanted to shoot you!" Jim said, astounded.

Danny brushed it off. His only concern was for Ginger. "He left her in there, Jim! He left her in there!"

Mary came over to Jim. He put a protective arm around her.

"Mary, have you seen Ginger? Ginger Logan?" Danny asked, hopeful.

She bit her lip and shook her head. Jim saw the panic in Danny's eyes and tried to reassure him. "Don't worry, buddy, we'll find her."

A fire alarm rang out three times, rattling their nerves.

Coast Guardsman Johnson ran out of the Broadway Lounge screaming. Shrieks rose up from the crowd when they realized he was on fire. Johnson dropped to the sidewalk and rolled around in a frenzy. Bobby leapt on him, smothering the flames.

Danny and Jim stared in shock. Mary buried her face in Jim's shoulder and sobbed. Jim sadly reminded Danny how the coastguardsman had happily scooped up their seats in the lounge for his date. They felt even worse for the guy when Mary cried, "He can't die. He saved my life!"

A doctor came out of the crowd and offered his aid to Johnson. Bobby stepped into the street to let the doctor take over. Jim stopped Bobby and asked him if the coastguardsman was still alive.

"Yup. But he might wish he wasn't," Bobby answered. Seeing the confusion on Jim's face, he explained, "If he hangs on, he'll be facing months of burn treatments, skin grafts.... He'll thank God for morphine." Jim nodded in agreement. The fireman went back to work.

Two policemen arrived on foot. Capt. Buccigross ordered them to help Fitzy keep the nervous onlookers calm. He then rejoined Chief Stickel.

The whine of sirens announced the arrival of Deputy Fire Chief John McDonough and his company. The direct, tough-as-nails veteran was in charge of the district that encompassed the Cocoanut Grove. He left his trucks and equipment on Piedmont Street to seek out the city's other deputy fire chief on Broadway. "Chief Stickel, what have we got?"

Chief Stickel didn't mince words. "It's a hot one, and there's a hell of a lot of people trapped inside. Police Captain Buccigross here tells me he believes it started in the main section of the club."

Chief McDonough's heart sank at the prospect of *that* nightmare. His dander rose. "Damn it!" he shouted. "I just knew something would happen here! I told them repeatedly not to overpack this place!"

Having heard McDonough's tirade, a deep sense

of foreboding began to overwhelm Danny.

McDonough told Stickel, "I'll go see if I can get in from Piedmont. Maybe we should call in a fourth alarm."

Chief Stickel ordered Chief Crowley to do so. Capt. Buccigross sent Fitzy with Chief McDonough.

Seeing McDonough and Fitzy heading to Piedmont, Welansky grumbled to Sal, "Go keep an eye on things." Sal felt a little uneasy, but he obeyed his boss' orders.

Mary, concerned that none of the firemen were checking the doors on Shawmut Street, brought it to Chief Stickel's attention. He beckoned Bobby, Arnie, and Charlie and said, "Young lady, lead these men to those doors."

Jim and Danny knew Mary was frightened, but they encouraged her to lend her assistance. The three firemen accompanied Mary to Shawmut.

Danny saw Sal follow Chief McDonough and Fitzy toward Piedmont Street. It dawned on him that they would be unlocking the door leading to the Melody Lounge. Danny needed to get in there to find Ginger. He grabbed his satchel. Jim knew what Danny was thinking. The two of them took off for Piedmont.

In the calm before the storm, four medics napped on cots in Massachusetts General Hospital's ambulance station. Two others played a competitive game of gin rummy. Everett leaned his small-framed body back in his chair and sheltered his cards from Howie's view. He adjusted his eyeglasses and scrutinized his hand. Howie puffed on a cigarette. He uncrossed his long, lanky legs, sat forward, and griped, "Come on, Everett! Play a card already! At this rate, we'll still be playing when our shift is over."

Everett raised his eyebrows in mock defiance. He cocked his head and teased, "Hey, don't rush me. I'm working out my strategy."

Howie heaved a sigh and stubbed out his cigarette. A perky little nurse burst in. Everett welcomed the intrusion. He flashed a charming smile and asked, "What's shaking, Mabel?"

Mabel didn't take the time to acknowledge his flirtation. Instead, she alerted all the medics in a tone that meant business, "Look alive, fellas!"

The sleeping medics woke abruptly and snapped to attention. Everett was surprised by the escalated sense of urgency coming from the normally unruffled nurse.

Mabel's voice rose feverishly as she told them, "Word just came in. The Cocoanut Grove is on fire! They're going to need every ambulance available!"

Trumpeters Ray and Pete climbed out the window

of the chorus girls' dressing room and up the fire escape to the roof. They assisted Kicky, Dot, and the other girls up after them. The musicians followed. Sammy went last to make sure they all got out safely.

Once Sammy reached the roof, Ray and Pete rushed over to him. Pete was shaking. His words spilled out in a torrent. "I thought we'd be able to get onto the roof next door, but it's too far to jump! What are we going to do, Sammy?"

The chorus girls and other musicians ran about, anxious to find a safe way down. Most of them flooded to the Piedmont Street side of the club to check things out. Kicky and Dot decided to rejoin the three trumpeters on the Shawmut Street side. The two frightened women, freezing in their skimpy costumes, clung to one another to share Dot's coat.

Ray noticed his feet were beginning to feel very warm. "Is it just me, or is this roof getting hot?"

Astonished to find the tiles beneath them melting, the five of them hopped from foot to foot on the sizzling roof. They looked across to the group on the Piedmont side and were stunned to see them leaping off.

Down below on Piedmont Street, Danny and Jim shadowed Sal who was following Chief McDonough and Fitzy. They were all shocked when the musicians and chorus girls landed on cars, one of them being Danny's, in the Grove's parking lot. Miraculously, those who had jumped only suffered minor scrapes and bruises. McDonough, satisfied that medical assistance wasn't required, continued on with Fitzy.

Sal trailed after them with Danny and Jim close behind.

A fire alarm echoed across the city four times.

Up on the Shawmut Street side of the roof, Pete stared wide-eyed, shocked by what he had just witnessed. He turned to the others in desperation and announced, "I think we're going to have to jump, too!"

Just the idea of it made Kicky's stomach lurch. She could hardly breathe. Attempting to alleviate Kicky's fears, Dot said, "Don't listen to him, sweetie. The firemen will get us down."

"But we're frying now!" Ray lamented.

"And I don't want to be a hamburger!" Pete added.

Ray and Pete nodded to each other in solidarity. They cradled their trumpets and stepped up onto the brick ledge.

"What are you doing? Wait!" Sammy shouted at them. But his words fell on deaf ears. Ray and Pete each took a deep breath and jumped off the roof together. Sammy's mouth gaped open. Kicky and Dot screamed.

The two trumpeters landed hard on the sidewalk just as Mary, Bobby, Arnie, and Charlie rounded the corner. Mary shrieked. She watched helplessly as Bobby and Arnie bolted to Ray and Pete who laid there moaning, clutching their legs and crumpled trumpets. Charlie looked down the street for other doors.

Shawmut was an old brick street that had a back-alley feel. Three signs advertising "DINE AND DANCE," "COCOANUT GROVE," and "VISIT THE MELODY LOUNGE" hung on the nightclub's brick backside. Ironically, while there were two service doors and the double dining room door, not one of them was a public entrance.

Smoke billowed out the other end of the club. Charlie hurried down the street to investigate. He quickly checked the stage door and the delivery door for heat. Although they were relatively cool to the touch, which indicated there was no fire behind them, he was annoyed to find them both locked. He continued toward the source of the smoke. A couple of people darted out through the burning dining room doorway with their hair and clothes on fire. Charlie was relieved when a fast-acting man rushed to them and patted out the flames.

A cacophony of sirens from emergency vehicles grew louder as they neared. Survivors standing in the street scattered to the sidewalk as ambulances arrived on the scene. Charlie grabbed a blanket from the first ambulance that stopped. He ran with it to the burning doorway and smothered the flames.

Everett and Howie jumped out of their ambulance and headed to Ray and Pete. Bobby and Arnie stepped aside and let the medics take over.

Above them on the rooftop, Dot yelled, "Help us, please! We're up here!" Mary gasped when she saw her coworkers trapped on the roof waving to get their attention.

Bobby looked up and shouted to them, "Don't jump! We'll get you down!" He raced back to Broadway and returned with a ladder. He hoisted it to the roof and, with the grace of an athlete, was up it in an instant.

Hesitant, Kicky told Dot, "You go first." Dot jumped into Bobby's arms. After helping her descend, Bobby hustled back up.

Sammy coaxed, "Come on, Kicks. You next."

Bobby saw Kicky's fear and sought to ease her anxiety. "Scared of heights, honey? Don't worry. I won't let you fall."

Kicky looked into his smiling blue eyes. Feeling assured, she climbed onto the ladder and into his arms. Bobby guided her down. Sammy followed them, unaided. Though still trembling, Kicky was relieved once they were all safe on the ground. Bobby approached an ambulance driver, brought back a blanket, and wrapped it around Kicky like a cloak.

"Thank you!" Kicky said breathlessly. She kissed Bobby's cheek.

Wowed, Bobby's eyes twinkled. He grinned and said, "Thank *you*."

She smiled and asked, "What's your name, hero?"

"Bobby."

"Everyone calls me Kicky."

"See you around, Kicky," Bobby said and tipped his helmet. He left to assist Charlie. Kicky gazed after him.

Sammy watched with concern as medics Everett and Howie placed Ray and Pete on stretchers and loaded them into their ambulance. Sammy looked around for anyone else he might know and was surprised to see Mickey wandering in a daze with a woman's fur coat draped over his shoulders. Mickey's clothes were burnt and his arms were bleeding. He seemed to be in shock. Public Safety Director Walsh also noticed this. He slapped Mickey and shook him into coherency. Sammy ran to Mickey's side.

Danny and Jim drew closer to the club's main entrance on Piedmont. They watched with apprehension as the Cocoanut Grove's neon sign sizzled, the marquee flickered, and both went out.

In the room beyond the kitchen, Ginger, Stanley, and the rest of the group scurried behind Henry and Lenny past a walk-in refrigerator and a freezer. The motors on the refrigeration units suddenly went quiet, and the lights went out.

Upstairs, the main room was now only lit by the hellish inferno that was ravaging everything and everyone.

CHAPTER FOURTEEN

The group in the refrigeration room was stunned to find themselves in pitch darkness. Ginger was amazed that she could no longer see Stanley standing right in front of her.

Henry flicked on his cigarette lighter. Its flame provided enough illumination for Ginger to see terror on the shadowed faces. Goody's cheeks were wet with tears. Billy was tense. College boy Ted was holding his wisp of a girlfriend, Helen, close. Susie had her arms wrapped around Mel's narrow waist and her face buried in his shoulder.

The light diminished as Henry started through the doorway to another room. Lenny was right behind him. Everyone else was about to follow until Lenny became apprehensive. He grabbed Henry's arm to hold him back. "Don't you feel that heat?"

"It's just the furnace," Billy reminded them.

"Are you sure that's all? What if that room is on fire now?" Lenny challenged.

A wave of uncertainty rippled through the rest of the group as they felt the heat, too.

"It's a waste of time anyway. I told you the doors are locked!" Billy said.

Henry would not be deterred. "We have to try."

"Well, I'm not taking the chance," Lenny declared.

"Suit yourself. If I get one of them open, I'll let you know." Henry pulled away from him. Weissy barged past Lenny and took off with Henry, leaving everyone else in the dark.

Henry and Weissy were relieved to find nothing burning in the next room. Billy had been right. The source of the heat was the furnace. Even though it had just shut down, it was still hot. They found the stairway that led to the delivery door. Using the flickering flame of Henry's lighter to see, they were able to make it up the steps and enter a smoke-filled corridor. Other employees gathering there were banging on the locked delivery door and pleading for help. It didn't bode well.

The group left behind in the refrigeration room was huddled together, too afraid to move. Billy flicked on his lighter and told everyone, "We should wait for the firemen. At least we can breathe in here."

"Yeah. But for how long?" Mel countered. He had expressed what many of them were worried about having witnessed others succumb to the lack of oxygen in the Melody Lounge.

"He's right. We can't just stand around!" Goody insisted.

Billy had an inspired idea. Moving to the walk-in refrigerator, he announced, "Hey, we can get in the icebox! We'll be safe in there. It's fireproof!"

"Good thinking, Billy!" Goody said and hurried over to him.

Billy held the refrigerator's hefty metal door open for Goody. He got inside after her, dousing his lighter both for safety and to conserve oxygen in the enclosed space. The chef and his kitchen staff rushed to join them. They heaved out crates of food to make more room and crammed in, too. Lenny squeezed in next. Stanley pushed Ginger forward, but Lenny got in her face and snarled, "Beat it! It's full!"

Stanley couldn't believe it. But Ginger was not surprised. She knew this was typical of Lenny.

Lenny started to close the door on them. Stanley fought him for it. Ted, the brawnier college boy, yanked it wide open and clocked Lenny right in the jaw. Lenny was furious. He popped Ted in the nose and squirmed away. He slammed the door and held it shut from within.

While Helen fretted over Ted, Stanley grabbed the handle and tugged to no avail. Ginger checked on Ted. He assured her his nose wasn't broken. Mel was livid and shouted obscenities. He kicked at the refrigerator door. "Ted, help me yank on this door. Maybe together we can wrestle it from him."

"Nah. He said it was full anyway," Ted lamented.

Susie whined, "Now what?"

"Maybe we should go the way those other guys went and look for that delivery door," Ted suggested.

"No! We all felt that heat!" Mel reminded him. "They never did come back for us. They're probably burnt to a crisp!"

The girls shuddered at the thought. No one spoke for a while. Ginger realized how eerily silent the building had become. Almost dreading to put it into words, she whispered, "I don't hear anything moving upstairs."

The dead calm was a new concern to everyone. Stanley shared a thought. "It might mean there's a way out upstairs now. Maybe we should check."

"It sure would help if we could see something," Mel complained.

"There might be a flashlight in the kitchen," Stanley offered.

Now that they had a plan, the small group set off with Stanley in the lead. Groping their way along the wall, they crept back toward the kitchen.

Across town, the Holy Cross Crusaders' victory celebration was coming to a close. The Boston College Eagles, dressed in modest suits and ties, looked somewhat out of place in the stately Parker House. But the affluent Holy Cross players and dinner hosts

Mayor Tobin and Fire Commissioner Reilly seemed very much at home in the nineteenth century luxury hotel with its opulent décor that reflected the elegance of a bygone era.

The Holy Cross players beamed as they posed for a team portrait. Newspapermen took photographs of Mayor Tobin and Commissioner Reilly congratulating the Crusaders. They also took candid shots of the quarterbacks of each team shaking hands with one another. Both teams' coaches, as well as B.C.'s Father Mike and the Holy Cross priest, looked on with pride.

Hearing the blare of sirens as fire trucks sped by the hotel, Commissioner Reilly boasted, "There go my boys!"

Mayor Tobin smiled and patted his chum on the back.

All eyes turned to a rookie policeman who rushed in and announced, "Commissioner, there's a four-alarm fire in progress at the Cocoanut Grove!"

The room was abuzz. Commissioner Reilly knew that if his boys had already called in a fourth alarm, it wasn't a good sign. He whispered something to Mayor Tobin. The mayor nodded in agreement. While Reilly spoke with the policeman, Tobin addressed their guests, "You'll have to excuse us, gentlemen. We need to get down there."

The mayor, the fire commissioner, and the policeman promptly left the room. Flynn, Ross, and the other newspapermen were hot on their heels. Concern spread rapidly among the attendees.

"I've got to get to the Grove! My sister and her

friend Rita went there tonight!" Andy told his buddies as he raced off. The players of both teams piled out after him. Father Mike, the Holy Cross priest, and the coaches were quick to follow.

Those who had escaped the danger via the revolving door lingered on Piedmont Street in front of the Cocoanut Grove. Distraught, some called out for loved ones from whom they had been separated. The wiry airman from the Melody Lounge, worrying about the fate of his buddy, paced incessantly. People were backing out of the stucco archways in front of the door, cringing and sobbing. A couple of them ran to the street and vomited. One woman fainted, and a man fell to his knees and prayed. Another woman cried, "God, help them! Help them!"

Chief McDonough and Fitzy rushed through an archway to the revolving door. Sal reluctantly followed. Danny and Jim searched for Ginger among those gathered. It didn't take long. There weren't that many. They saw McDonough come away from the entrance looking grim and Fitzy lower his head in prayer. When Sal returned, he just stood there in stunned silence. Concerned by their reactions, Danny and Jim decided to take a look for themselves.

What they saw astounded them. The jammed-shut revolving door was packed with dead and dying patrons. Contorted hands and feet were sticking out freakishly along its edges. Bodies were smoldering. Skin was melting off the desperate faces mashed against the glass. In the dark, behind the plate glass door next to it, lay a great mound. What that consisted of, they did not even want to imagine. Jim shuddered to his core. Danny stifled a cry and had to look away, unable to bear the thought that Ginger could be trapped in there.

Chief McDonough ordered Danny and Jim away from the entrance. With steely resolve, he put his men to work. The firemen unfurled hoses and hooked them up to hydrants and a water tower truck. They quickly cooled down the revolving door. But it was going to be a difficult task to get people out from between the glass sections without injuring them further.

Danny was immobilized by overwhelming emotion. Jim took out his notepad. He could barely write because his hands were shaking so much. He closed his eyes, drew in a deep breath, and forced himself to do his job.

More units of policemen arrived on the scene to care for those gathered out front as well as handle a growing crowd of curiosity seekers. Fitzy pitched in. Emergency vehicles continued to pull up in front of the club. Medics jumped out, unloaded stretchers, and began tending to the injured who had escaped. Chief McDonough headed to the corner door.

With an ear-piercing siren, a fire engine blasted down Piedmont Street. It sideswiped several parked cars, startling everyone. People scattered in all directions.

"Jesus Christ!" McDonough spat.

Rattled, the fire chief tugged on the corner door. Sal went over and started to withdraw his keys, but, before he was able to produce them, McDonough bellowed, "Why the hell is this door locked? That's a direct violation of fire regulations!"

Sal slyly calculated the situation and realized that he could get hung out to dry. Deciding not to give the chief any ammunition, he left the keys in his pocket.

McDonough ordered two firemen to bust the door open with a battering ram. Smoke poured out. Danny and Jim, thinking they could gain entrance to the Melody Lounge now, rushed over. The chief shined a flashlight inside and yelled back to his men, "They're piled up at this door, too!"

Hope sank like a stone in the pit of Danny's stomach. Jim was determined to stay strong for Danny even though it was obvious it was not going to be easy to rescue Ginger.

Sal was shocked to learn that this part of the club had also been affected. He grimaced at the sight of the bodies and worried about Rita and Ginger. He attempted to slip into the sea of gathering onlookers, but Danny grabbed hold of him and threatened, "I swear to God, Sal, if Ginger is still in there…."

Sal forcefully shrugged Danny off.

Jim added a warning, "Don't forget, you son of a bitch, we saw you lock that door."

Overhearing Jim's words, McDonough glared at Sal. He made a mental note to remember who was responsible and then refocused on the task at hand.

Sal could have pounded Jim into the ground for opening his trap in front of the chief, but he didn't want to draw any more attention. Instead, he just walked away. He pressed on toward Broadway, scanning the crowd for Rita and Ginger. He hoped they'd gotten out somehow. A momentary pang of guilt made him glance back at the club's corner door.

Danny moved closer to the corner doorway and peered past Chief McDonough. The number of bodies overwhelmed him.

"What do you think you're doing?" the fire chief snapped as he eyed Danny. "Nobody's getting in here, especially a cripple!" Spying the camera satchel and press pass, he added, "And no pictures! Back up, mister."

Jim steered Danny away. Danny cried, "Jim, did you see all those bodies in there? They were blocking the stairs!"

"Get ahold of yourself, Danny."

"How could she have gotten up those stairs, Jim? How?"

Jim saw that Danny was spiraling out of control. He tried to be the voice of reason. "Calm down, Danny, or you won't be any help to her when we do find her."

"You think she could be okay?" Danny asked, searching for reassurance.

"Sure. She might still be in the Melody Lounge waiting to be rescued. How about I take some notes, and you get on the horn to the paper? This is big news!"

Danny stared at him like he had two heads. "I'm not leaving. You go! I have to look for Ginger!"

Jim took a deep breath and tried again. "Danny, give the firemen time to get inside. We'll know more then. Don't worry, buddy, we'll find her."

Stanley, Ginger, and the college kids rummaged through drawers in the dark kitchen. A sickening stench accompanied thick smoke that now wafted down the stairs. The only way the group could stay focused was to deny what their senses were telling them about the fate of others in the club above them.

They were surprised when someone clomped down the stairs and cried, "Oh my God! Oh my God! Oh my God!"

Stanley located a flashlight at last. He aimed its beam at the figure. Recognizing the busboy, he called out, "Tony!"

Startled, Tony squinted against the light. He blurted out, "Everything's on fire up there! The doorway to Shawmut Street's on fire! And the revolving door is stuck!"

Stanley blanched. "What? You mean there's no way out upstairs?"

"No, I don't think so," Tony whimpered and shook uncontrollably. He hid his face in his hands. "Everybody's dying up there!"

Everyone in the kitchen reeled from Tony's news.

Tony darted past them into the refrigeration room. Stanley called to him, "Tony! Where you going?"

Flushed and coughing, Tony yanked on the refrigerator door handle. "Oh, God, I'm so hot! Why won't this open?"

"Scram!" Lenny shouted from within. "There's not enough air in here as it is!"

"Lenny? You crumb. Let me in!" Tony pounded on the door. After a couple of minutes, he gave up. Gasping for breath, he rushed to the freezer and hauled out a five-gallon vat of ice cream. He ripped off the lid, plunged his face into the melting ice cream, and sighed in relief.

Stanley was concerned about his distraught friend. He called to Tony and begged him to come back into the kitchen. At least they'd be together.

Helen and Susie were racked with fear again, knowing there was no escape upstairs. Ted and Mel were also frightened but put on a brave front to console their girlfriends.

Ginger's heart quickened, and her mind raced. Her eyes stung from smoke and tears. She wondered how long it would be safe in the kitchen. She closed her eyes and tried to calm herself. She wouldn't give up hope. She couldn't. But frightful imaginings of what was happening above in the main club overtook her thoughts, especially after having been surrounded by so many dead bodies in the Melody Lounge. She began to question if she'd even live through this nightmare. She agonized over how unfair it was that she might not get the chance to have a future with Danny, now that she'd reconnected with him. Tears rolled down her cheeks as the grim reality of that possibility sunk in.

Many injured and dead lay in the street outside the Broadway Lounge. Those still alive desperately awaited medical attention. Firemen continued to drag out victims. Capt. Buccigross and other policemen had their hands full with the growing number of bystanders jostling to get a good look. As additional policemen arrived, he dispatched them to help control the crowd.

Welansky, Sharps, and Byrne stood by stoically. Welansky spotted Sal making his way back. His gut told him his brother's bootlicker was squirming inside. Sal's step lacked its usual bravado. He almost seemed like somebody who didn't want to be noticed. The news couldn't be good. But as Sal approached, Welansky asked him anyway, "How'd it go?"

Sal couldn't look him in the eye. "Not too many people got out. And that fire chief was pretty steamed that the door to the lounge was locked."

Welansky sighed. "We better go fill Barney in."

"But I haven't had a chance to look for my sister. Or my girl," Sal protested weakly.

Welansky set him straight. "Leave that to the firemen, Sal. If you know what's good for you, you'll quit kvetching and come with me. This is Barney's joint. We gotta find out what needs doing. But we'll have to take your car. Mine's blocked in."

Welansky bid farewell to Sharps and Byrne. Torn, Sal glanced back at the club. As a fire alarm sounded five times, he dutifully led Welansky toward the parking garage.

Bobby, Arnie, and other axe-wielding firemen smashed storefront-type windows on the Shawmut Street side of the building. They were disgusted. They couldn't believe their efforts to break through were being hindered by wood panels used to cleverly conceal the windows from the inside. Time was ticking away and every moment counted. Lives were at stake. They kept at it until they managed to hack open the panels. As the fire within received fresh oxygen, smoke and flames roared out. The firemen were forced to draw back. Additional firemen aimed water at the windows. The spray cascaded down onto the brick sidewalk and almost instantly created an icy glaze.

A double bass came crashing through the stage door, splitting it open from inside and releasing a cloud of smoke. A musician ran out, lugging the instrument. Several other musicians and terrified chorus girls dashed out behind him. Coughing and gagging, they gathered together in the street with Kicky, Dot, and Mary. Everyone embraced, grateful to be alive.

In his office at the *Boston City Press*, Eddie Eisner plopped a couple of Alka-Seltzer tablets into a glass of water. He sat at his desk and waited for the fizzing to stop before chugging it down. He listened to the coverage of the fire on the radio as he sifted through Jim's file on the Cocoanut Grove. The intense editor was hungry for information. He studied Danny's photo of Sal paying the city official for the phony safety inspection certificate. His wheels were turning. He speculated that this fire was, in fact, the end result of that bribe. Eddie hadn't been this revved up since he was a young reporter himself.

Danny waited impatiently outside a phone booth up the street from the mayhem at the Cocoanut Grove. He puffed on a cigarette like a lot of other anxious people in the long line behind him. He knew he needed to call this in to the paper but was frustrated that it was taking so long.

When a sobbing woman finally exited the phone booth, Danny quickly crushed out his cigarette and fumbled with the door. Once inside, he dropped a nickel in the slot and dialed. Eddie picked up on the first ring. Danny was surprised to hear his voice, figuring it had to be close to midnight. "You're still there, Eddie?"

"I'm always here, McGuire."

Eddie was relieved to know that Danny and Jim were all right. He told Danny that the news of the fire was all over the wire but urged him to recount everything he knew.

"It's bad, Eddie. The joint was packed!" Danny said. He rattled on, bringing his boss up to speed.

Eddie began to drill him. "Any idea on a possible body count?"

"Could be in the hundreds. A lot of the doors were locked, and that revolving...." Danny choked up. "That damn revolving door got stuck, and they're all jammed in it! Makes me sick just thinking about it." He rubbed his face with a shaky hand, trying to erase the horror of that image.

"What about Buck Jones?"

"I don't know. I think he was still in there when I left. So many people are trapped in there."

Eddie sighed and deflated against the back of his chair. He jotted down a few notes before starting in again. "Have you gotten any pictures?"

Danny winced at the idea of it. "Oh, Eddie, you don't know how gruesome it is. I know some of these people!"

"It's going to be tough. But this story is bigger than you."

"Eddie, my girl's in there!"

"I'm sorry to hear that, son." Eddie felt for the kid, but he also needed him to focus. "Listen, McGuire. This may be the biggest story of your life. And you might be able to tie this in to what you and Reed have been working on about the corruption at the Grove. Good job getting that shot today, by the way. I see they were issued several warnings for substandard electrical work. This fire could be connected. This is your chance to bust that story wide open."

Danny was overcome by a host of emotions. He held the receiver to his forehead as he wrestled with his thoughts. Someone rapped on the phone booth. He felt guilty that he'd occupied it for so long. He heard Eddie calling his name and muttered, "I'm here."

"Flynn and Ross are on their way there from the Parker House," Eddie informed him. "I need all of you to get everything you can and hand it off to the runners."

Danny acquiesced, "Okay, Eddie. I'm on it."

CHAPTER FIFTEEN

Public Safety Director Walsh approached Chief McDonough on Piedmont Street and relayed what he had experienced inside the Grove. McDonough shook his head in disbelief. When Commissioner Reilly and Mayor Tobin arrived, the deputy fire chief unleashed his frustration on his boss. "Commissioner, bodies are blocking every entryway because all the doors were locked!"

Tobin shot a worried look to Reilly and Walsh. The commissioner sighed in disgust at the stupidity of the brazen safety violation by the club's management.

McDonough continued, "We have to remove them before we can even get in. You better decide where we're going to put them."

Mayor Tobin thought for a moment before he responded, "I'll commandeer that vacant store across the street as a temporary morgue."

"That might work for a little while," McDonough agreed. "But you don't understand. There's likely to be hundreds. We're going to need something much bigger and with better ventilation."

Tobin reeled at the potential scope of the situation.

Commissioner Reilly asked the mayor, "Maurice, what about that parking garage down the street?"

Although the idea of bodies laid out on the garage floor caused Mayor Tobin to shudder, he assured him he'd see to it.

Commissioner Reilly informed the fire chief, "I've seen to having companies from all the neighboring towns dispatched."

Mayor Tobin added, "And I've got plenty of police officers reporting to the scene." He turned to Walsh and said, "It's not a drill this time, John. I need you to direct the Civil Defense Headquarters to organize the Red Cross. The hospitals are going to have their hands full. And I'm afraid we may to have to call in the military for this one. It's a darn good thing you ran those Civil Defense drills last week. Hopefully, everyone who participated is ready now to handle an emergency of this magnitude."

Jim was standing between two parked cars close behind them and heard the whole exchange. He was surprised to learn that they felt this fire warranted military assistance. This was big!

The dinner guests from the celebration at the Parker House began to congregate on Piedmont. The coaches and priests were stunned. Andy and the rest of the football players gawked, slack-jawed. Flynn, Ross, and other reporters dug right in to cover the story. Flynn approached Jim, who filled him in on what was known so far.

Father Mike looked to the heavens and spoke in his thick Irish brogue, "Father, I thank You now for the Holy Cross win. In Your infinite wisdom, You kept all of the boys safe." He blessed himself and kissed the thick gold cross that hung from his neck.

"God works in mysterious ways," the Holy Cross priest affirmed solemnly. He blessed himself and kissed his own cross. Realizing they were the first on the scene able to offer spiritual comfort, the two priests consoled survivors and prayed with them.

Andy scouted through the mob of onlookers. A lump formed in his throat as his eyes passed over victims lying on the sidewalk. Unable to locate his sister and Rita, it troubled him to think they might not have gotten out yet. He forged a path to the revolving door, expecting to be able to search the club. He was shocked by the horror. It was beyond his worst nightmare.

Fitzy stepped in front of Andy to block his way. "Back up, Andy. The firemen are going to get everybody out."

Jim glanced up from his notes when he heard Fitzy and drew Andy aside. Andy was visibly shaken. Jim empathized, "I know. It's awful."

"Have you seen Ginger?" Andy asked. "She was here with Rita."

"Yeah, I know. I saw them inside earlier. But I haven't seen them out here yet, and I've been looking."

"Aw, geez! Do you think they're still in there?"

"I sure hope not." Jim looked away to hide his own

anxiety. In an effort to keep Andy from dwelling on the grisly sight at the door, Jim suggested, "How about you look over on Shawmut? People might have gotten out that way. I'll stay here and keep an eye out. I'm waiting for Danny anyway."

The blood drained from Andy's face. "Is he in the club?"

Jim shook his head. "No. No."

Andy breathed a sigh of relief.

Jim explained, "He's beside himself worrying about Ginger. I sent him off to make a phone call to keep him from looking at that." He indicated the grim scene at the revolving door. Jim had noticed Andy's puzzled expression at the mention of Danny's feelings for Ginger and clarified, "Yeah, he's never stopped loving her."

Andy nodded, not entirely surprised. "Does she know?"

"Yup. Now we just need to find her. Let me know how it looks on Shawmut."

Andy summoned a few of his buddies and sped off down the street with them.

Jim spotted Lynn Andrews, the house photographer, returning. He was aware she had to leave the premises each night to develop pictures she had taken and knew she must have come back to deliver ones her customers had ordered. He approached her, hoping to learn the names of the patrons she had photographed earlier that evening.

Lynn surveyed the scene in a state of shock. She seemed almost apologetic when she told Jim that she had been gone less than an hour. She could not believe what had happened during that time. She gazed down sadly at her picture envelope, wondering about the fate of those customers.

The disruptive B.C. fan and his pals had gone to a bar a few blocks away. News of the fire had sent them racing back. They were now kind of glad that Sal had tossed them out earlier.

Firemen began smashing storefront-type windows on the Piedmont side of the Grove. Here, their efforts were hampered by iron grills that covered the glass.

Policemen labored to hold back spectators who continued to flock to the scene of the fire. Fitzy couldn't understand their morbid curiosity. It never ceased to amaze him how fast crowds gathered to see blood, guts, and gore. The officers, insisting people had to stay back as a matter of safety, were met with protests.

Flames shot forth, driving the firemen back. Smoke poured into the street from broken and blackened windows. Smoldering materials inside the nightclub burst into flames. Water was blasted in.

Danny hobbled back from the phone booth as fast as he could. He was perturbed to see Jim chatting with Lynn. He rushed up and dragged Jim away, demanding, "Why aren't you looking for Ginger?"

"I *have* been looking for her! So's Andy!" Jim snapped. "Did you call it in?"

Danny just nodded. He stood there hypnotized by the intensity of all the action.

The wiry airman and other military men who had been in the club or had rushed to the scene aided firemen and policemen in removing victims from the corner door. It was a grim job identifying the living from the dead. Bodies were unceremoniously stacked up like cordwood on the sidewalk before others brought them to the vacant store. Those still alive were laid on the icy cobblestone street to await medics. Father Mike and the Holy Cross priest added administering Last Rites to their tasks.

Floodlights were set up to illuminate the stuck revolving door. Firemen worked feverishly to dismantle it. Along with each heavy glass partition, trapped bodies had to be removed. When they tore away the last section, twenty-foot flames shot out, forcing the firemen back. Thick smoke engulfed everything. Countless bodies piled in the foyer spilled out like sacks of grain. It overwhelmed even the most seasoned firemen to see resolute survivors, desperate to reach safety, crawling out over the dead.

Onlookers were shaken to the core. The nightmare they were witnessing was beyond anything they ever could have imagined. Jim stared numbly. Tears ran down Danny's face. His mind couldn't function. He couldn't admit that Ginger might be dead. Wrenched by Danny's pain, Jim put a hand on his friend's shoulder to comfort him. But reality screamed all around Danny, and Jim's reassurances weren't helping anymore.

The naval officer who had reprimanded Danny for spilling his wife's drink was standing nearby. He was visibly rattled. Jim spoke gently to him. "Excuse me, sir. Can you tell me what happened inside?"

Danny listened in as the naval officer, still in disbelief, answered, "I was holding my wife's hand the whole time! We were right at the door. Right at the door! My wristwatch came off and … and I lost her."

Danny and Jim were humbled by the officer's fragility.

Fitzy carried out the man's wife and laid her on the sidewalk then went back in through an archway. The naval officer hurried over to her and dropped to his knees. He took her hand. His wristwatch tumbled out. He held her lifeless body to his chest and sobbed.

Jim swallowed hard. Out of respect, he averted his eyes from the grief-stricken man. Danny teared up again.

Jim saw that the firemen were ready to break through the single plate glass door next to the revolving door. If Ginger was in there, he wanted to know first so that he could cushion the blow for Danny. He needed to distract him. Jim spotted Fitzy bringing an injured person to medics in the street. He suggested to Danny that he ask the cop if he had any news about Ginger. And, while he was at it, see if he had any details on the fire.

Danny's heart leapt at the idea that Fitzy might know something to help him find Ginger. He stopped Fitzy in the street and bombarded him with questions.

Jim watched as the plate glass door was smashed open. He moved closer to get a better look. He cringed at the sight of Rosie's dead body in its threshold. Bodies lay in a tangled mound behind her. Choked up, he backed away.

Trying to immediately identify Ginger in that pile would be impossible. Jim was desperate now to get answers for Danny. Seeking any sign of hope, he took a chance and approached Chief McDonough, who was coming from the corner door carrying a body. "Chief, can you tell me what it looks like in there?"

McDonough was annoyed when he saw Jim's press pass. "If it's a big story you're after, I can tell you this. There's nobody left alive in that Melody Lounge."

Jim blanched. His belief that Ginger might still be alive was waning. He spotted Danny on his way back, shaking his head. Obviously, Danny had found out nothing more from Fitzy. Jim was determined to keep the fire chief's bad news regarding the Melody Lounge from Danny. He pulled himself together just as Danny joined him and proposed, "How about we check over on Shawmut? Maybe Andy's found her."

Jim started down the street without waiting for an answer. With renewed faith, Danny fell in right behind him. As they passed the parking lot out front, firemen blasted their hoses at the club. Danny winced to see his Packard and other cars being pummeled with water.

The stench in the smoky kitchen unnerved Ginger. She shook off her despair, dried her tears, and tried to think logically. There had to be some way to get out of the building.

Stanley suddenly remembered there was a

window used to ventilate the kitchen in the summertime. He panned the flashlight beam along the wall above the sink. It fell upon a small window near the ceiling.

Ginger and the college kids hooted with newfound hope. Tony heard their excitement and ran in from the refrigeration room, ice cream still stuck to his face.

Ginger held the flashlight as Stanley climbed up and straddled the sink. He struggled to pry open the narrow basement window. It wouldn't budge. Stanley banged on the frame in frustration. "It's stuck!" he griped. "I'm going to try to break it." He smacked his fist against the glass. When it did not give way, he nearly fell.

"Be careful, Stanley!" Ginger cautioned him. "Don't use your hand! Use this." She handed him the heavy metal flashlight.

Coughing on smoke, everyone watched Stanley in eager anticipation. They collectively willed the window to break. Stanley whacked hard at the glass. The strong blow shattered it. When cold air rushed in, everyone cheered.

Stanley used the flashlight to hammer out most of the shards. He handed it to Ted, hoisted himself up, and crawled through the tight opening. Smoke followed him out the window. He stood up and gulped in fresh air, glad to be outside at last. Broken glass littered the icy ground and crunched beneath his feet. The strobing lights of emergency vehicles flashed in the sky above him. Sirens echoed in the streets. He glanced around and realized he was in the dark alley behind the nightclub. Although it was closed off by an apartment building, he knew the way through.

Ted directed Mel to go out next. He shone the flashlight as Mel shimmied up. Once outside, Mel called down, "Okay! Help the girls up!"

Susie appeared at the window. Mel and Stanley yanked her out. Ted gave his nervous girlfriend a kiss and boosted her up. Helen grabbed waiting hands that pulled her through. Tony was ready to assist Ginger, but she hesitated. She was thinking of Goody, Billy, and the others. "What about the people in the refrigerator?" she asked.

"They wanted to wait for the firemen, so let them!" Ted curtly remarked. Angry that they had kept him out of the refrigerator, Tony was in total agreement. Ted urged Ginger, "Come on! Time's a wasting!"

Ginger allowed them to hoist her up. She grabbed the sill but lost her grip. Tony steadied her. She swiped at tears and tried again. Stanley reached in to pull her out. She handed him her purse. He placed it on the ground. He grabbed her hands and helped her squirm through the window. A small piece of jagged glass left in the frame scratched her leg. Though she had torn one of her coveted stockings, she was grateful to be out.

Stanley helped Ginger to her feet. Unsteady on the icy ground in her high heels, she held onto him until she regained her footing. She picked up her purse and went to join the shivering college girls.

Tony squeezed through the window next. Ted wriggled out last with great agility, bringing the flashlight. Everyone was giddy that they had finally escaped.

Ginger gave Stanley a big hug and thanked him for helping them all get out. He smiled at her humbly before explaining to the group, "The only way to the street is through that apartment house over there. Come on!"

Stanley took the lit flashlight from Ted and led everyone across the slippery alley to the back door of the old brick apartment house.

Henry, Weissy, and other employees still waiting to be rescued were having trouble breathing in the smoky corridor. Henry kicked at the locked delivery door that led to Shawmut Street. Exhausted, he hoarsely called for help. He prayed someone would finally hear him over the noise outside. Weissy, keeping the damp towel to his face, stayed determined. He continued to pound his fist on the unrelenting door.

They were all greatly relieved to hear a voice shouting, "We'll get you out! We're going to break the door down with a battering ram! Stand back!"

The employees in the corridor scurried away from the door. With a loud crack, it smashed open. They staggered out through the smoke, coughing profusely. Weissy thanked Bobby and Arnie for getting them out and informed them about the people downstairs in the kitchen.

Mary watched the rescue from the street. She gave each employee a hug as they passed by. She was glad to see Jim and Danny finally coming through the crowd that had gathered on Shawmut. She ran into Jim's open arms.

Anxious, Danny asked, "Mary, have you seen Ginger yet?"

Mary shook her head. She saw Danny's agony, and her eyes welled up. Sadness weighed heavily on Jim. He caught sight of Andy still searching for Ginger and felt even worse.

At the corner of Shawmut and Broadway, Chief Stickel told Charlie, "We've got to get the boys up on the roof to start venting this place."

Charlie was in complete agreement but expressed his own concern, "And we still have a heck of a lot of people to get out."

"Well, here comes some help for you, Charlie." Chief Stickel indicated veteran fire captain "Iron Mike" Foley approaching with his newly arriving company of firemen.

Stickel greeted the captain, "Glad you're here, Mike. I need Engine Two to give Charlie some assistance. There's a double door down there, but one side is locked. Bust the damn thing open and get those people out of that doorway." Chief Stickel gave him a solemn look and lowered his voice. "God only knows what we've got inside."

Capt. Foley acknowledged this with a grimace.

Stickel leaned toward Foley and asked, "Mike, wasn't your daughter Edyth supposed to be here tonight?"

Iron Mike fought hard to hold back the depth of his emotions. "I don't know. B.C. lost, so I'm not sure she came."

Showing his support, Stickel patted his friend's shoulder before Foley and his men followed Charlie down the street.

Aware that the firemen were moving to an open exit, Andy and his fellow football players gathered close by to observe the action. Andy noticed Danny, Jim, and Mary coming over, too. He and Danny exchanged a nod of recognition.

A few people were still managing to get out, one at a time, via the dining room doorway. Danny, Jim, and Mary watched intently for any familiar face. They were relieved to see Frank exit unharmed. Mary ran over and hugged him. Next came the handsome army private who had danced with Ginger, followed by the sailor who had been enamored with Dot.

Fred stumbled out. Charlie got there just in time to catch him. The elderly man called out, "Gladys! Where are you?" as he tried to get back inside.

Charlie hung onto the trembling man and said, "Sir, please. Stand aside and let us get to her."

Capt. Foley and his men broke down the second door, making the opening wider at last. Scads of people had piled on top of one another in the threshold during their fight to escape through the narrow exit. Knowing help had arrived, they begged to be rescued. Firemen dove in and began dragging out victims from the doorway. The entrance needed to be cleared if they had any hope of getting inside.

Andy and other football players rushed up and helped them. Jim, Frank, Weissy, Henry, the army private, Dot's sailor, and several more men also lent a hand. Danny did his best despite his disability.

Jim carried out Gladys. As soon as Fred saw her, he trotted along behind him. Jim laid Gladys in the street away from the frantic rescue effort. Fred kissed her hand, grateful she was alive. He looked up at Jim, misty-eyed, and said, "Bless you, my boy."

One of the football players, in his youthful exuberance, yanked a small woman in a frilly cocktail dress from the top of the pile. Mary was horrified when the woman was catapulted out and landed hard in the gutter right in front of her.

The army private labored to haul out a rotund man. Danny, hurrying to back out of his way, tripped over a dead woman and fell to the ground. Cringing, he struggled to get to his feet.

Charlie reached down and gave Danny a hand up. Noticing the leg brace, he advised, "Maybe you ought to stay out of this, son. We have enough injured people to deal with right now."

Smarting with embarrassment, Danny hobbled to the street. He spotted Mr. Marshall rushing to the scene with a crate of medical supplies from his pharmacy. Danny wasn't surprised. The conscientious druggist always had compassion for those in pain. It touched Danny's heart to see how many people were showing up to provide whatever help they could.

The relentless rescue and recovery effort on

Shawmut was much like those on Piedmont and Broadway. The injured were brought into the street to await medical attention. The deceased were left on the sidewalk with little deliberation before eventually being carted off to a temporary morgue. Priests, ministers, and rabbis offered comfort and prayers.

Weissy and Henry each carried an injured woman out to the street. Weissy suddenly collapsed, overcome with dizziness. Alarmed, Henry hovered over him. He gently slapped Weissy's face in an attempt to revive him. Weissy caught his breath, and Henry helped him to his feet. "Are you okay?" Henry asked.

"I'll be all right," Weissy answered, trying to sound confident as he brushed slush off his clothes. He looked around at the faces in the crowd then said, "I want to go look for my Uncle Jimmy. I want to make sure he's okay."

Henry nodded but watched with concern as Weissy disappeared down the street. Not knowing what else to do, he joined Kicky, Dot, and the other chorus girls huddled together with Mickey and Sammy nearby. When Bobby and Arnie escorted Billy, Goody, Lenny, and the kitchen staff out through the smashed-in delivery door, everyone was thrilled. Henry ran over to Lenny. Mickey went to chat with Billy and Goody. Kicky reached a hand out from inside the blanket that Bobby had given her. She caught Bobby's arm and praised, "You really are a hero." He grinned and shied away to rejoin Arnie.

Chief Stickel gave Bobby and Arnie new orders. The two young firemen leaned a ladder against the building. They dragged hoses up to the roof. A few other firemen did the same. They spread out and inspected its condition. Many of the tiles had melted. Fire was spurting up all along the section that could be retracted in the summer months. Some of the firemen began dousing the flames. Arnie, now knowing what they were dealing with, let Stickel know. The chief organized more hose men on both sides of the club to cool off the roof.

When Ginger, Stanley, Tony, and the college kids exited the apartment house onto Shawmut, they were astonished to see a myriad of emergency vehicles, legions of firemen, and so many people in the street. They watched in awe as the roof of the club was bombarded with water from a multitude of hoses.

Helen clung to Ted as they followed Mel and Susie toward the Grove. The four college kids merged with the hordes of spectators to get a closer look.

Tony was terrified by everything he saw. He ran away without a word to Stanley and Ginger.

Overwhelmed by the destruction, Ginger burst into tears. Stanley stared at the ground, his stomach in knots. He looked up and spotted Billy and Goody chatting with Mickey at the edge of the crowd. "Hey, it looks like the people from the refrigerator made it out!"

"Thank God. I hope Kicky got out … and Rita … and Sal," Ginger said.

Stanley took a breath to steady his nerves. He tried to console her. "Come on, Ginger. Sal's probably out front looking for you."

Stanley guided Ginger up the street away from the numerous emergency vehicles and the throng of people gathered between them and Broadway. As a result, Ginger never saw Danny, Jim, Mary, Andy, or Kicky right there among the dense crowd on the backside of the club.

CHAPTER SIXTEEN

A street lamp on Shawmut illuminated the now-cleared threshold that led into the Grove's dining room. Through the opening, undefined mounds were silhouetted by the glow of fire within. Those frantic to find loved ones tried to rush in. Policemen pushed them back for their own safety, despite loud protests.

Charlie and a young fireman peered inside. They were jolted to find bodies piled up shoulder high on either side of the opening and beyond. They shined their flashlights on the faces but detected no signs of life. It was obvious that some had succumbed to severe burns, while others had suffocated under all the crushing weight. In addition, all had been unable to benefit from any fresh air because so many people had been blocking the open exit. Charlie could only imagine the kind of fear that drove people to such desperate measures that they would climb on top of dozens of dead bodies even when they saw others' attempts to escape had been futile.

The two firemen continued to inspect the interior from the doorway, their flashlight beams cutting through dense smoke. Active flames were on the ceiling and in some sections of the room. Haunting cries and moans from unseen victims still clinging to life permeated the silence. Contorted bodies were sprawled everywhere. It sent chills up the firemen's spines. The young fireman was so overcome by it all, he backed away and vomited in the gutter.

Charlie went to check on him. The veteran's eyes welled with tears. His voice broke as he let the rookie know, "In all my years, I've never seen anything this bad. You'd better go tell Chief Crowley we're going to need a lot of help."

Danny, Jim, and Mary were rubbernecking like the rest of the onlookers in the street. Danny was on pins and needles. It frustrated him that his search for Ginger had come to a halt. He knew Jim was right, he had to let the firemen do their job. So, he resigned himself to wait it out. First chance he got, though, he'd be in there looking.

The roof had cooled down enough to be vented. Bobby, Arnie, and the other hose men shut off their hoses and stood at the ready. Five firemen with axes started hacking holes. The fire within rose up, feeding on fresh oxygen, and threatened the axe-wielding firemen. They jumped back as flames shot high into the sky.

There was a collective gasp from the spectators below. They remained riveted by the firemen's harrowing efforts.

Bobby, Arnie, and the other hose men quickly doused the fire. The axe-wielding firemen returned to creating vents. A thunderous crack emanated from beneath them. They all knew what that meant. They abruptly stopped hacking. The roof started to vibrate. The axe men glanced to the hose men, but no one had time to react. Loud cracking resounded. The center of the roof fractured and gave way. The axe-wielding firemen were sucked down through the barrage of flames that jettisoned up. Bobby, Arnie, and the others scrambled away. They forced themselves to concentrate on putting out the blaze. Once they had it under control, the hose men stared down into the abyss, shaken.

Shrieks and groans convulsed from the crowd. Lenny and Henry gaped in awe. Kicky hung onto Dot, concerned for Bobby's safety. Danny feared what the result of the roof collapsing could mean for anyone still inside. Seeing the look of dread on Danny's face, Jim shut his eyes tight and pulled Mary close.

Bobby and Arnie bounded down the ladder. Kicky pushed her way toward them, grateful Bobby was safe. But he and Arnie were on a mission. Intent on reaching their trapped comrades, they maneuvered through the mass of onlookers and around bodies now stacked up in rows on the sidewalk. They joined Charlie and George at the double doorway to the dining room, where Chief Crowley was addressing Capt. Foley and his men.

Crowley was all worked up. Devastating losses at a restaurant fire in East Boston two weeks before were fresh in his mind. "We just lost six men in the Luongo fire, and I'll be damned if we lose any more!" he bellowed. "We've got to get in there, pronto! We've already removed a lot of bodies just to clear a path. But there are still a hell of a lot of people to get out and now our guys, too! George, get in there with a hose. I'll stay close behind you with Charlie, Bobby, and Arnie until we know what we're dealing with. Mike, you and your men stay put until I give the word."

George dragged in a hose. Chief Crowley, Charlie, Bobby, and Arnie hustled in behind him beaming wheat lights and flashlights through the heavy smoke. George extinguished burning furniture and décor to adeptly create a safe pathway. The men made their way into the dining and dancing area, stepping around bodies and toppled furniture. The sheer volume of the dead and dying astounded them.

Ginger and Stanley headed toward the front of the club in search of Sal. It was so cold their breath was visible in the night air. Ginger hugged her body to stay warm.

Smoke lingered in the air. The drone of fire truck and ambulance motors reverberated off the buildings on Piedmont Street. Emergency lights strobed relentlessly. Policemen, firemen, and rescuers shouted back and forth to one another above the din. Medical personnel scurried about, struggling to keep up with the growing number of injured.

Tears choked Ginger as the scope of the tragedy began to register. Dead bodies lay in rows along the sidewalk, some with their elegant evening attire or brand-new military uniforms shredded or entirely burned off. Many victims were burnt beyond recognition. Dozens had seared skin or a reddish glow and were smeared with blood and soot. Others appeared to be sleeping, covered in pale ash. Ginger could not stop shivering from the shock of it all.

Stanley had never seen a dead body in his entire life. Now they were everywhere, and it was horrifying. The thought crossed his mind that this was probably what a battlefield looked like. He'd never really given that a thought when he'd idolized older kids signing up to be heroes. Now, the idea sickened him. He wanted to run away. The realization that he might be held responsible for this fire began to overwhelm him, too. Stanley tried not to cry. His voice cracked as he confessed, "Ginger. I didn't know when I lit the match...."

Ginger's heart went out to him. She took his hand and said gently, "Stanley. It's not your fault."

He lowered his eyes. Even though she had attempted to make him feel better, it wasn't really helping. He still felt awful.

Newly arriving army and Red Cross medics rushed by toting stretchers and medical supplies. Chief McDonough climbed up onto the hood of a police car. He shouted into a bullhorn, "Attention everyone! The Red Cross is setting up in the Film Exchange building on Broadway. Anyone with medical training, please report and lend a hand. We can use all the help we can get."

Ginger informed Stanley that she was going to the Red Cross station. She knew she could put what she had learned in nursing school to good use. She could tell Stanley was still rattled and unsure what he should do, so she advised, "Maybe you ought to go home now. When your parents hear there was a fire, they'll be worried about you."

It seemed a little selfish to Stanley to just take off, but he was relieved at the thought of going home. "You're right. I should go home. Let me walk you over to Broadway first."

Ginger and Stanley navigated past fire equipment, ambulances, and clusters of curiosity seekers on Piedmont. They were stunned to see gaping holes where the doors of the nightclub once stood.

A fireman helped a man out to the street. Gulping for air, the survivor dropped to his knees. Ginger and Stanley gasped as another fireman hosed down smoldering bodies. To their horror, they realized the victims weren't all dead. Ginger shivered as the residual water formed an icy coating on the cobblestones.

On Shawmut, reporters and photographers scrambled to cover the story. Young runners from newspaper offices stood by to collect notes and sheet film holders and then rush them back to their editors.

Danny wasn't interested in taking any pictures. All he could think about was Ginger. Jim, however, was intent on getting something into the paper. He kept on Danny until he relented.

Danny captured images of the fire-ravaged Cocoanut Grove, the valiant firemen in action, and the despair on the faces of the onlookers. But he drew the line when it came to photographing the severely injured and the dead, finding that too distasteful and disrespectful.

Despite Mary clinging to him, Jim recorded the unfolding events with furious speed. The point of his pencil snapped. He cursed. Luckily, he kept a spare in his suit jacket pocket.

When Jim and Danny were satisfied that they had enough coverage to send back to Eddie, they handed off their work to their runner. The boy restocked Danny with a stack of fresh sheet film holders and flashbulbs before hurrying to return to the paper.

"I hope when that roof gave way, it didn't take the booze in the ceiling with it," Jim griped.

Danny was incredulous. "The booze? Jim! Ginger is still in there!"

Even though Jim felt like a jerk, he said in his own defense, "We don't know that for sure, Danny." He knew he was probably offering false hope. He swallowed hard. In the back of his mind, he had already accepted Ginger was dead. But Danny didn't know that, and Jim didn't want him to. Jim thought he'd better keep up the front for as long as possible. After all, he had no actual proof, and Danny would demand it.

Danny wished he could believe Ginger might still be all right. But his hope waned with every hour that passed. He wouldn't rest until he saw her with his own eyes.

Chief Crowley called Capt. Foley and his men into the dining room. Frank snuck in behind them. The sailor who had a crush on Dot and the soldier who had danced with Ginger followed. Danny saw his chance and lunged for the doorway.

Jim grabbed hold of him. "Are you crazy? The roof just collapsed!"

"I don't care!" Danny yelled as he tried to push past him.

Jim's jaw clenched. He was determined to stop Danny. Through gritted teeth, he said, "Stay here. I'll go."

Mary held Jim back. "No, Jimmy! It's too dangerous!"

Danny pulled Mary away. As Jim headed for the doorway, Danny called after him, "Find her, Jim!" Mary started to cry. Danny felt responsible for her tears. He offered her his handkerchief. Grateful, she took it and dabbed at her eyes.

Inside, flames licked at Jim as he trod carefully across the dance floor. The place was in shambles. Fabric, decorations, and even bodies burning made the air noxious. He looked around in despair. There was no way to tell where Ginger and Rita might be.

Ironically, he was unaware that he'd walked right past Rita as she squirmed beneath the body of the drunken sailor.

Capt. Foley and his men searched for anyone still alive. Chief Crowley, George, Charlie, Bobby, and Arnie fought to get to the firemen who had plunged through the roof. Miraculously, the bodies and debris below had cushioned their fall. A couple of the men were already getting to their feet. The others needed some assistance but had not sustained any life-threatening injuries. Bobby and Arnie helped a limping fireman out to a medic and then dashed back inside.

Jim recoiled at the sight of victims crawling over the dead through pools of water as they inched toward the open doors. A delirious, moaning woman clawed at his legs. He lifted her into his arms. Gasping and fighting to catch his breath, he trailed after the soldier and the sailor who were already lugging victims out. He didn't notice Frank was no longer with them.

Jim felt the woman he was carrying go limp and wondered if she had just died in his arms. He choked back a sob as he gently laid her in the street where other victims awaited medics. He attempted to reenter the building along with the soldier and the sailor. More volunteers, eager to help, joined them.

"Christ Almighty!" Chief Crowley growled when he spotted them at the door. "Charlie, keep those civilians outside!"

Charlie went to the doorway and pleaded with the would-be rescuers, "Really, fellas. We don't need any more casualties."

A police lieutenant marched over. He conferred with Charlie before announcing, "We can only allow in military personnel and those trained in first aid, like bus and cab drivers."

Dot's sailor, the young soldier, and other military men were ushered in. Jim and the civilians who'd been helping protested. They pressed forward to get past the stern lieutenant. He put his hands up to stop them and barked, "Back up, all of you!"

"But we're trying to help!" Jim argued.

The police lieutenant stared him down. "Don't make me arrest you!" Jim reluctantly retreated.

Chief Stickel greeted a hulking army sergeant arriving with a group of soldiers. The sergeant assigned a number of his men to herd onlookers away from the building and a few to form a barricade at the doorway. Army medics pitched in to help the hospital medics deal with the overwhelming number of victims.

Jim made his way over to Danny and Mary. Danny looked to him expectantly, but Jim was coughing too hard to give him an answer.

"Are you okay, Jimmy?" Mary fretted.

Jim shrugged off her concern. "I'm fine." He saw Danny staring at him, impatient for any word on Ginger. "I'm sorry, buddy. You can't tell one person from another in there."

Danny smacked his fist into his palm in frustration. He had to find Ginger. But cops and firemen were at every door, and they weren't going to let him in, especially with his brace.

Kicky spotted Mary with Danny and Jim and hurried over to them. Jim embraced her and said, "Mary told me you were on the roof! Glad to know you're okay. Sure wouldn't want anything to happen to those million dollar gams."

Danny gave Kicky a quick hug and asked if she'd seen Ginger.

Kicky grew anxious. "I was hoping you knew where she was. I haven't seen her since I left her in the Melody Lounge."

Jim winced. He rubbed his eyes to cover up his fear.

Danny begged Kicky, "If you do see her, can you tell her I'm here and looking for her? I've got to find her. I've just got to."

"I sure will, Danny," Kicky promised and gave him another hug. She nodded her goodbyes to Jim and Mary before returning to Dot and the other chorus girls.

"Jim, you heard what Kicky said. Ginger was in the Melody Lounge. We've got to get back to Piedmont!" Danny insisted.

Jim was dreading the moment when Danny would finally learn the awful truth about the people in the Melody Lounge. He tried to stall him. "In a minute. Get more pictures," Jim mumbled. He scribbled notes, intentionally ignoring Danny.

"Can you forget the damn story for five minutes?" Danny snapped.

"Danny, this is big! And Eddie's waiting," Jim said

without looking up.

Danny glared at him. Defiant, he sought out Andy. Danny was relieved that Ginger's brother no longer held any animosity toward him. It didn't take much convincing to enlist his aid to begin searching for Ginger again. Danny and Andy headed toward Broadway, two men on a mission.

They were nearly plowed into by Salvation Army personnel hurrying by with blankets and hot coffee. Soldiers and sailors administering artificial respiration to victims presented additional obstacles. And Danny had to be extra cautious as he stepped over icy debris and fire hoses frozen to the ground.

Jim cursed under his breath when he realized Danny had taken off without him. Clasping Mary's hand, he said, "Come on, honey," and led her in pursuit of Danny and Andy.

The recent Civil Defense drills had prepared local citizens to be ready should a wartime disaster strike. Over on Piedmont, leaders organized military men and civilians into a line. Ginger and Stanley were amazed to see a human chain being formed to pass stretchers bearing the injured overhead along the length of the street and around to Broadway.

Since the blaze in the new lounge was now out, the fire trucks on Broadway were moved to open the street for further rescue efforts. Every ambulance was already in use. Undaunted, stalwart policemen began flagging down cars, taxi cabs, milk trucks, and even newspaper trucks to transport the injured to hospitals as fast as possible.

As Ginger and Stanley crossed the street from the Grove to the Film Exchange building, they had to dodge a pickup truck leaving in a hurry and were almost hit by a cab before it screeched to a halt. Once they were safe on the opposite side, Ginger gave Stanley a warm hug and bid him goodbye. She climbed the stairs and went inside.

Because of their Civil Defense training, volunteers were quick to arrive and deal with this crisis in an efficient manner. Soldiers shoved shelving units loaded with cans of film up against the walls. Military medics carried in crate after crate of supplies. Citizens at the ready hurried to create a makeshift medical station and spread blankets out on the floor. Red Cross nurses set up trays of bandages, saline, syringes, and bottles of morphine.

As news of the fire reached them, doctors and nurses from hospitals in the areas around Boston and beyond came to lend a hand. Many off-duty practitioners also responded. And, as luck would have it, a medical convention was in town. Attendees answered the call as well. A few medical professionals who had been in the Cocoanut Grove and managed to escape offered their skills. They knew better than most how much they would be needed.

Ginger was given a Red Cross armband and an apron. She was directed to the restroom where she could wash up.

Jim and Mary rounded the corner of Broadway. Jim was surprised to find the entrance to the club unguarded. He took a chance and glanced in at the smoking, charred remains of the lounge. He scanned the street and realized the authorities were preoccupied with the transport of victims. He was puzzled when he saw Danny and Andy crossing the street, until he spotted a soldier placing a Red Cross flag outside the Film Exchange building. He and Mary rushed to catch up with them, also anxious to see if Ginger was inside.

The four of them entered the busy, makeshift medical station. No patients had been brought in yet. Danny made sure Ginger wasn't among the volunteers. Disheartened when he didn't find her, he headed out the door. Jim, Mary, and Andy followed. Little did they know, Ginger had been in the restroom. She had been pinning her hair back in place and scrubbing the soot from her hands and face.

Mary and Andy plodded in silence behind Danny. Jim walked beside him without saying a word.

"I really hoped I'd find her in there," Danny finally said. "Even if she was injured, at least I'd know she was alive."

Jim nodded and muttered, "Yeah. Me, too."

Danny searched the faces of every victim and every volunteer in the stretcher chain that came around the corner from Piedmont. "You know, Danny, she might have been taken to the hospital already," Jim told him.

Danny considered this. "Maybe. But I need to find out if she ever got out of the Melody Lounge. If she's still in there, we need to make sure she gets to the hospital." Jim's stomach squirmed as he turned the corner onto Piedmont with Danny. They made their way up the street along with Mary and Andy.

Danny and Jim realized immediately that they would not be able to get through any entrance on this side of the club because there was too much activity still going on. Soldiers parted the crowd as firemen hauled out bodies via the cavernous hole where the revolving door had been and through the archways to the sidewalk. One man was laid right in front of Danny, Jim, Mary, and Andy. He was badly burnt and unresponsive. His fancy cowboy boots stood out conspicuously.

"Oh, no!" Mary cried.

Andy stared at Buck Jones in disbelief. Danny blanched. Jim gazed at Buck somberly. He nudged Danny. "Take his picture before they cart him away."

Danny was outraged. "What? Are you kidding me?"

"Danny, he's a big movie star. People need to see what happened to him because of those greedy S.O.B.s!" Jim insisted.

"Jim…." Danny protested weakly.

"Take the goddamn picture!"

Danny groaned as he loaded a film sheet holder

and a flashbulb into his camera. He reluctantly snapped the photo before Everett and Howie got there to examine Buck.

Danny, Jim, Mary, and Andy were glad to hear the two medics determine that Buck was alive. Soldiers brought Buck to the street and laid him on a stretcher to await his turn in the chain.

Jim caught a couple of men looting jewelry and money from bodies heaped on the sidewalk. He ran toward them, yelling, "Hey! Get away from them! What the hell is wrong with you?"

Policemen nearby were alerted by Jim's shouts and chased after the thieves.

Jim shook his head, wondering how the looters could have so little respect for the dead. These were people, for crying out loud! He held his breath and forced himself to look at the individuals lying there in a haphazard stack. He was stunned to identify a friend among them.

Arthur was severely burnt. His bloated face was beet red. Jim turned away, tears stinging his eyes. He removed his fedora with a shaky hand and held the hat to his chest in reverence.

Danny, noticing Jim's reaction, went straight over to him. Andy and Mary followed.

"Arthur," Jim murmured hoarsely as he pointed out Arthur's body. Danny was heartsick. Mary sobbed on Jim's shoulder. Andy, seeing the anguish on Danny and Jim's faces, realized they must have known this man well. He stood by, quiet and respectful.

Danny fumed, "All he had to do was finish his

shift, and he would have been done with this joint! Why'd he have to die?"

"Bastards!" Jim spat. "I'm taking them down if it's the last thing I ever do!" he vowed.

Danny was now with Jim one hundred percent.

Jim soothed Mary until her tears abated. He leaned over to Danny and told him, "That stash of booze is the ticket. I've got to find out if it survived."

Danny agreed, "And we've got to find Ginger!"

"Right. Okay, then. Let's sneak in through the Broadway Lounge," Jim proposed. "When Mary and I went by it before, it was unguarded."

Mary's apprehension showed on her face.

Andy asked warily, "Won't they throw us out?"

"Nah. Danny and I just need to hide our press passes. If anybody asks, we're all cabbies helping with first aid," Jim told him.

Andy nodded in agreement.

Jim turned to Danny. "Put your camera away." Danny looked down at his brace. He raised an eyebrow at Jim. Jim waved it off. "Don't worry about it. It's dark in there."

Jim and Danny removed their press passes from their hats and pocketed them. Danny secured his camera in the satchel. Mary clutched Jim's arm in an attempt to keep him from going.

"It'll be fine," Jim told Mary confidently. He put an arm around her and ushered her along.

On Broadway, rescuers were still busy commandeering vehicles to transport victims. Andy was able to creep up to the club's entrance without being noticed. He snuck a peek into the lounge. The coast was clear. He beckoned Danny and Jim to follow as he slipped inside. Danny, checking first to be sure no one was watching, ducked in behind Andy.

"Jimmy, please don't go in there!" Mary begged.

Jim gave Mary a hug to reassure her. He kissed her cheek and said, "Wait here for me, honey."

CHAPTER SEVENTEEN

Once inside the Broadway Lounge, Danny, Jim, and Andy erupted into fits of coughing. Acrid smoke hung in the air like a filmy veil. Although light streamed in from a streetlamp through holes where the block glass windows had been, it was difficult to make anything out. It took a few minutes for their eyes to adjust.

Andy was astonished to see the destruction. Danny and Jim could not believe the dramatic change to the posh new lounge. All that was left of the inward opening door was a bashed-up doorframe. Big chunks of glass and debris lay on the floor beneath the missing windows. The tables and chairs were piled up against the walls, many of them smashed to pieces. The fashionable bar was now blackened and littered with broken glass.

Danny touched a barstool. "Hard to believe we were just sitting here."

Jim nodded. He sighed as he thought about Tiny, the affable bartender. He told Danny, "Mary said Tiny was trapped behind the bar."

Danny voiced what they were both thinking, "I wonder if he's still alive."

Andy cleared his throat and suggested, "Guys, we should get moving."

Danny and Jim quickly refocused. They followed Andy into the main room. Jim took up the rear in order to look out for Danny.

The fire had been extinguished. The stench from burnt bodies gagged them. It was a smell that would haunt them for the rest of their lives. Floodlights eerily illuminated the smoky, smoldering remains of the swanky club. They were struck by the stillness of the place, so lively a couple of hours before. The only sound now was the tick, tick, ticking of watches.

Danny and Jim were stunned by the devastation at Arthur's end of the Caricature Bar. The area where they had sat most of the night was completely cooked. Charred bodies were slumped over the bar. Danny shuddered. His words were barely audible. "Jesus, Jim. That could have been us."

"Arthur didn't stand a chance," Jim lamented.

They surveyed the main room and noticed several firemen silently checking the building's stability. Jim pointed out the massive pile of roof debris on the dance floor. Danny winced, imagining what it must have been like for anyone who had been beneath it when it came down.

Jim was perplexed by what had burned and what had not. Tables to their right under the canopy were not even scorched, and the far end of the Caricature

Bar seemed untouched. From a distance, the Terrace looked totally ravaged, yet many of the tables and chairs in the dining area below it appeared unscathed. Regardless of the reason, people's fates were determined by their locations and the bizarre path the fire had taken. He recorded these peculiarities on his notepad.

Andy, Danny, and Jim crept along the pathway. Victims were sprawled over tables. Bodies were lying entwined with one another, entangled beneath furniture. It was like a macabre scene out of a horror movie but far worse to them because this was real. Danny tried to fight off the thought that Ginger may have suffered the same fate. Rattled, he tripped over a discarded fire extinguisher and reached out to break his fall. His hands landed upon a lifeless woman draped over a table. He recoiled, stumbling backward.

Jim's vigilance paid off. He managed to catch Danny and steady him on his feet. Andy spun around to see what had happened. Sullen-faced, Danny straightened his topcoat to camouflage his embarrassment.

"Danny, you sure you can do this?" Jim whispered. Danny shot Jim a cold look. Voices coming from the Piedmont Street entrance prompted Jim to pull Danny and Andy into the shadows.

Charlie, Bobby, and Arnie trooped in along with other firemen, military men, and some civilians. Their mission to get the injured out to the stretcher chain was, for the most part, complete, but they continued to search for anyone left alive. The removal of the dead could wait. They began making a ruckus, tossing furniture and the rubble from the caved-in roof into a pile. All the while, water dripped steadily onto them from the hole in the ceiling.

Charlie suddenly collapsed. Bobby and Arnie rushed to his side. They checked his vital signs. Bobby said, "I think we'd better get him to that Red Cross station." Arnie agreed and helped Bobby carry Charlie out.

Seeing what had happened to Charlie made Andy frantic. "What are we standing here for? We're wasting time! We need to look for Ginger!" He boldly headed to the dance floor.

Jim and Danny started after him. As they reached the steps to the Caricature Bar near the foyer, Jim held Danny back. "Stay here and wait for me. I've got to check to see if the booze survived," Jim insisted.

Danny was aggravated that Jim was still putting the story before Ginger and frustrated that navigating around the rubble on his own would be a challenge.

The glamorous woman who'd had eyes for Danny lay dead near the stairs of the Caricature Bar. Unnerved, Jim carefully stepped around her and up onto the platform. It was strewn with shards of glass. He made his way to the burnt end of the bar. It was disconcerting to see the group of fun-loving soldiers and flirtatious women sitting there, motionless, some still holding their drinks. He knew they must be dead, though they were hardly singed. Yet beyond them, others were nearly incinerated. The whole scene gave Jim the willies, but he was determined to accomplish his goal.

Inside the makeshift Red Cross station, patients were coughing, gasping, and spitting up blood or black, sooty phlegm. Those with severe burns were screaming in agony. Others, who had suffered injuries as a result of being trampled, were moaning in pain. Doctors and nurses worked tirelessly, doing their best to treat them all. Unfortunately, numerous victims perished before they could even be examined.

For doctors, the first order of business was to alleviate pain. The drug of choice was morphine. To eliminate the possibility of an overdose, Ginger and other female aides used their own lipstick to mark an "M" on the forehead of any patient given some.

Kicky and Dot could not bring themselves to leave behind the tragic situation at the Cocoanut Grove. The fates of too many of their friends were still unknown. It gnawed at Kicky that she had not been able to find Ginger.

The news that a Red Cross station had been set up in the Film Exchange building made its way to them on Shawmut. Kicky and Dot headed there, hoping to get some answers. The frantic activity of the stretcher chain had slowed some on Broadway by one o'clock in the morning. Even so, the two chorus girls did not notice Mary outside the lounge nervously waiting for Jim.

Upon entering the Red Cross station, Kicky and Dot stopped in their tracks. They were shaken to see and hear so much suffering. They obediently stepped aside as soldiers brought in one fire victim after another. Several people skirted past them, desperately searching for missing loved ones.

Kicky and Dot were surprised to see Ginger tending to a patient and were relieved to find her safe. Ginger looked up instinctively and was thrilled to see them at the door. When she finished with her patient, she hurried over, gave each chorus girl a hug, and said, "Thank God you both made it out!"

"Are you okay, kiddo?" Kicky asked.

"Yes," Ginger assured her.

"We were stuck on the roof!" Dot told her.

Ginger gasped. She explained that she'd escaped from the basement.

Kicky praised Ginger's nursing skills.

"I'm doing my best," Ginger replied. Hearing the desperate cries of the patients and knowing she was needed, Ginger asked anxiously, "Have you seen Sal and Rita?"

Dot shook her head. "Not yet."

Ginger frowned. Despite how she felt about Sal, she hoped he and Rita had gotten out. She closed her eyes and shuddered, praying they had. Her focus shifted abruptly when Kicky told her, "I'm glad we found you. Danny's crazy with worry looking for you."

Ginger knew how she would feel if the situation was reversed. She would be frantic if she was looking for Danny. She pleaded with Kicky, "Can you please tell him where I am? I can't leave right now."

"Of course, kiddo," Kicky said and gave Ginger's hand a reassuring squeeze.

Dot piped in, "Is there anything else we can do to help?"

"The Salvation Army is distributing coats and blankets to keep the survivors warm. Can you lend a hand with that?"

Kicky nodded. "Sure thing. We'll round up the girls and get right on it."

Ginger was about to return to her duties when Bobby and Arnie burst in carrying Charlie. She directed them to lay Charlie on a blanket. She was concerned. Charlie's face was bright red, and he was coughing up black, sooty phlegm. Bobby and Arnie stepped back to allow a doctor to examine him.

Kicky caught Bobby's eye. There was a spark between them. He sensed her empathy for him.

Ginger removed Charlie's helmet. She whispered to the doctor, "His face is so red."

The doctor was solemn. "I've seen a lot of this tonight. It's an indication that he's been exposed to toxic fumes."

Jim checked out the ceiling panel with three stars above the bar. It was still intact. He made a note about the strange twist of fate. While most of the club had been destroyed, the section of the ceiling which held the incriminating evidence had endured. What a stroke of luck!

Danny was sick of wasting precious time waiting for Jim. They needed to find Ginger, and they needed to find her now! God only knew how she might be suffering. She could be in terrible pain. She could be burnt. Or she could be crushed and have broken bones. Or she could be having trouble breathing like so many people he'd seen. He couldn't stand it anymore.

Danny cupped his hand over his mouth to muffle the sound of his coughs and limped to the dance floor. The last thing he needed was to draw attention to himself and get thrown out because of his bum leg. But he really didn't need to worry. The clatter of wreckage being tossed about, mingling with the shouts of firemen and soldiers, created a constant din. The rescuers were simply too busy to take notice of him.

Jim glanced into the Piedmont Bar. Bodies lay in heaps, arms reaching out toward the windows behind the bar where just outside, a glowing streetlamp had teased them with freedom. Charred hands clung to iron grills that had prevented an escape route. Bills and coins were scattered all over the floor. Jim described it all on his notepad and became incensed. It was obvious that the owners of the club were more concerned with losing money than losing lives.

As Danny neared the Terrace, he was startled to see bodies dangling over its railing and tangled beneath its blackened, toppled tables. He was glad Buck had already been removed from this nightmare.

Creepier still were victims sitting upright in chairs along the dance floor as if engaged in conversation, not burnt but not moving.

Under the dented canopy across the room, the entire wedding party was dead. The sight of the bride resting against her groom's chest cleft a deep sadness in Danny's heart and made him shiver. They had been on the threshold of life, and it had been snuffed out in an instant. What a way to end up. Some wedding night. What if this had been *his* wedding celebration? That could have been Ginger on *his* shoulder! The mere thought of that made him seethe.

The harsh smoke inside the Cocoanut Grove was getting to Jim. He coughed several times. Feeling phlegm rising in his throat, he withdrew his handkerchief and coughed into it. He was alarmed to see that the phlegm he had expelled was black and sooty.

Danny made his way toward Andy, who coughed repeatedly as he continued to hunt through debris. Danny was mindful to step around hunks of the fallen-in roof. He stopped short.

Jim headed for the platform stairs and was irritated to find that Danny had gone to the dance floor without him. Broken glass and china crunched underfoot as he hastened to join him. He started to tell Danny that the hidden booze seemed undamaged but realized Danny wasn't listening. Jim looked down to see what had captured Danny's attention. Frank was dead, lying on the floor with his eyes wide open. His face and hands were burnt, and his tuxedo was in tatters.

Jim muttered, "Damn it all, Frank." He turned to Danny and confessed in a voice tinged with guilt, "I had no idea he didn't come out with the rest of us."

Andy heard a moan from a woman trapped beneath a lifeless sailor. The strapping football player dragged the body aside to free her. Stunned, he cried out, "It's Rita! She's alive!"

Danny's heart leapt. Rita had survived! He was filled with renewed hope that Ginger had, too. He and Jim rushed over. Rita moaned again when Andy scooped her up. She was weak and coughed profusely. Danny looked at her sadly before frantically searching through the debris nearby. Jim, knowing exactly what Danny was thinking, pitched in.

Rita tried to wrap her arms around Andy's neck. Her face was bright red. She was wet and sooty. Her dress was torn, and her shoes were missing. Her gardenia was crushed in her hair. She looked up at him glassy-eyed and squeaked, "Andy. You came."

Andy smiled at the irony of it.

Rita's words were labored, "I thought … I was … a goner."

"You'll be okay now," Andy assured her. He told

Danny and Jim, "I need to get her to a doctor. Keep looking for Ginger. Please!"

Danny knew Rita was weak, but, before he lost his chance, he had to ask her. "Rita, where's Ginger?"

Rita whimpered, "Melody … Lounge."

Jim blanched. Danny had his answer, and nothing would stop him now.

Andy headed toward the exit to Shawmut Street. The effort of struggling to breathe while carrying Rita triggered more coughing from him.

Danny set off for the foyer. Jim blocked his way. Danny fought to get past him. The dance floor began to creak and groan. The firemen snapped to attention, but Jim and Danny were so caught up, they didn't notice. Danny was desperate. "Get out of my way, Jim! You heard Rita. Ginger was in the Melody Lounge!"

Jim knew it was time to come clean if he was going to prevent his buddy from doing something reckless. He grasped Danny's shoulders. Though he spoke with authority, tears filled Jim's eyes. "Listen to me, Danny. One of the fire chiefs told me everybody in the Melody Lounge is…." Jim almost couldn't bring himself to say it. "Danny, they're all dead."

Danny shot back angrily, "You knew that all this time and were just coddling me?"

Loud rumbling echoed beneath them. Jim and Danny exchanged worried looks. The dance floor cracked open. Rescuers ran in every direction. Jim instinctively leapt away, but Danny's attempt to flee was impeded by his crippled leg. A section of the floor caved in. Danny started to fall through. He flailed his arms, trying to hang onto anything that would keep him from slipping further.

Jim dove across the floor. He grabbed hold of Danny, determined not to let him go. Jim yanked with all his might and struggled to drag Danny clear. They scrambled away just as bodies, furniture, and rubble slid down into the chasm.

Jim was wheezing as he got to his feet. Danny was gasping. Jim gave him a hand up. They caught their breath and straightened their clothes. Danny adjusted his satchel. Grateful, he patted Jim on the back. Jim tipped his hat to Danny and said, "Well, I guess that makes us even."

They headed to the foyer together. Danny veered off in the direction of the corridor to the Melody Lounge. Jim gripped him by the shoulders of his topcoat and shoved him toward the exit. "That does it! Get the hell out of this building right now!"

"But, Jim, she's still down there!" Danny cried.

With a heavy sigh, Jim shook his head.

"Rita was alive. Ginger might be, too. And even if she isn't," Danny's voice cracked, "I can't just leave her down there."

Jim understood but wasn't about to let his buddy see her like that. "I'll go take a look."

"No! She's my girl."

"Danny, it'll be dangerous for a guy with two good legs. Go on outside and let me check things out." Jim pushed a reluctant Danny out to Piedmont.

CHAPTER EIGHTEEN

On Broadway, a siren blared as an ambulance sped away with the last victim from the stretcher chain. It had been an enormous undertaking getting the hundreds of injured transported to area hospitals. Heaving a collective sigh of relief, the chain of volunteers disbanded. Soldiers could take any other injured survivors found to the Red Cross station. Ambulances would collect them from there.

Mary paced in front of the Broadway Lounge. Her nerves were on edge knowing policemen and firemen no longer had to focus on activity in the street. She was afraid, if they went inside, Jimmy, Danny, and Andy might get nabbed.

Kicky and Dot emerged from the Film Exchange building. Concerned when she spotted Mary alone, Kicky told Dot she wanted to check on her. Dot volunteered to start gathering the other chorus girls to help distribute blankets and coats. Kicky reminded her to also keep an eye out for Danny. They exchanged a quick hug before Dot headed off.

Kicky crossed the street. She approached Mary and asked, "What are you doing here all by yourself?"

Teary-eyed, Mary turned to her and whined, "Oh, Kicky." She pulled Jim's topcoat more tightly around herself and fretted, "Jimmy's inside with Danny and Ginger's brother Andy!"

"What? Why?"

"They're looking for Ginger," Mary explained.

"Oh, for heaven's sake! Ginger's already out!" Kicky told her.

Mary was beside herself to think the guys were risking their lives for nothing. She burst into sobs. Kicky suggested, "Let's go find a fireman to get them the heck out of there."

"But Jimmy told me to wait here," Mary protested as she sniffed back tears.

"Better to get them out before they get hurt, kiddo."

In the Red Cross station, Ginger took Charlie's blood pressure. Satisfied, she sponged the soot from his flushed face. Charlie gave her a grateful smile.

Bobby and Arnie stood nearby. Worried, Bobby fidgeted with his helmet in his hands while Arnie watched Ginger's every move. Once she was done, she assured the pair of waiting firemen, "He'll be all right now. The medics will get him to the hospital soon."

Arnie chided Charlie, "Well, I guess we'd better get back and do your job for you, Charlie."

Charlie managed a weak chuckle.

"See you later, Charlie." Bobby nodded to Charlie with warm regard. Donning his helmet, Bobby tipped it to Ginger, smiled, and said, "Thanks for taking care of him, miss."

Andy, carrying Rita, ran by Kicky and Mary. They were upset to see her condition. It made Mary even more frightened for Jim. She called out to Andy, "Are Jimmy and Danny still in there?"

He glanced back at her and hollered, "Yes!"

Andy hustled up the steps of the Film Exchange building and almost collided with Bobby and Arnie in the doorway.

Bobby and Arnie descended the stairs and crossed the street. Kicky rushed up to them and appealed to Bobby, "I need your help. Two friends of mine snuck back into the club."

Bobby's face darkened. Arnie groaned.

Kicky continued, "One of them thinks his girl is trapped inside. I told him earlier the last place I saw her was in the Melody Lounge. And, Bobby, he's a cripple."

"Aw, hell!" Bobby lamented. "Don't tell me. The two guys from the *City Press*."

"Yeah," Kicky muttered.

"Which way did they go in?" Arnie asked wearily.

Kicky pointed to the Broadway Lounge entrance. Without another word, Bobby and Arnie trudged past Mary into the lounge. Mary was grateful, even if Jimmy and Danny got in trouble, the firemen would make sure they were safe.

"Look at you," Kicky said to Mary. "You're freezing. Let's go over to the Red Cross station. We can get warmed up and check on Rita."

Mary didn't want to leave her post, but Kicky was right. She was cold. She followed Kicky across the street and into the Film Exchange building where they found Andy hovering over Rita.

Rita was lying among the many victims on the floor. Andy was perspiring and winded from the exertion of carrying her there. He started to cough. When he caught his breath, he crouched beside Rita. She was trembling and taking in ragged breaths. Andy held her hand to soothe her. She smiled at him weakly.

Kicky was upset to see Rita looking so flushed. She whispered to Andy, "How's she doing?"

"I don't know," Andy said, rubbing the back of his neck. He looked around for someone to come to Rita's aid. He spied Ginger overseeing medics as they carried Charlie out on a stretcher. He was elated to find her unharmed. "Sis!" Andy called. "Thank God!"

Ginger hastened to him. As he gave her a hug, he burst into a bout of coughing. Ginger was concerned. But Andy drew her attention to Rita who was coughing feebly. Ginger was shocked to see her in such serious shape. "Rita? Oh, my goodness!"

"She's having trouble breathing," Andy told his sister, worried.

Rita continued to cough and began to shiver uncontrollably.

Ginger had seen these symptoms in others that night and knew Rita's condition was grave. She knelt next to Rita and checked her pulse. As she had done for so many other patients upon learning their identity, Ginger pulled a slip of paper from her apron pocket and wrote the patient's name and address on it. She pinned it to Rita's dress and then tucked a blanket around her.

Andy crouched beside Rita and held her hand again.

"Salvi," Rita moaned, her voice barely audible.

"I haven't seen him yet," Ginger told her gently.

Mary informed them, "He got out before the firemen got here."

Knowing that Sal had survived brought Rita comfort.

Keeping her voice low so Rita wouldn't hear, Mary added bitterly, "And he never even tried to get any of the rest of us out."

Ginger couldn't believe Sal had been out all this time and hadn't helped a soul.

It was total mayhem outside Massachusetts

General Hospital. Screaming sirens announced the quick succession of ambulances as they came and went. An endless stream of cars and trucks of every type pulled up and parked haphazardly. Soldiers helped doctors, nurses, and orderlies get fire victims onto gurneys and rush them inside. People who were frantic to obtain treatment for their injured loved ones didn't wait. They hurried into the hospital carrying them in their arms.

Across the street, Sal sat behind the wheel of his Cadillac. He and Jimmy Welansky observed the chaos while they listened to the radio for the latest news about the fire. The keyed-up announcer reported, "Cowboy movie star Buck Jones, who was dining at the nightclub with a group of individuals from the motion picture industry, has been found and transported to Massachusetts General Hospital. His condition is still unknown. Mass General has received a good number of the injured, but, by all reports, Boston City Hospital is overwhelmed with victims. Meanwhile, the death toll is mounting. It may well be in the hundreds. Many are wondering if the Cocoanut Grove's management will be cited for criminal negligence."

Welansky grunted and snapped off the radio.

Sal was alarmed to think they might go down for this. He turned to Welansky and asked, "What are we gonna do? Shouldn't we go back in and let your brother know?"

"Nah," Welansky answered with a cocky smirk. "Barney's gonna have another heart attack if he hears this. He really stepped in it this time. We better go wake up his lawyer."

Jim moved through the Cocoanut Grove foyer, carefully stepping over bodies and coughing to clear his lungs. He came across a young woman in one of the phone booths. She was staring blankly. Hopeful she had somehow survived, Jim opened the door. He recoiled when she slumped forward, lifeless, the receiver melted to her ear. Once he got over the shock of it, he recorded the incident and pocketed his notepad.

He started for the corridor to the Melody Lounge. He saw a woman's body slumped over the coat checkroom counter and recognized her copper-colored hair. Fearing the worst but determined to make sure, Jim approached and took Marilyn's wrist. He was not surprised when he didn't find a pulse. Still, it hit him hard. He reverently stroked her hair.

Jim added her name to his notepad's list of the dead he had been able to identify. He reluctantly moved on. He made it to the corridor before being seized by a fit of coughing. He began to choke. He couldn't catch his breath. Dizziness overtook him. Knowing he needed fresh air, he staggered back toward the opening to Piedmont Street.

Danny noticed there was a lot less activity now on Piedmont Street. The backlog of injured no longer lay in the street. He watched in a daze as soldiers hauled away the remaining dead bodies from the sidewalk. Because of the numbing cold and not much left to keep them interested, the number of gawking onlookers had dwindled.

For most of the evening, Fitzy had remained on Piedmont handling crowd control. He was now seeing to it that bodies got taken to temporary morgues. And, when any new survivors were discovered, he made sure they got to the Red Cross station.

Two military men hustled by Danny toting a seriously burnt soldier on a stretcher. Danny watched them transport the victim down the street to Fitzy who directed them where to go. The scene jolted Danny into a vivid memory of that terrible night on Guadalcanal. He had been taking a picture of a burnt and bloody soldier being carted away from the fighting on a stretcher. When he'd heard the whistling of an incoming shell, he'd instinctively leapt on Jim to shield him from the explosion.

Danny's body tensed at the recall of the searing pain he'd felt. He tried to shake off the emotional impact it had left on him and clear his mind of the horrors he had seen. He could not believe he had to witness such carnage again and in his hometown, no less. Danny started to get antsy. He contemplated going back inside to see if Jim had found Ginger but shook his head in frustration and cursed his crippled leg.

Jim's evasive behavior had irritated Danny all night long. It wasn't like Jim to be so uncaring. This was Ginger after all, someone Danny loved. Jim had known her for years, and he'd always been fond of her. And then it hit him. His best friend had believed for hours that Ginger was probably dead and just couldn't tell him.

Danny wasn't going to dwell on that possibility until he had proof. He spoke with a fireman and was told the bodies from the Melody Lounge had been taken to the vacant store across the street and a parking garage around the corner. Danny closed his eyes not wanting to think about bodies crudely laid out on the cold cement floors of the garage. When he opened them again, he saw a gardenia floating down the gutter. The idea that it might be Ginger's sent a shiver up his spine. Through misty eyes, he glanced over at the store. He didn't want to believe she could be in that makeshift morgue, but he had to rule it out. He took a deep breath and crossed the street.

The bizarre twist of fate was unsettling to Danny. Soldiers were now stoically standing guard right where he had been that morning to get the photo of Sal. Steeling himself, he shuffled in behind others also searching for people they knew. The stench inside nearly knocked him over. Row after row of dead bodies covered the floor.

Danny moved apprehensively from body to body.

He was jarred when he came across Katherine, the Grove's cashier, among them.

The woman in front of him broke down. She had found her husband. Her grief cut through Danny like a knife. He prayed to God he wouldn't have to experience that kind of pain. Then he came upon a dead woman in a blue dress. His heart raced. He edged closer to get a look at her face. Relief flooded over him. It wasn't Ginger. But he'd had enough. Overwhelmed, he made for the door.

Bobby and Arnie scanned the Broadway Lounge for Danny and Jim before continuing on to the main room. They played their flashlight beams along the pathway, still littered with bodies, below the Caricature Bar. They scanned the room and were shocked to find a portion of the dance floor had collapsed during their absence.

Rescuers had no choice but to skirt around the cavernous hole to continue removing the dead and the rare survivor from the club. They took great care for fear that any further structural instability would hinder their efforts.

Unable to locate Danny and Jim in the main room, Bobby and Arnie started for the Melody Lounge. They heard coughing in the foyer and quickened their pace. They spotted Jim stumbling toward the revolving door opening, flushed and gasping. The two firemen called to him. Jim did not respond. They hurried over. Before they could reach him, Jim collapsed.

Arnie told Bobby, "Get him out of here. I'll go check the Melody Lounge for his friend."

Bobby brought Jim outside and laid him on the sidewalk. He loosened Jim's tie. Concerned by Jim's labored breathing, Bobby flagged over Howie, who was still on the scene doing triage.

Fitzy, who had returned to the front of the club, wanted to know where the latest victim needed to be moved. He approached Bobby and Howie. He was stunned to see who was lying there. "Mary, Mother of God, not Jim Reed!"

Bobby heaved a sigh. "And his crippled partner is still in there somewhere."

Fitzy fussed, removing his cap and wiping his brow in exasperation. "Jesus, Mary, and Joseph! Those two. Always in trouble since they was knee-high." When he spotted Danny heading toward him from the store/morgue, Fitzy was relieved. He alerted Bobby, who went back into the club to tell Arnie.

Howie examined Jim and explained his condition to Fitzy before moving off to check on someone else. Fitzy glanced down at Jim with a pained expression and then over to Danny.

Puzzled by the look on Fitzy's face, Danny was slow to approach him. He became momentarily paralyzed when he saw Jim lying there motionless. He crept up with trepidation and studied Jim to find out if he was breathing. Jim's eyes flashed open. Startled, Danny yelled, "Jim! You bastard! You scared the shit out of me!"

Fitzy winced at Danny's words. He stepped aside to give them a moment.

Danny grilled Jim, "What's the matter with you? Are you okay? Did you make it down to the Melody Lounge?"

Jim's face was cherry red. Between weak coughs, his breathing was ragged.

Danny was baffled. He didn't understand what the heck had happened to Jim. The more Jim struggled, the more Danny's anxiety rose. "Oh my God, Jim!"

Jim feebly tried to speak. Although it was a challenge for Danny, he managed to sit down next to Jim on the cold sidewalk. He leaned in close to listen. Jim sputtered, "You … weren't here … save me … this ti—"

His words scared Danny. "Cut it out," Danny said, scowling.

Jim futilely attempted to reach for his notepad. "Story … up to you … now."

"No! No, it's you and me," Danny objected tearfully. "We're going to do the story together."

Tears trickled from Jim's eyes. He coughed uncontrollably and started to choke. Dark phlegm dripped from his mouth.

"Jim! Jim!" Danny shouted in alarm. He looked about wildly for help and hollered, "I need a medic over here!"

Fitzy brought over Father Mike. The Boston College priest immediately recognized Jim. He sighed as he thought how sad it was that the world would be losing a young man with such potential.

"I called for a medic, not a priest!" Danny spat. Fitzy attempted to help him to his feet, but Danny shrugged him off.

Fitzy stood by quietly as Father Mike knelt beside Jim and anointed him. Danny stared in disbelief. Fitzy watched, mournful. The priest solemnly administered Last Rites. As Father Mike made the Sign of the Cross over Jim, Fitzy blessed himself.

Jim's eyes fluttered and closed for the last time. With a gurgle, he exhaled his final breath.

Danny was in a state of shock.

Father Mike placed Jim's hands atop his chest, one over the other, and gave them a gentle, goodbye pat. Before moving on to give Last Rites to another, he tried to offer comfort. He put a hand on Danny's shoulder and said, "Jim's with God now, son."

Danny was unwilling to accept that this was the end. He shook Jim's lifeless body. "Jim! No! Come on! Wake up, Jim!"

Fitzy was wrenched by Danny's heartbreak. He knew Danny and Jim had been like brothers. He tried to pull Danny away, but Danny resisted.

Behind them, Bobby and Arnie exited the club.

Fitzy strove to reason with Danny. "Stop it, Danny. He's gone. Let the poor man rest in peace."

"No, Fitzy, he can't be gone! He was fine a few minutes ago when I left him in there!"

Bobby and Arnie felt bad for Danny. Arnie offered him an explanation. "Unfortunately, I think the guy might have breathed in some toxic fumes."

"But he wasn't even in the fire!" Danny argued.

"Yeah, but it's still smoldering. You breathe in enough of that crap and...." Arnie patted Danny's shoulder. "I'm sorry, pal."

Danny couldn't believe it. He hated that he had made Jim stay in there looking for Ginger while he was safe outside. Jim might still be alive if he had been able to do it himself. Danny pounded his fists on his brace, angry with himself and plagued with guilt.

Enraged, Danny looked up at the sky. He could not understand why God had him save Jim at Guadalcanal and ruin his own life, only to have Jim die *now*. Why would God take Jim after he risked his life trying to find Ginger? And what if Sal had survived, but Ginger's life was taken? He couldn't stand to think about it. When he thought of all the people who had died or been hurt, he could not fathom what kind of God would allow such suffering. All they had been doing was enjoying a night on the town. And many of them were those who were willing to sacrifice their lives for their country. Everything—*everything*—seemed so senseless. Gulping back sobs, Danny broke down.

Fitzy, again, offered to help Danny up. Danny wiped away his tears. His voice was hoarse as he said, "Give me another minute, Fitzy. I need to collect Jim's stuff."

Fitzy backed away and motioned for Bobby and Arnie to follow him to the street.

Danny swallowed hard. He muttered to Jim, "I'm going to make sure no one steals these." His hands shook as he confiscated Jim's wallet and Boston College ring. He found his car keys, too. He pocketed everything. He unfastened Jim's watch and put it on. "Looks like I have a watch now, Jim," he said ruefully. He withdrew Jim's press pass from the suit coat pocket and clipped it to a lapel to ensure Jim would be identified correctly.

Finally, he retrieved the one thing Jim valued most. Just holding the notepad filled Danny with anguish. The fact that Jim would never be able to finish the story after all the hard work he had done was agonizing. As Danny grappled with this, a powerful sense of determination overtook him. The injustice of it all piqued his indignation and fueled his passion. He made a decision. He patted Jim's press pass and assured him, "You can rest easy, buddy. I'll finish it."

Danny secured the notepad within the inner breast pocket of his suit coat. He struggled to get up. When he grabbed his camera satchel, Jim's words echoed in his mind insisting, "People need to see what happened to him because of those greedy S.O.B.s!"

Danny gritted his teeth and prepared his camera. With a deep breath, he slowly raised it and snapped a photo of Jim. "I'll make sure you're never forgotten."

He took one long, last look at his friend and whispered, "See you when I see you, Jim."

CHAPTER NINETEEN

A doctor in the Red Cross station put a stethoscope to Rita's chest and listened to her labored breathing. He gave Ginger a somber look before going to examine a patient nearby. Ginger was determined not to cry. She needed to remain calm for Rita. She gently smoothed Rita's hair. "Just rest now, honey."

Rita gazed up at Ginger, grateful for her comfort. But, within minutes, Rita began gasping for air. Her eyes opened wide before slowly closing. When she became completely still, Ginger checked her pulse then started weeping.

Andy asked softly, "Is she … dead?"

Ginger nodded. Mary burst into tears. Kicky hugged them both.

"But why, Sis? I thought once I got Rita out, she'd be okay."

"The poisonous fumes in there are so deadly, Andy, some people have died almost instantly after inhaling them. They're toxic even now," Ginger told him.

"What?" Andy asked in alarm. The news seemed to trigger his own coughs. Though he tried, he was unable to suppress them.

Kicky and Mary watched him with concern. Ginger brought back the doctor. Andy tried to push past him. Ginger stopped her brother in his tracks. "Where do you think you're going? You need to get checked out!"

Andy protested through a fit of coughing, "But Ginger, Danny and Jim are still looking for you in there!"

Ginger was aghast.

Kicky jumped in to reassure her. "It's all right, sweetie. I sent a couple of firemen in to get them."

Ginger appreciated what Kicky had done, but she couldn't keep from worrying.

The doctor listened to Andy's chest. "Son, get yourself to a hospital and let them take an x-ray of those lungs," he advised. "The sooner you find out if you need treatment, the better your chances of avoiding any lasting damage."

Andy heeded the doctor's warning. He looked to Ginger and said, "I can take care of myself, Sis. You go see to Danny and Jim."

Ginger gave Andy a protective hug. She looked around and assessed that there were enough nurses to care for the few remaining patients to be seen. She explained to the doctor that she had to leave and took off with Kicky and Mary.

Danny was in a daze. The entire night felt surreal. In a matter of hours, his whole life had changed *again*. He had gone from the elation of having the love of his life back in his arms to the devastation of having to accept that she might be dead. And just when he thought things couldn't get any worse, he'd lost his best friend. Things would never be the same. He took a deep breath to compose himself and headed into the street to speak with Fitzy.

The good-hearted policeman was engaged in conversation with Bobby and Arnie. Danny approached just as Bobby set off toward Broadway. Fitzy looked Danny in the eye and said, "Such a shame about Jim. He was a stand-up guy."

Danny's stomach lurched. It was going to take a long time before he could accept that Jim was really gone. He just couldn't wrap his head around it. He cleared his throat. "Fitzy, please don't let them take Jim to that … garage. Let me give his family a call. I'm sure they'll want O'Brien's Funeral Home to come pick him up."

"I'll make sure of it, Danny."

Danny nodded his thanks to Fitzy. He turned to Arnie, dreading to learn the truth. But he had to know. "So, I guess it's true then? Everybody who was in the Melody Lounge died?"

Arnie nodded sadly. "Yup. Just about everybody."

Danny closed his eyes, fighting back tears.

A short way up the street, Bobby spotted Kicky heading his way with Mary and Ginger. He hastened to stop them before they came upon Jim. "I'm sorry to have to tell you this, ladies. That reporter friend of yours, Jim Reed?" Bobby paused before gently informing them, "He didn't make it." He pointed out Jim's body.

"No!" Mary groaned and clutched her stomach. "Not Jimmy!"

The color drained from Ginger's face. She stared numbly at the lifeless form lying on the sidewalk. Of all the bodies she'd seen that night, this one affected her the most. It was inconceivable to her that Jim was dead.

Kicky felt Ginger's pain and knew what she feared. And her heart ached for Mary.

Danny was shocked to see Mary run past him, drop down, and sob on Jim's chest. Watching her grieve was torture. It made his own pain harder to bear.

Ginger was filled with anguish. Jimmy had been inside that dangerous place looking for her and so had Danny! Her pulse raced as she imagined the worst. If Jimmy was dead, then Danny must be, too. Pouncing on Bobby in a panic, she demanded, "Danny! Where's Danny?"

"The photographer in the leg brace?" Bobby asked. He gestured toward Danny and said, "He's right over there."

Ginger's heart leapt. Relief flooded over her. She

ran to Danny shouting his name.

Danny heard her calling him and spun around. He could not believe his eyes. "Ginger!"

Danny slipped the satchel from his shoulder to the ground. Ginger fell into his waiting arms. He hugged her fiercely. He touched her face to convince himself she was real. His eyes filled up when he saw the mangled gardenia still in her hair, remembering his despair over the one floating in the gutter.

"Oh, Danny," Ginger said with a sigh.

Danny whispered, "I was so afraid you were...."

They shared desperate kisses. She cupped his face in her hands, grateful he was alive. She collapsed into him and wept. The floodgates opened, and Danny sobbed. They cried in each other's arms.

A lump caught in Fitzy's throat when he saw that Danny had found Ginger at last. It felt like a ray of hope on this otherwise grim night.

Bobby walked Kicky over to Mary. Kicky did her best to console her. They helped her to her feet. Mary, still wearing Jim's topcoat, removed it and spread it over him like a warm blanket. Kicky looked around for Ginger and saw that she was safe with Danny. Satisfied, she and Bobby ushered Mary back toward Broadway.

Ginger let go of Danny and went over to view Jim's body. Danny picked up his satchel and followed. Ginger gazed down at Jim, tears spilling from her eyes. "Oh, Danny. He didn't need to die! You guys didn't need to look for me. I had already made it out."

Danny could not bear to think about that nor could

he stand to hear her feeling responsible for Jim's death. He pulled her in close. He stroked her hair and held her for a long time.

Ginger crouched next to Jim. She brought two fingers to her lips, kissed them, and touched them to his cheek. Her words were barely a whisper. "I can't believe he's…."

Danny noticed her shivering and put his satchel down. He removed his topcoat and draped it around her. Grateful, she rose and kissed his cheek. As he bent over for the satchel, he let out a hoarse cough that made her anxious.

Ginger grasped his arm. "Danny, are you okay? Can you breathe okay?" Before he could answer, she added, "Maybe you should go to the hospital."

"I'm all right, Ginger," Danny assured her. "I've had enough of hospitals." He looked over his shoulder at Jim then put his arm around Ginger. "Come on, sweetheart. Let me get you away from here. With Piedmont closed, we won't be able to move my car just yet. But maybe we can find someplace to rest for a while."

Ginger leaned her head against Danny's shoulder, and he escorted her down the street. Cold and weary, they walked to an all-night diner a few streets away from the Grove. It looked warm and inviting, but Ginger was anxious to call home from the phone booth outside. Danny smoked his last cigarette while she ensured her parents that she and Andy were safe. Danny wanted to get her settled inside the diner before he made the dreaded call to Jim's parents.

The place was teeming with nervous people sipping coffee and chattering about the fire. Some were in tears. When two soldiers exited a booth, Danny was quick to scoop it up. Although the olive-green vinyl seat was cracked, Ginger appreciated the chance to finally sit down. Her feet ached from standing in her high heels all night long.

Danny put his satchel on the bench opposite her. Ginger gave his hand a supportive squeeze. She watched him trudge off. He stopped to buy cigarettes from a vending machine near the door, opened the pack, and lit one up. She knew he was stalling. Her eyes filled with tears. Telling Jim's parents that their son was dead was going to be one of the hardest things Danny would ever have to do.

The reality that she would never see Jim again began to sink in. She would never again get to laugh at his goofy jokes and harmless teasing. And even though she was often annoyed by his demands on Danny's time, she would miss that charming smile. She felt bad that she'd scolded him for lying to her, and now she would never get the chance to tell him she forgave him. Ginger broke down in sobs.

A warm-hearted, matronly waitress, wearing a pale green uniform with a white apron, approached Ginger's table with a pot of coffee. Noticing the state Ginger was in, she asked, "Did you lose somebody, too, honey? I'm so sorry. What can I get for you?"

Ginger gulped, sniffed back tears, and dabbed at her eyes with a napkin. "Two cups of coffee, please." Now a bit more composed, she saw how tired the busy waitress looked as the woman flipped over both jadeite mugs on the table and filled them with coffee. Empathizing, Ginger said, "You sure have got your hands full in here tonight."

"Well, this is one of the only places people can go. Everybody's cars are blocked in. And you can forget about a cab," the waitress said.

Ginger smiled and thanked her.

"Think nothing of it, honey. A hot cup of joe is the least we can do with everything people are going through." She gave Ginger a sympathetic smile and moved on to help other customers.

Ginger stirred sugar and cream into each mug. She sipped on her coffee, luxuriating in the sweet comfort it provided as she kept an eye on the door for Danny.

Voicing the words "Jim is dead" to Jim's mother had made it all too real for Danny. He walked slowly to the booth, removed his fedora, and placed it down on top of his satchel. He slid in beside Ginger and buried his face in his hands.

She wanted to say something to comfort him, but there were no words. He seemed so broken. Her heart ached for him. She rubbed his back to console him.

After a few minutes, Danny wiped his eyes. He took a gulp of his coffee. It tasted good, despite having gone cold. But he really could have used a stiff shot of Dewars now.

They drank coffee and sadly shared their stories about what each of them had been through that night and discovered who else they'd lost. Ginger was devastated to learn of Arthur's death. Danny was surprised to find out Rita didn't make it. When Ginger let Danny know that she'd heard Sal made it out, Danny didn't bother to mention the fight he'd had with him. He steered the conversation to Buck Jones. He told her he wasn't sure if the movie star would survive. Ginger prayed that he would.

A man, looking shell-shocked, entered the diner. He approached a middle-aged couple who were sitting in the booth behind Danny and Ginger. He took the woman's hand and muttered something. She burst into a loud, agonizing wail that rattled those around them. Danny and Ginger glanced at one another knowingly. It seemed everyone in Boston was feeling the pain of loss that night.

Danny gave Ginger a comforting hug. The waitress stopped by and refilled their mugs with hot coffee. Now that Ginger was warm again and able to stop running on adrenaline, she curled up against Danny.

He withdrew Jim's notepad from his breast pocket and rested it reverently on the table. This was the last thing Jim would ever write. As difficult as it would be, he knew he had to look through it in order to fulfill his promise to Jim. Summoning strength, Danny opened the notepad and began to read through Jim's notes.

Deciphering his buddy's shorthand was fairly easy. He quickly caught on to Jim's use of comical, abbreviated nicknames. Jim had referred to Barney Welansky as "W1." In his observations regarding the meeting with Byrne and Buccigross, Jim had referred to Barney's brother Jimmy as "W2." Danny had to stifle a laugh when he realized that "SOB" stood for "son of a bitch," Jim's favorite name for Sal.

Ginger shifted her weight and dozed off. The warmth of her body next to his and knowing she was safe brought Danny a sense of peace. Danny lit a cigarette and reviewed Jim's quotes from Buck Jones. It saddened him that Buck, feeling under the weather, had not even wanted to go to the Grove.

Danny was glad Jim had taken down all the information on both the electrical wiring permit and the fire safety inspection certificate. He was sure that Jim's record of what was written on those documents would come in handy. And, as additional proof, Danny had photographic evidence of them.

He leafed through several pages describing the fire. He came across a list of those Jim had known who had died. He was sad to see Rosie's and Marilyn's names on the list. As he thought about the vivacious redhead who'd had a crush on Jim, he got a lump in his throat. He read Jim's somber retelling of having seen Rosie's dead body in the threshold of the single plate glass door. Danny thought of the sweet, little coat check girl who had always had a smile for him. He couldn't believe Jim hadn't said anything to him about seeing Rosie when they were on Piedmont. It irked him that, since his injury, Jim was always trying to protect him from anything upsetting. Then reality hit him like a punch to the gut. Jim would never be able to do that again.

The waitress quietly refilled Danny's mug without asking. Danny sipped his coffee, yawned, and rubbed his eyes but continued to read. He stopped on a page where Jim had written *D take pix: Cases of booze—No tax seals!!! Bars on windows in Piedmont Bar—No escape!!!*

By the time Danny was finished reviewing Jim's notes, it was dawn. The diner was quiet. He checked the time on Jim's wristwatch with a melancholy smile. Ginger was sound asleep, wrapped up in his topcoat, resting her back against the wall. Not wanting to disturb her, Danny tore a page from the notepad and wrote an explanation about where he would be when she woke up.

He rose and flexed his aching shoulders. He counted how many unused sheet film holders he had left, inserted one in his camera, then hung it from his neck by its strap. After leaving the note and some money on the table, Danny tenderly kissed the top of Ginger's head. He donned his hat, picked up his satchel, and exited the diner, resolved to finish the job.

CHAPTER TWENTY

Danny limped along stiffly in the early morning light. His breath was visible in the frosty air. The streets surrounding the Cocoanut Grove were eerily silent, a striking contrast to the noise and chaos of the night before. A long line of mourners moved stoically in and out of the parking garage being used as a temporary morgue. It sent a chill through him when a truck laden with pine box coffins pulled up in front of it. He knew Jim would want him to record these solemn reminders, so he raised his camera and captured the heartrending image.

Danny made his way to Piedmont Street. He wasn't surprised that it was already lined with vehicles belonging to a variety of city, state, and national officials. He glanced over at his own car in the Grove's parking lot. Like all the others left there, it had an icy sheen.

He stopped at the burnt-out windows and soot-blackened walls of the club. Visions of so many who had perished came flooding back to him in explicit detail as he photographed the debris that littered the sidewalk. Amongst broken chairs and scattered sheet music lay shoes, gloves, hats, handbags, eyeglasses, and other personal items left behind by souls who would never need them again.

Up ahead, Commissioner Reilly, Public Safety Director Walsh, Deputy Fire Chiefs Stickel and McDonough, other fire investigators, F.B.I. agents, and police detectives were inspecting what was left of the revolving door mechanisms. Danny bristled at the sight of Sal and Welansky, freshly groomed and accompanied by a slick lawyer. He shoved in another sheet film holder and got a shot of the three of them watching the proceedings with smug indifference. Sal turned to him, filled with disdain.

The investigators finished their initial examination and gathered in the street to share their expertise. After snapping a picture of the group, Danny took Chief Stickel aside. Sal was able to overhear their conversation. Danny didn't really care.

"Chief, I'm Danny McGuire from the *Boston City Press*. My partner…." The words caught in his throat. "My partner and I covered the car fire on Stuart Street last night."

Eyeing him wearily, Stickel nodded. "Yes, I remember."

In an effort to grab the chief's interest, Danny led with, "Jim and I were working on a story about the shady practices that went on here."

The muscles in Sal's shoulders grew tense. He

nudged Welansky, who listened in as well.

Danny could see that Chief Stickel's curiosity was piqued. But, before explaining more, Danny respectfully asked, "By the way, are all your men okay?"

The veteran fire chief got emotional. "I don't know how, but, by the grace of God, all my men came out of it alive. Even those who fell through the roof."

Danny gave Stickel a moment to refocus before launching in. "Jim and I uncovered that the wiring inspector from the fire department issued more than one warning to the Grove regarding substandard electrical work. And yesterday morning, I witnessed a city official taking a bribe for a permit that concealed the fact that an unlicensed electrician did wiring in the Broadway Lounge. I managed to get a picture of the payoff."

Sal's eyes bugged out. He was livid.

It galled Chief Stickel to know that, besides keeping exits locked, other underhanded business practices of the nightclub's management may have led to this disaster. He sighed in disgust. He knew, if they had political connections, bringing them to justice was going to be an uphill battle.

Danny cleared his throat to ensure the chief's full attention. With great satisfaction, he delivered the most crucial information of all. "We also learned there's a stash of liquor without tax seals in the ceiling. And I happen to know it survived the fire."

Stickel lit up. This news was powerful. There was physical evidence; actual proof of breaking the law.

They needed to jump on this before it could disappear. One way or another, justice would be served.

Danny plunged in. "Will you allow me inside to show you that booze and get a picture of it?"

Sal fumed. He wasn't about to let that gimp take him down. Although Welansky was also aware of Danny's disclosure, he kept a poker face. The only giveaway was the tightening of his jaw.

Chief Stickel was cognizant of Danny's disability. But considering what was at stake, he ushered him to the club's entrance anyway.

Danny shuddered when he passed the area of sidewalk where Jim's body had lain. As he moved through the center archway, he thought about waiting in line there the night before. He paused at the opening where the revolving door had stood. Under his breath, he said, "No waiting now, Jim."

Danny followed the fire chief into the foyer. He was relieved to find that there were no more dead bodies in the club. The coatrack lay in disarray, its coats burnt and soggy. A deep sadness came over him. He remembered that Jim had written how Rosie had been trapped at this very spot. Thanks to Sal, yet another exit had remained locked.

Chief Stickel allowed Danny to lead the way to the Caricature Bar to show him the illegal cache. Rays of sunlight beamed down through holes in the roof onto the floor still strewn with broken furniture. Danny climbed the steps of the platform. A lump formed in his throat. Personal belongings, including cigarette cases and lighters, lay scattered on the bar along with tumbled and shattered bar glasses. A hollow ache filled his chest. The faces of the customers who had been around him flashed in his mind. These things probably belonged to them. He wondered how many of those people were dead now.

At the far end of the bar near the Broadway Lounge, Danny pointed out the ceiling panel with three stars to the chief. Wanting to be ready, Danny prepared his camera.

Chief Stickel was eager to see the stash for himself. He searched for something to stand on and found the metal stepladder in the utility closet. He set it up behind the bar amidst smashed liquor bottles and mounted its steps. He opened the panel, pulled down the trapdoor, and poked his head up inside. The chief was astonished by how many cases of liquor there were. "Holy mackerel! There must be hundreds of them!" He grabbed a bottle from an open crate and inspected it. Sure enough, there was no tax seal. He let out a long whistle then called down to Danny, "You best take that picture."

Stickel descended the ladder. He held it steady for Danny to climb up, take the shot, and come back down. Stickel thanked him and asked him to wait there. "I need to get a police officer to write this up and take your statement. Don't touch anything, and be very careful where you step."

While Danny waited, he stared at the burnt stools on which he and Jim had started out the night. He couldn't believe that the last debate they would ever have would be about a martini. He shook his head as he remembered how their favorite bartender had taken Jim's side, and how Arthur had been so happy to see that he still carried the picture of Ginger. He would be forever grateful to Arthur for setting him straight about her dilemma with Sal. It was unimaginable that Jim and Arthur were both gone.

Misty-eyed, Danny moved around to the other side of the bar. He had two sheet film holders left. He used one to photograph the barred windows in the Piedmont Bar that Jim had mentioned in his notes. He deposited it safely in his satchel and reloaded his camera.

Danny grew impatient. He stepped down off the Caricature Bar platform and wandered into the dining area. He surveyed the room and was amazed at the incredible amount of destruction. Because finding Ginger was his singular focus the last time he was in there, he had not really been aware of the extent of it all. Everything that had made the nightclub the talk of the town was in shambles. The once-majestic palm trees were now burnt, lonely sentinels overlooking what remained of the dance floor. Musicians' podiums, conga drums, speakers, a microphone, and other items from the stage had been thrown into piles with chairs, tables, and dinnerware. It was sad to think that he and Ginger would never again enjoy another night out at the Cocoanut Grove.

Sal stormed in. He made a racket stomping over debris and jarred Danny out of his thoughts. He growled, "What are you doing in here, McGuire?"

Danny was indignant. "My job. What are *you*

doing in here?"

Sal lunged for Danny and grabbed him by the lapels of his suit coat. "Nobody throws a sucker punch at Sal Russo and gets away with it!" He held Danny with one hand and threw a punch with the other.

Danny blocked it and broke free. He saw Sal unbutton his coat and knew he was planning to pull his handgun. Danny couldn't believe the absurd lengths Sal would go to in his arrogance. "What are you going to do, Sal? Gun me down with all those cops right outside?" Danny chided. He jabbed a finger into Sal's chest. "The jig is up! I'm going to expose you and all the rest of the crooks that ran this joint. You're going to lose everything, Sal. Everything you think makes you somebody."

"You think so, pal?" Sal spat. He grabbed Danny's hand, twisted his arm behind his back, and boasted smugly, "I'm no chump. I got friends in places you can only dream of."

Sal reached over Danny's shoulder with his free hand. He snatched the camera and tried to flip the strap up and over Danny's head. Though encumbered by the satchel, Danny managed to keep him from getting the camera.

Sal didn't quit. He shoved Danny hard, sending him crashing to the floor. The camera's flash reflector broke off. It gave Sal great satisfaction to see that Danny was furious.

Incensed, Danny quickly got his good leg under him and started to rise. Sal kicked him back down, drew his handgun, and aimed it at him. Danny tensed, wondering if the hothead might actually pull the trigger this time. Not waiting to find out, Danny glanced around for anything he could use to defend himself. He spied the leg of a busted chair. He nabbed it and swung it forcefully at Sal's knees.

Sal yelped, stumbled forward, and clutched his throbbing knee. In the process, he dropped his gun. It hit the floor and slid out of reach. As Sal rubbed away the pain, he kept eyes full of venom on Danny.

The irony of the situation did not escape Danny. He had to endure that kind of pain every single day. Now Sal was getting a taste of it. Danny calculated the distance to the gun and thought about going for it. But before he could make his move, they heard someone entering. Sal scooped up the gun and slipped it back into his shoulder holster.

Chief Stickel had returned with Fitzy. Seeing Danny on the floor, Fitzy rushed over to make sure he was okay. He helped him to his feet. Danny fixed an accusatory glare on Sal. Fitzy looked back and forth between them. He was well aware of their mutual dislike for one another. Knowing that Sal never hesitated to draw his gun to impose his will, Fitzy eyed Sal with warranted suspicion.

The fire chief, none too pleased that Sal had entered without approval, laid down the law. "Sir, you have no permission to be in here. In view of all that's gone on in this establishment, it could be seen as an attempt to tamper with evidence. You need to leave right now."

Sal was steamed. He wasn't accustomed to letting

authorities push him around. He tried to brush off the reprimand, but his stomach was squirming. That was a new sensation for him. He had always been so confident. But ever since he'd heard that radio broadcaster say charges of criminal negligence might be thrown at the club's management, he'd been running scared. He didn't want to end up in the slammer like his old man.

Sal rolled his shoulders to shrug off his tension. He avoided eye contact with Fitzy. He didn't want the cop thinking up anything to pin on him. Acting nonchalant, he straightened his tie and strolled out of the club. Chief Stickel followed right behind him.

With Sal gone, Danny regained his composure. He turned to Fitzy and asked, "Have you been here all night?"

"It's my beat. I need to stay on top of it. You and Jim sniff this out?"

Danny nodded.

"Always where the action is, eh?" Fitzy asked sadly.

Danny winced. He knew Fitzy was referring to Jim's comment at the car fire. It had always been Jim's way of describing the life of a reporter.

Fitzy pulled out a notepad and a fountain pen. "Are you ready to give me a statement about that liquor, Danny?"

Danny started in with conviction.

Ginger headed up Piedmont Street in search of Danny. The bright sunshine felt strangely inappropriate to her, given the deep sense of mourning that hung in the air. She weaved past ambitious newspapermen now gathered outside the ruins of the nightclub hungry for information from the investigators. The destruction in the light of day was chilling. Ginger instinctively drew Danny's topcoat tighter.

Kicky and Bobby strolled by arm-in-arm, somberly surveying the damage to the Grove. Ginger was surprised to see them together. They had both changed into casual attire and warm winter coats. Before Ginger got the chance to speak with them, they disappeared around the corner.

She noticed Lenny and Henry had also shown up. Despite how Lenny had treated her, Ginger was glad to see that he and Henry had gotten out safely. But, as she drew near and overheard them discussing the fire, it sickened her to learn they had been drawn back by a ghoulish fascination.

Ginger spotted Sal, and her heart went cold. He and Welansky were being interrogated. Some other man was answering for them. It annoyed her when Lenny and Henry crept up close to their bosses hoping, no doubt, to hear all the morbid details.

Sal became aware of Ginger watching him from the street. A sense of relief washed over him to know she was alive and well. The interrogator stepped away to speak with investigators. Welansky conferred with his lawyer. Sal saw this as an opportunity to talk to Ginger. His attempt was thwarted, however, when Danny emerged from the club and joined her. Sal's blood boiled.

Lenny shifted his focus to the lovers' triangle, deviously anticipating the inevitable fireworks. He whispered a heads-up to Henry.

Sal was enraged that Danny had squealed to the fire chief and that the gimp had the gall to try and steal Ginger away from him. He got in Danny's face and spat, "You got a pretty big mouth, pal, and I don't like it!"

Sal's temper unnerved Ginger, but Danny just smirked.

With a dangerous edge in his voice, Sal questioned Danny, "How'd you find out about that booze? Arthur fingered us, didn't he?"

Angry at the mention of Arthur, Danny shouted back, "Yeah! Not like you can do anything to him. He's dead!"

Ginger was surprised by Danny's ferocity.

Danny was fed up with Sal and continued to let him have it. "A lot of people are dead. All because you bastards had to be so damned greedy. You kept the doors locked. Nobody could get out! You let them die. You let them *all* die! You goddamn murderer!"

Heads turned in their direction. Ginger held her breath, awaiting Sal's reaction.

Sal's eyes blazed. He grabbed Danny by his lapels.

Lenny and Henry were enjoying the action.

Indignant, Danny shook Sal off.

Sal was acutely aware that Welansky and the lawyer were staring at him. So, instead of grabbing Danny again, he snarled, "This isn't over."

Danny fiercely stood his ground. "Oh, it's over."

Ginger couldn't stand any more. "Will you two stop it! How can you act like this after losing people you loved?"

Danny was embarrassed that she had needed to remind him.

Ginger saw confusion on Sal's face. "For heaven's sake, Sal, don't you even know your sister died last night?"

Lenny was shocked by Ginger's words. He hung his head mournfully.

"Rita's not dead," Sal scoffed.

Danny stuck the knife in and twisted it. "Yeah. She is. Poor Rita died needlessly, locked in there like everybody else!"

"What do you mean?" Sal growled, believing Danny was just busting his chops. Danny looked to Ginger in exasperation. Sal stared at her for confirmation.

"Sal, I was with her in the Red Cross station when she took her last breath," Ginger said gently.

"Dio mio!" Sal cried. He glared at Danny until the pain and guilt of losing his sister consumed him. He knew he should have made sure she was all right. He was her big brother, after all, and it was his responsibility to look out for her. His mother would

never forgive him. Sal's bravado sagged.

Ginger watched sadly as Sal blinked back tears.

"And Jim's dead, too," Danny added bitterly. "He was looking for Ginger like you should have been!"

The shame of it all cut Sal to the quick. He could not deal with the truth that, when it counted, he had not acted like a man. It broke him. Sal watched without protest as Danny wrapped a protective arm around Ginger and steered her away.

Danny and Ginger were weary to the bone. He was glad that the ice had melted off the cars in the parking lot. The last thing he was in the mood for was scraping his windshield. He stored his camera in his satchel and secured the bag behind the driver's seat. It felt good to get the weight off his neck and shoulders.

Danny turned to Ginger and pulled her close. He whispered, "I was so worried I'd lost you forever." He kissed her with all the pent-up yearning in his heart. She willingly surrendered. Their kiss was long and smoldering.

"I've waited a long time for that," Ginger confessed.

Danny gave her an impish smile. "Me, too. How did I ever think I could live without you? We need to get that ring back on your finger."

Ginger beamed.

He kissed her again.

Ginger scrutinized his necktie. She straightened it. "This is a handsome tie. Did Jimmy help you pick it out?"

Danny's voice cracked as he answered, "Yeah."

Feeling his sadness, she welled up with tears. "He was a good influence on you."

Danny touched the tie with a wistful smile. "The guy always did have class."

Ginger cupped his cheek tenderly.

Grateful for her comfort, Danny hugged her close. "Ready to go home?"

"More than ready."

"You'll have to drive," Danny told her self-consciously.

"I can do that. On one condition," she said mischievously.

"What's that?"

"You stop thinking of yourself as only half a man."

Danny's eyes twinkled. "I can do that, sweetheart."

Ginger gave him a peck on the cheek. She slipped into the driver's seat. Danny shut her door, went around the car, and eased his way into the passenger side.

They drove away in the brilliant sunlight, leaving behind the burnt-out shell of the Cocoanut Grove.

EPILOGUE

The Cocoanut Grove Fire on November 28, 1942 claimed the lives of 490 people, including legendary cowboy movie star Buck Jones. Hundreds more were injured. Everyone in the Boston area knew someone that was there that night, whether in the fire or as part of the rescue effort.

Though widely accepted, it was never proven that the match lit by Stanley (Tomaszewski) actually caused the inferno. In recent years, there has been speculation that faulty wiring sparked methyl chloride gas leaking from the nightclub's refrigerant system. Firsthand accounts about the ball of blue flames that sped through the club tend to support that theory.

There turned out to be 4,000 cases of liquor without tax seals hidden in the space above the ceiling of the Caricature Bar. They were auctioned off, raising $171,000, with the intent that the proceeds should go to the fire victims. But $100,000 went to the federal government to settle Cocoanut Grove owner Barney

Welansky's tax evasion charges on the liquor. All other plaintiffs had to make do with a small percentage of the remaining $71,000. In the end, survivors received a mere $160 apiece for pain and suffering.

Barney Welansky was the only person ever convicted on charges related to the fire. Despite having been in the hospital at the time of the tragedy, he was found guilty of involuntary manslaughter and reckless conduct. In 1943, he was sentenced to 12–15 years in prison. But he served just 3 years and 7 months. Welansky was dying of cancer and, as a result, was pardoned by Governor Maurice Tobin (the former mayor of Boston).

There was a silver lining, however, to the catastrophic fire. The multitude of victims presented Boston hospitals with the opportunity to try out newly developed burn care treatments. The first humans to ever receive penicillin were 13 of the survivors. Merck and Company rushed a 32-liter supply from New Jersey to Boston. The new antibiotic proved its merit in combating the staphylococcus bacteria that often infects skin grafts. The longstanding use of tannic acid was replaced by petroleum jelly-covered soft gauze. Innovative techniques in fluid resuscitation were introduced by Massachusetts General Hospital surgeons Francis Daniels Moore and Oliver Cope. Also, the first major utilization of the blood bank was implemented. These medical advancements, still in use today, were very successful and became invaluable during World War II for treating wounded soldiers.

The tragedy also led to some of the earliest

systematic investigations of grief and survivor's guilt as well as post-traumatic stress disorder. Boston psychiatrist Erich Lindemann published the significant paper "Symptomatology and Management of Acute Grief" after analyzing families and relatives of those who had died in the fire. Austrian psychiatric and neurological researcher Alexandra Adler conducted a pioneering study of post-traumatic stress disorder while working in Boston with more than 500 of the survivors. She published the notable paper "Neuropsychiatric Complications in Victims of Boston's Cocoanut Grove Disaster."

In addition to the strides made in the medical community, official reports of the incidents at the Cocoanut Grove prompted tougher enforcement of fire safety codes. The inaccessibility of the club's exits brought forth new laws requiring all public buildings to have outward opening doors, especially on either side of any revolving door, and to keep them unlocked during hours of operation. Because highly flammable decorations had escalated the peril, use of fire retardant, non-toxic materials became mandatory in all indoor public gathering places. The intensity of the fire and the speed at which it traveled throughout the nightclub inspired the importance of sprinkler systems. Thankfully, their installation eventually became commonplace.

The lessons learned from the Cocoanut Grove Fire are still studied by nurses, doctors, and firefighters today. For example, it became apparent how much a standardized system of triaging mass casualties was needed. And, because history has shown that fires of this type continue to happen, fire companies must stay prepared to handle such conditions as overcrowding, limited exits, flammable materials, toxic fumes, and, now, even pyrotechnics.

The Cocoanut Grove Fire remains the deadliest nightclub fire in history. Out of respect for all who had been affected, no entertainment establishment in the city of Boston has ever again been named "Cocoanut Grove."

READING GROUP QUESTIONS

1. Before reading *A Fire That Still Burns,* had you ever heard about the Cocoanut Grove Fire?

2. In the 1940's, people dressed to the nines to enjoy the Cocoanut Grove nightclub's exotic setting, live orchestra, captivating entertainment, dining and dancing, and multiple lounges. Do you wish places like this existed today?

3. If you had been in the Cocoanut Grove when the fire started, what would you have done?

4. After experiencing the fire via this book, will you be more cognizant of where exits are located in public buildings?

5. Do you feel the authors' approach of following the reporters through the 24-hour period was a good way to tell the story?

6. Which characters do you think were real people and which do you think were fictitious?

7. Whose story tugged at your heart the most?

8. Which character's death did you find the most upsetting?

9. Do you believe Sal got his just desserts?

10. Overall, do you think justice was served?

11. Some people, by a stroke of luck, were unable to make it to the Cocoanut Grove on the night of the tragedy, while others unfortunately happened to be there when the fire broke out. Do you know of other incidents where fate intervened?

12. Were you surprised to find out that so many innovative medical treatments came into mainstream use as a direct result of the Cocoanut Grove Fire? Are you aware that what has been learned from the fire is still studied by nurses, doctors, firefighters, and police officers to this very day?

ACKNOWLEDGEMENTS

This book is dedicated to the 490 souls who lost their lives as a result of the Cocoanut Grove Fire, to all those who participated in the rescue efforts, and to those in the medical field who tirelessly assisted survivors with the long process of healing both physically and emotionally.

Thank you to our editors Dr. Jeff Levin at FirstEditing and author, editor, and writing teacher Stephanie Schorow for their assistance and expertise.

We would like to express our deepest appreciation to everyone from whom we gained invaluable information in our pursuit of writing this story.

We are indebted to the late Edward Keyes, whose fabulous book *Cocoanut Grove* sparked our fascination. With a multitude of anecdotes, he vividly brought the experience of the fire to life. We are grateful as well to three other authors, whose books were marvelous sources of research and inspiration: the late Paul Benzaquin for his riveting *Holocaust!*, John C. Esposito for his absorbing *Fire in the Grove*, and Stephanie Schorow for her well-crafted and fact-filled *The Cocoanut Grove Fire* and her updated version *The Cocoanut Grove Nightclub Fire: A Boston Tragedy.*

We are thankful to the Boston Public Library for allowing us to view their files of newspaper coverage, fire reports, and photographs of the Cocoanut Grove Fire. We must credit the National Fire Protection Association, the Cocoanut Grove Coalition, the Boston Fire Historical Society, and the Boston Fire Museum for making so much information available to us and anyone else who wishes to learn about the fire. We appreciate retired Boston Fire Department firefighter and photographer Bill Noonan for giving us his input regarding press cameras used in 1942.

We applaud the *Boston Globe,* the *Boston Herald,* and the *Patriot Ledger* for outstanding newspaper coverage of the fire in 1942, investigative reporting thereafter, and sustained coverage on anniversaries since. Special thanks to Jeremy C. Fox, correspondent for the *Boston Globe,* for his article in July 2012 that informed us about the existence of the Cocoanut Grove Coalition. We hope he will be flattered (not bemoan) that we usurped the article's title for our novel.

Finally, we extend our sincerest gratitude to our friend Mike Foley, author and retired Boston Fire Department lieutenant, for sharing his extensive knowledge of firefighting and for giving us continual support and encouragement as we wrote and published this book.

ABOUT THE AUTHORS

Denise M. McShane was born and raised in her beloved Boston, Massachusetts. She now lives in Stoughton, Massachusetts with her husband, Paul.

Betty Lynn Nye was born a New Englander but currently resides in Charlottesville, Virginia with her husband, Bob.

For as long as we can remember, we have both been captivated by books, movies, and television series. Individually, we have composed many songs, poems, and short stories, but we found that when we combined our efforts writing screenplays it enhanced our creativity. And working together on this novel, although challenging, was extremely gratifying.

We truly enjoy sharing the excitement of developing new stories, the thrill of discovering unexpected background research, and the exhilaration of spinning our words into magic to awaken emotions and touch the spirit.

dbmasterpieces.com

www.ingramcontent.com/pod-product-compliance
Lightning Source LLC
Chambersburg PA
CBHW031208020726
47499CB00002B/538

* 9 7 9 8 2 1 8 1 4 4 8 6 9 *